M000046973

# AVA HARRISON

*Illicit: A Novel*
Copyright © 2017 by Ava Harrison
Published by AH Publishing

ISBN: 978-0-9963585-9-0

All rights reserved. No part of this book may be reproduced or transmitted in any form by any means, including photocopying, recording or by information storage and retrieval system without the written permission of the author, except for the use of brief quotations in a book review.

This book is a work of fiction. Names, characters, places and incidents are products of the author's imagination or are used fictitiously. Any resemblance to actual persons, living or dead, events or locations is entirely coincidental.

The author acknowledges the trademark status and trademark owners of various products, brands, and/or restaurants referenced in the work of fiction, which have been used without permission. The publication/use of these trademarks is not authorized, associated with, or sponsored by the trademark owners.

**Illicit: A Novel**
Cover Design: By Hang Le
Photographer: Wong Sim
Cover Model: Chad Hurst
Interior Design: Champagne Formats

Editors: Ellie McLove, Love N. Books
Brenda Letendre, Write Girl Editing Services
Content Editor: Jennifer Roberts-Hall, Indie After Hours
Proofreader: Marla Selkow Esposito

Dedicated to those looking for *home.*

# PROLOGUE

'VE STOPPED WISHING FOR EXTRAORDINARY.

I've stopped wishing for that one moment so profound it will change everything. I know it will never happen, so there's no point in dreaming.

But like all things in life, extraordinary happens when you least expect it, and in the blink of an eye, everything can change.

# CHAPTER ONE

## Lynn

I GAZE OUT AT THE VAST OCEAN BEFORE ME. THE WATER LAPS against the shore like a graceful song to my ears, quietly whispering a melody I once loved, but it does nothing to calm my nerves. Waves roll in, and with each pass of the water, the sand below me scratches beneath my bare feet. I close my eyes to take in the peace, but the visions behind my eyelids are still there, and the pain of his betrayal continues to etch away at me.

As usual, nothing has gone according to my plan. I'm not sure what I expected, but it certainly wasn't what I got.

I never really liked him.

*So why did it hurt so much?*

Life has taught me hard lessons. I learned long ago that I could never rely on anyone to be there for me, but even after everything I've been through, I still need to know I mean something to someone. That someone out there cares.

It certainly isn't my parents. Although my father tries, ever since he left when I was ten it hasn't been the same. And my mom . . . well, my mom is currently in the midst of becoming Mrs. Someone for the fourth time. I'm her perfectly created specimen. The daughter she flaunts at the parties she attends.

When I was eleven, Mom was trying to land a British Duke, which required extensive travel to Europe. To this day, I'm not sure why she dragged me along. In the end, all we had to show for the experience was me being held back a grade. So, even though I'm already eighteen, I'm only a senior in high school.

Turning my head to look over my shoulder, I gaze at the house in the distance. Right up the beach is the house party we decided to crash. Bridget's older sister rented the house for the summer with a bunch of her college buddies. We knew a ton of Cranbrook Alumni, including my boyfriend, Matthew—well, *ex-boyfriend* now—would also be there.

At the last minute, Bridget and I decided to pack a bag and join the fun. Although everyone at the party was significantly older than us, we knew we'd be welcome. It would be everyone's last hurrah. I couldn't wait to get there and spend some time with Matt before school started, but it turned out he wasn't missing me as much as I missed him.

*My feet were cemented to the floor as I took in the sight before me. There, standing at the edge of the bed, was my boyfriend and a blonde I didn't know. I couldn't move as I watched him thrust in and out of her from behind. The sickly sweet smell of sex permeated the air.*

*I was afraid I'd be sick.*

*"Matt." His movements stopped at the sound of my voice.*

*"Oh, shit," he said as he pulled out of her and faced me. His face contorted into a look of shock. "Fuck. I didn't know you'd be here." My mouth dropped open. Did he just say that? Every muscle*

*in my body flinched as anger filled my blood. A tense silence enveloped the room. It was as if a fierce storm was about to blow.*

*"You didn't know I would be here?"*

*He made no move to cover himself or his whore. Instead, I was forced to look at the woman he cheated on me with. Model tall with bones sticking out of her hips—the complete opposite of me. Her hair was the shade of blond only present in a bottle, and she had lips that looked as if they had recently been injected with fillers. Shaking my head, I turned my attention back to Matt, whose dick was still hard. His mouth hung open, obviously thinking of a way to respond to my question. He let out an audible sigh and then—finally—reached for a sheet to cover the evidence of his tryst.*

*"Listen, Lynn. I'm sorry you found out this way, but maybe it's for the best."*

*My stomach tightened, and anger coiled inside me. "For the best? What the fuck, Matt? We've been together for months!"*

*"Yeah, but now I'm going away to college, and I'm not sure how I can go that long without you. You don't get it since you're still in high school. But I have needs."*

*"Needs? You know what? No. No! You don't get to put this on me like it's my fault you're a lying, cheating dick. Have a nice life."*

*"Lynn—"*

*I stormed out the door.*

I take a deep breath, and the smell of the ocean rushes up through my nose. Its salty and pungent fragrance should act as a balm, an elixir that soothes me, but I'm too destroyed for something that simple to work. I exhale the emotion collecting inside me.

All I can do now is pray for a miracle to save my night.

# CHAPTER TWO

## Carson

ANOTHER FUCKING PARTY.

I'm so sick of this shit. If there's one thing I won't miss it's the drunk, self-indulgent idiots getting high and fucking anything with a hole. *Not that I don't like fucking, but I have some standards . . .*

I reach for a bottle of Grey Goose on the counter and search for a spot where I can be alone and drown out the noise these children are making.

*Why the hell am I here again?*

Oh, yes. *Dylan.* It's his last party before he starts law school. Unlike him, I'm over this college shit, but he insisted on one last *rager.* Normally, I wouldn't have bothered, but the guilt he laid on was even too thick for me to say no to.

I'm too old for this crap.

My real life starts on Monday. After four years of college, my head stuck in the books trying to get my shit together, I finally have a degree to show for it. I'm ready for the next stage, but I still have a few more days before this new phase of my life starts, so I guess there's no harm in one more night of oblivion. But unlike these people, I would prefer to spend it alone.

Looking from right to left, it's apparent there is no place for me to hide. Then, from the corner of my eye, I spot the door to the beach. *There.* That's where I'll find peace. Everyone is too busy getting drunk inside to be out there. It's the perfect place. With a deep breath, I stroll toward the sliding door, and on the way grab a blanket lying across the back of the couch. *Might need that.* Over the loud thumping music there's no creaking noise when I pull the glass door open, but as I step outside and close it behind me, the sound echoes against the new silence of the night. The summer heat slaps my face as I search for a secluded area on the deck. Then, I notice the path leading down to the water.

Bingo.

With every step I take, the party becomes a distant hum, but when I finally reach the sand, I see I'm not alone. A little way down the beach, sitting where the sand almost meets the water is a girl. I only catch glimpses of her face from this angle, but each time her light hair is rustled by the wind, the exposed skin on the back of her neck peeks out. *She's beautiful.* Even though my view is obstructed by the distance and angle, it doesn't take much to realize that she is breathtaking. Ethereal . . . like a goddess. I stare at her some more and find that although I came here to be alone, I no longer want to be. The fact she's here has me welcoming the company, or more like *her* company. I lift the bottle to my mouth and take a long swig.

*This should be interesting.*

# CHAPTER THREE

Lynn

URYING MY HANDS DEEP IN THE COOL, COARSE SAND that's still pulpy from the retreating tide, I recline and shut my eyes. Other than the ocean, the beach is silent. I'm not sure how long I sit here, but eventually my shoulders uncoil and the corded muscles loosen from my earlier tension.

"Not in the mood to party?"

I jump at the sound.

He chuckles. "Sorry. I didn't mean to startle you."

I peer up at the stranger interrupting my solitude. My breath catches in my throat. His stance is confident, and he has an air about him that sends a chill down my spine. The glare of the moon shimmers in his eyes. They appear dark and ominous. A burning, faraway look reflects back at me. A look I know too well. I see it in the mirror every day when I don't want to be home; when I don't want to be alone. He stares back in waiting silence, then inclines his head as he continues to assess me. It's as if he feels my pain and matches it. *Maybe, just maybe*, he understands me.

But how could he? He doesn't know me, or anything about me.

The thought of him being like me, feeling like me, sets my skin on fire from embarrassment and elates me at the same time. It makes no sense to feel these two emotions together, but nonetheless, a heat spreads across my cheeks and down to my collarbone. His eyes glisten as the moonlight continues to reflect off them, reminding me of a night at sea. His gaze sweeps down and then lingers, undressing me with his eyes and searching within my soul for my secrets.

He's beautiful.

Devastatingly beautiful.

A gust of wind whips around us, and his untamable brown locks become even more unruly as they drift across his brows. All thoughts of anything but running my fingers through his tousled hair fade away. I chastise myself for my thoughts. I shouldn't even be considering hooking up with someone when my boyfriend just cheated on me.

Thank God we're cloaked in darkness because the black night hides my blush. I have never been so attracted to anyone in my life. Maybe it's that I'm vulnerable after what Matt did to me, but staring at him has my pulse beating erratically.

He smiles, and I can't pull my gaze away. It's as if my world is on pause.

"So, no party?" he repeats, and I realize I never answered his original question.

I mutter, "No," still lost in his stare.

"Mind if I sit down?" His voice is gentle and makes me feel at ease.

I nod, and he lowers his body to the ground, spreading his

long legs in front of him. With a turn of his head toward me, he lifts a bottle of vodka. "Want a sip?"

"I'm normally not much of a vodka drinker." Lifting one hand, I reach toward him. "Okay, I'm not at all a vodka drinker, but after the night I've had, I wouldn't mind taking the edge off."

He hands me the bottle, and our fingers brush. His are cool and smooth. The gentle encounter makes me hyper aware of the close proximity of our bodies. I lift the bottle to my mouth and take a sip. The cool liquid burns my tongue and sears my throat on its way down. Not my poison, but it does the trick. Our fingers meet again as he grasps the bottle from me and props it in the sand beside us. This time the contact causes my body to shiver. I notice he has a blanket in his hand, but instead of sitting on it he lays it down beside the bottle.

"What brings you out here to the beach all alone?"

"The wild festivities sucked." My hands dredge in the sand by my feet. As I lift them, the grains pass through my fingers.

"And you're not in the mood to get drunk and act like an asshole like the rest of them?" he asks, his voice all velvety and smooth.

"Oh, God, no."

He laughs at my answer. It's a hearty laugh that makes my own lips want to part, but I don't let them.

"I hear that."

I lift an eyebrow. "I take it you didn't enjoy the party either?"

"That obvious?" Sarcasm drips off his words and I nod in understanding.

"If you hate them so much, what brings *you* to a lame ass party?" I can't help but mock him. His answer intrigues me.

"What can I say . . . Last party of the season. Had to make an appearance. I'm over it, though. School starts in one day. I'm ready to get to it already."

"Yeah, I totally get that," I mutter.

"What's your name?"

"Lynn."

He stretches his hand out and I take it. His fingers wrap around mine and I feel a surge of energy go through me. "Well, it's nice to meet you, Lynn. I'm Carson."

"Nice to meet you, too, Carson."

Pulling his hand from my grasp, he leans away. I grip the base of the cool glass and take another swig. The taste burns its way down and makes me feel warm inside. As the liquid pools in my stomach, it lessens the misery from Matt's rejection swirling inside me.

"Okay, Lynn. From the look on your face and your obvious disdain . . . why did you really leave? Because it's got to be something more than the party being lame." He shrugs matter-of-factly before turning toward me and inclining his head. "What happened?"

My body stiffens. *A perfect Barbie replaced me.* "I don't want to talk about it, okay?"

"I understand." He leans back on his elbows, his face still focused on me. "So, if you don't want to talk to me about what's got you so upset, let's talk about something else."

I groan. "Or we can just sit in silence."

"But that wouldn't be quite as fun, now would it?"

"I guess not."

"You know, you'll probably never see me again after tonight. I'm the perfect person to vent to." The baritone of his voice reverberates through my body. "If you won't tell me why you left, then tell me one fun fact about yourself."

He's right, what he just said. This is my chance to just talk and have someone listen with no judgment or expectations. I look up to the sky and let out a sigh. Plus, talking to this guy is a much better choice than hiding from Matt.

"Fine. Hmm, one fun fact . . ." As my eyes gaze overhead, I come up with a relatively easy answer. "I'm mildly obsessed with the stars."

"Any reason why?"

"Growing up, I moved around a lot. I never felt I had a home. But no matter where I was—what city I was in—the stars were always the same. Even if some aren't visible, you know they're there. You know what I mean?" For some reason, it feels good to tell him this. Refreshing in a way. It's not often anyone asks me questions about my home life, but sitting here telling this stranger feels cathartic.

"I didn't move around a lot but I understand the feeling of liking consistency in life." He reaches out his hand and takes the bottle back, pausing for a swig from it. "I know a thing or two about stars," he says as he looks up to the sky.

"Do you now?"

"Yep." He sits up tall and puffs out his chest, then turns toward me and smirks.

*Wow.* That smirk makes me want to relax, have fun. Forget everything that happened tonight and just enjoy the moment. I take a deep breath and try my best.

"Okay, big shot, what's that one over there?" I ask.

"That constellation is Cassiopeia," he responds candidly.

"Cassiopeia?"

"Do you know anything about mythology?"

"No, not really."

"Have you ever heard about Perseus?"

"Wait, isn't he the one in the movie with the hot guy . . ."

He grunts from beside me and I stifle a laugh. "Yes, he's the hot guy from the movie. He's also the one who killed Medusa to save Andromeda, the woman he loved. Remember?"

"Um, yeah, sure."

"Okay, so where was I?"

"Telling me a really long story," I chide.

"Hardy har har. Okay, yeah, so Cassiopeia was Andromeda's mother. She was also married to the King of Ethiopia. She was an incredibly vain woman and believed she was above everyone and so was her daughter. One day she said her daughter was more beautiful than the goddess Juno. The gods decided to punish the country for this comment and let loose a sea monster to kill everyone. When given the choice to sacrifice her daughter Andromeda, and thus, save herself, she chose that route. Luckily for Andromeda, Perseus saved her, but still—"

"Holy shit. Sounds like my mom." Our eyes meet and he furrows his brow. "She would easily sacrifice my well-being to make her life better," I clarify, and he bites his lip in thought.

"I'm no stranger to crazy parents," he mutters. I cock my head at him and wonder if he'll clarify what he means, but after a few seconds of complete silence, I look back up to the sky. I guess he's like me and doesn't want to talk about it either.

"Then what happened?"

"After her daughter was saved, she was punished by being placed in the sky as a constellation in such a way that her head was upside down half the time . . . forever to be humiliated."

"That's pretty anticlimactic if you ask me. Where's the humiliation in that? If my mom did that to me . . ." I take a deep breath. "I guess I wouldn't do anything, either. At least this way, she hangs upside down half the year for eternity. That's got to suck. Maybe next time my mom pisses me off, I can do that."

I laugh, but I'm only partly kidding. It would be nice to hold my mother accountable for her actions. However, that would require her to be around, not traveling the world and leaving me to raise myself.

"If only it were that easy, right?" he says, and I give him a half smile. *It's time to change the topic.* Talking about my mom is not the way I want to spend my evening. Hanging with Matt and his bimbo would be more fun.

"What about you, Carson? Any weird things I should know? I mean, we'll probably never see each other again? So you might as well tell me all of your secrets."

He eyes me for a minute, and then shakes his head. "Nope."

"Oh, come on. That's not fair. I told you mine." I pout and bat my eyelashes.

"I hate clowns," he blurts out and I bust into a fit of giggles. "Like, despise them."

"Really?"

His firm mouth curls as if it wants to smile, but he's fighting it. A small dimple gives him away, though.

"Have you seen *It*?"

"You know that's just a movie, right? Clowns are just normal people in a costume." I laugh as I shake my head.

"Doesn't stop me from hating them."

"Any reason for this 'hate'?" I air quote, obviously poking fun at him. From the corner of my eye, I can see his lips purse, holding back a laugh.

"Not that I can remember. Maybe I was tortured as a child."

"Maybe," I say and wait for him to laugh. But when he doesn't, I narrow my eyes at him. "Wait, were you?" I shift toward him with one eyebrow raised.

"No. I do have mommy issues too, but *she* never *tortured*

*me,*" he air quotes and I nod, but there is no mistaking the hollow look in his blue eyes. I can feel my own pain lodge in my chest at the thought.

"I feel you. Guess no life is perfect."

"Ain't that the truth? I'll toast to that."

I reach for the bottle and take another big gulp.

"Why constellations?" I ask him, looking back up to the spot he had pointed to before.

"Why not?"

"There has to be a reason?" He shrugs at my question. "You can tell me," I say.

"Okay, fine. I guess it's because it makes something beautiful from chaos. Two points in the sky. Two stars otherwise not connected. Then an imaginary line connects them and everything makes sense." There's a deep significance to his words.

We sit for a while, neither of us speaking as we continue to share the bottle. After my last sip, I balance the bottle in the sand. I've had enough to take the edge off. Any more and I'll be a sloppy drunk, and unlike most of the girls at the party, I don't enjoy praying to the porcelain god.

A loud crash from within the house breaks the silence between us. Both our heads turn in unison to investigate.

"God, they really aren't the most mature, are they?" Carson says, shaking his head.

"I know. Sometimes I can't believe I dated one of them."

"You dated one from that bunch?" he asks, looking at me now.

I shrug. "Yes, unfortunately. Matthew Robinson. Do you know him? He was at the party tonight."

"Can't say that I do. Should I?"

*Thank God.* I don't think I could continue to sit here if they were friends. As cool as Carson seems to be, that would be too much to bear after tonight's fiasco. "Oh, God, no. You're much better off. He's not worth knowing, trust me." I glance back at the house. "He's kind of the reason I'm out here."

"What happened?" His voice is soft over the lapping of the waves and I take a deep breath.

"I walked in on him fucking another girl," I blurt in a shrill voice before I can change my mind. I turn my head to him and his mouth is hanging open, probably from my bluntness. It makes me laugh. "Truth?"

"Always. No reason to ever lie."

"I never really liked him all that much, but it was nice to have someone. I have my best friend Bridget, but with my mom . . ." I trail off.

"I understand. My parents aren't the best, either." His gaze finds mine. "Okay, enough of this serious shit."

I nod, and then point a hand up to another cluster of stars.

"What's that one over there?"

Hours must pass, but it doesn't feel like it. We talk about everything and nothing. He shares the mythology stories that correspond with each constellation, and I marvel at how knowledgeable he is. It's comfortable with him and even though we don't know each other, when I talked about my mother . . . it was as if he understood me. A yawn escapes and with that he jumps to his feet.

"You're falling asleep listening to my stories. Come on, let's do something fun."

"Like what?"

He looks back at the house and then toward the ocean. His lips turn up and form a smile. "We could go back into the party?"

The idea of seeing Matt has my blood running cold.

"Yeah, that's not an option," I say, and he expels a giant puff of air he must have been holding in.

"Oh, thank God. I don't know what I would have done if you said yes to that."

"Nothing to fear there. What are the other options?"

He lifts his eyebrow, and I playfully feign shock. "What? I was just going to say I could bore you with more of my fears."

We both stare at the beach in front of us. All of a sudden, he turns to face me. Excitement shines in his eyes. "Let's go for a swim." He reaches a hand out to grab mine.

I stare at his large palm, then the vast ocean, and then back at him. "Now? But we can't see. Won't that be dangerous?"

"The moon is bright enough. We won't go in too deep. Come on, it'll be fun." The corners of his eyes crinkle as he smiles at me. "A lot more fun than that party. Plus, this is my last weekend before I have to become an adult with responsibilities. Have a little fun with me. Live a little, Lynn."

I turn my head to gaze into the Atlantic. As the moon gleams across the water, I realize he's right. It's definitely bright enough to swim, and seeing as this night has already gone off plan, I should have as much fun as possible rather than dwell on some douche who can't keep his dick in his pants.

"I don't have a bathing suit on." A dimple forms in his right cheek.

"Dream on." I laugh.

"Go in your clothes. It's so damn hot, they'll dry within minutes."

"Okay," I say, but then I look down at my outfit and shake my head no. "But not this skirt." It's my favorite, and the short strands of layered chiffon would never hold up against the salty water. Running my hands down my torso, I unzip my skirt. The material hits the sand, and although I know that amidst the crashing of the waves nothing can be heard, it echoes in my mind. Nervous tension courses through me and then fills the space between us. With timid steps, I walk ankle deep into the water. It's the perfect temperature.

I watch as he dives under and emerges a few seconds later. "It's fucking amazing. Just jump in."

I walk in deeper and finally immerse myself. It really is amazing.

"Isn't it perfect?"

I smile. It really is perfect and having him with me even more so.

"You're really beautiful when you smile." His words pull me from my daze. I must look like a lunatic smiling so wide. My heart hammers in my chest. I shake my head and pick my brain for a snarky response.

"Does that mean I'm not beautiful when I don't?"

"You know what I meant."

"Do I?" I tease, and he moves toward me.

"Stop being a smart-ass or I'll dunk you."

"You wouldn't dare." I try to move away but Carson's arms wrap around my middle. His fingers splay against my ribs, and the feel of his skin on mine drives me crazy. It makes me crave every inch of his skin against mine.

Our eyes lock, and as Carson's grip around me tightens, I brace myself to go into the cold water. On instinct, my eyes close and I wait to be submerged. When nothing happens, I re-open them and am met with his gaze still fixed on me. A wave of feelings pushes through me.

I'm trapped between opposing thoughts.

Need and hesitation.

I should probably put space between us, but after Matt's betrayal, the idea of being wanted, of letting go and just doing something crazy with a stranger, is all encompassing. I can no longer think straight. Carson's expression grows serious and everything—all the thoughts inside me—melt away as his fingers touch my jaw. With all my inhibitions now gone, my lids flutter closed as he strokes my skin.

Our faces are inches apart. We're so close I feel his breath tickling my lips on each exhale. The feeling flowing through me is monumental. I feel paralyzed by it.

Unable to move.

Unable to even breathe.

My desire for this stranger is painful. Opening my eyes, I peer into his. His pupils are large and edged with desire, and his gaze is intense as I wait for one of us to make a move. For one of us to throw caution to the wind and seal our fate. The urge to be kissed takes over every facet of my mind.

Dropping my gaze, I take in his deliciously full lips. I need to kiss him. Need to feel his mouth on mine. Need to get lost in him.

"God, you're beautiful." His voice breaks with huskiness.

A ragged breath escapes my trembling lips as his thumbs tip my head back and he descends. His lips brush mine, soft and pliable. They coax my own open, and as his tongue sweeps against me, I am lost to this man.

Completely and utterly lost.

I have no choice but to surrender to him.

His large hand cups my face as he deepens the kiss. The soft caress of his mouth becomes firmer. The kiss is no longer sweet—it's fast and rough. A kiss demanding we're both equal partners in this.

Matt always complained that I never initiated sex, and that when we had sex I wasn't into it. I never understood what he meant, but now, kissing Carson, I get it. This is what a kiss should be like.

Hungry.

Desperate.

Primal.

Carson pulls me roughly to his body, almost violently, and I melt against him. "Need you," he growls.

I know what he needs and I need it, too, the way I need oxygen to live. I need his hands to touch me, his mouth to kiss me, and most of all, I need to feel him inside me.

"Yes," I plead. He answers by sweeping me weightlessly into his arms and bringing us out of the ocean and onto the beach. Lowering me to the sand, he rolls his body over mine. The feel of him on me is like a blanket of comfort that I have always sought. It's perfect.

He buries his nose in my neck, and then his lips drop delicate kisses down a path to my collarbone. When they reach the strap of my camisole, he drops the flimsy material covering me.

Exposing me.

Strong hands cup my breasts, as warm lips trail down until they reach the hollow of my chest. His mouth takes possession of me, finding each peak and licking and sucking until my body quivers with need. His mouth meets mine again, and our tongues collide at a faster clip.

Carson hooks one finger into my wet panties, and pulls them down my thighs. Once completely stripped, I lie naked on the blanket instead of sand. His eyes roam my body as he leans over me like a predator stalking his prey. Parting my legs, he angles his body between them and kisses all the way up until he meets the inside of my thighs. Slowly, he makes his way up to the bundle of nerves inside me and I jerk away, closing my thighs as embarrassment fills me, but he tightens his grip around me.

"No, I need to taste you."

He licks up my seam, and I'm surprised when a moan escapes. All thoughts of halting this delicious torture fade with each swipe of his tongue. The back and forth motion is almost my undoing. I hang on by a thread until he begins to flick and then suck in a maddening pace that has me gripping the blanket and falling over the edge. With one last kiss, Carson climbs up my body until his hard length concealed by wet boxer teases at my entrance.

"Are you sure?" he mumbles against my neck.

*Am I?* I might never see him again, but at this moment, it doesn't matter. I have never wanted something or someone so much.

"Yes," I pant.

"Thank God," he moans as he reaches across the blanket and into his shorts pocket, grabbing a condom. Pulling off his wet boxers, he rolls the condom on himself and positions his body once again, the tip of him teasing my opening. When I think I can't take much more of this torture, he pushes inside my slick heat. The feel of him sinking inside me elicits a moan of pleasure, but Carson silences me with his mouth as he pulls out and then thrusts back in. My thighs clamp around his lean waist, and my back arches up to meet each of his strokes. He lifts my knee to his shoulder for deeper penetration, and the new angle makes me succumb to the blinding euphoria that's been building inside me. As I ride my high, I feel him push forward a few more times until his body jerks within me, following me over into the bliss.

———————

The fragrance of salt wafting in the air brings me out of my post orgasmic haze. Opening my eyes, I see Carson smiling down at me.

"That was incredible. *You're* incredible."

My face warms at his words, and I'm thankful that in the dark of the night he can't see the blush that must be spreading against my cheeks. He lifts off me and flops down beside me on the blanket. His chest rises and falls as I regulate my own breathing.

"You really are." Carson's voice sounds lazy. Stealing a glance, I notice his lids are shut. The even rhythm of his breathing indicates that he's fallen asleep. I quietly slip my clothes back on.

*Now what?*

When he wakes, will he politely tell me he has to go? Will he ask for my number? Oh, God, what if he doesn't? What if he never wants to see me again? What if I'm just another slut who slept with him on the first night? I feel sick at the thought. I need to leave before he awakens.

I pick up my bag and grab my phone. 4:25 a.m. *Fuck.* There are a couple of missed texts from Bridget.

**Bridget: Where you at?**

**Bridget: Everyone at the party is talking about what Matt did! What a dick. U okay?**

My stomach drops. Knowing I'm the big gossip of the night has me mentally refusing to go back in to search for Bridget. Since this message was only sent an hour ago, I decide to answer and make sure she's still around before I go. I can't leave without her.

**Me: Fine, but I need to get out of here. You ready?**

**Bridget: Sure thing. Meet me by the car.**

I look down at Carson one last time. I contemplate leaving a note but shake the idea out of my mind. It's better to just cut my losses. This is for the best. One night, no strings attached. I just ended one crap relationship, no way am I jumping into something else. Why would I bother? As amazing as Carson seems, I'm sure he would disappoint me. Leave me. Eventually, everyone does.

I see Bridget standing by my mom's car in the driveway. "You cool to drive?" she hollers.

I calculate how long it's been since I had a drink. A few hours, at least. "Yep. We can drive up to my mom's place. They're in the south of France right now." I roll my eyes.

As I turn on the car, I pray she doesn't ask me details of my night, and luck is on my side. By the time we pull out of the driveway, Bridget is already sound asleep.

# CHAPTER FOUR

## Lynn

THE EARLY MORNING SUN CASCADES ACROSS THE room, bathing me in iridescent streams of white light. It filters through my thin eyelids, causing me to flicker them open. With a stretch of my arms and a giant yawn, I check the clock. It's a little after nine in the morning. Turning to my left, I find Bridget still asleep in the other queen bed in the room. My stomach rumbles as I wring the last bit of remaining sleep from my body. *God, am I hungry.*

"Bridge?"

"Hmm," she grumbles from under the pillow.

"Food?"

"Hmm . . . what?" It's obvious she's talking in her sleep. Oh, well, she'll come down when she wakes. I stand from the bed and make my way toward the door.

"I'm going to brush my teeth then head downstairs. If you need me, holler." She probably doesn't hear me, but still worth trying one more time.

After freshening up in the bathroom, I head downstairs. The house is peaceful. The only sound filtering through the air is the soft hum of the air conditioner. Mom and Richard are away, and I'm lucky enough to have the key and permission to use the property. There's not much my mother does for me, but access to a sweet place in the Hamptons is acceptable. Thank God for some things. After last night, heading back to the city is daunting.

*Carson . . .*

Was I wrong to run off? My body tingles at the thought of his hands on my skin. I was such a coward, and now I'll never see him again. I didn't even catch his last name. Maybe it's for the best, though. After Matt, jumping into a new relationship, even if it's only sexual, isn't a good idea. No, this is better. No connections, no strings, no expectation. With a shake of my head, I set out to make breakfast instead of dwelling on things I can't change.

Pulling out some eggs, a fork and a bowl, I begin to whisk. Once the eggs are on the stove, I pop a K-Cup in the Keurig and make myself a cup. The air becomes thick with the robust scent of coffee, and my mouth begins to water. With just one sip, my taste buds come alive as it bathes my mouth and then my throat with the perfect amount of warmth and bitterness to start my day right. As I'm placing the food on the table, Bridget stumbles in, looking a little worse for the wear.

"I feel awful," Bridget groans as she plops down on the chair and burrows her head in her disheveled hair. Her sandy blonde locks look extra dirty today. Between the beach air and a night of partying, I'm not at all surprised by her appearance this morning. "Like a freight train hit me. I'm not as hung over as I am beat the fuck up tired."

"Beat the fuck up? Is that even a sentence?" I laugh.

She narrows her eyes at me. "Yes." Her one-word answer makes me chuckle even more.

"I'm not sure how much you drank, but when I saw you at the end of the night you were exhausted. We weren't even out of the driveway before you passed out dead asleep. I almost had to carry you into the house."

"Wow." Her torso shudders. "How did you even get me inside?"

"Slowly. Very slowly. And good thing I hit the gym this summer, because pulling you was like lifting dead weight." I laugh and she groans.

"I swear I might die. I really am so tired. It's like I didn't sleep at all."

"I promise you won't die. And I can also promise that you did, in fact, sleep. You're just very hungover. Here, take my coffee. I already took a sip, but by the look on your face, I'm guessing you don't care."

"You sure?" She squints her eyes at me.

"Yeah, you need it more than I do. I'll make myself another one." After my new cup is brewed, I take the seat across from her and serve myself some eggs.

"So, what happened to you last night?" she asks between sips of coffee.

*Oh, God*, I so did not want to get into this with her right now. "Besides walking in on Matt fucking some fake blonde with a bad boob job?"

Her mouth drops open, and a series of coughs follows next. "Oh, shit. Yeah." She grimaces. "I forgot about that."

"I wish *I* could forget about that."

"What a scum bag."

"You think?"

"He's the worst. So where did you go?"

"I couldn't take it, so I just hung outside."

"Alone?"

My stomach muscles tighten. I should tell her about Carson. It was a magical evening, and how something so bad could turn out so perfect was beyond me. But I don't want to share it with anyone. Not even my best friend. Instead of opening my mouth and divulging everything, all I do is nod and quickly change the subject.

"Enough about me, tell me about you. I saw you with Mason."

Her cheeks turn crimson as a large smile spreads across her face. "You did?" She's full fledge blushing now, and it's super cute.

I can't help but allow my lips to turn up. "Yeah, you guys looked totally into each other. Tell me what happened."

"We made out," she blurts.

"Oh, I know," I chide.

"You do?" she squeals.

"I saw you two going at it, so it didn't take a rocket scientist." I laugh. "So now what?"

"He's going to college." Her brow furrows.

I can understand her reluctance. Matt is starting college too, and I obviously wasn't important enough for him to stay faithful to or at least try. But Bridget is different, and maybe it could work out for them. Meeting Carson last night made me realize that crazy things can happen. Why not for Bridget?

"So."

"What chance do we have if he's in college? I'm here, and he's there."

"Bridge, he's not that far. It's like an hour to Princeton. If you want to make it work, it will."

"You think?" Her eyes look hopeful, so I plaster on the biggest, fakest smile I can muster.

"Yes, I do. Listen, just because it didn't work with Matt and me, doesn't mean it won't work out for you. Matt just decided I wasn't worth it."

"You are worth it," she says firmly.

"I know." I lean back in my chair and close my eyes on a sigh.

"Do you?"

*No, I didn't know.* All my life it's been evident that I'm not. If Mom and Dad have taught me anything, it's that I'm not worth the time and inconvenience.

"You're worth it to me."

I reopen my eyes and draw my lips in thoughtfully. "I know," I finally say to appease her, even if I don't mean it. We sit in silence for a few minutes, each lost in our own thoughts. After I take a sip of my coffee, I turn my head back in her direction.

"So, what do you want to do today?" I ask.

"Choices?" She perks an eyebrow up at me.

"Today's Sunday, so we have the farmers market. Bike into town—"

"Bike into town? You're kidding, right? I'm too tired to walk to the bathroom, let alone get on a bicycle." She tilts her head to the side and scrunches her nose. "But I could totally go for some macaroons. I bet they would make me feel better."

I shake my head at her. "Only you." I laugh. "Only you think of macaroons as a hangover cure. Maybe you should just take some Motrin."

She throws her head back in a fit of giggles and the sound makes me smile brighter. Being with Bridget is easy. She gets me. I don't have to try with her. There's a connection there, as if we are kindred spirits. As if we are family. I don't know what I would do without her.

After we finish breakfast, I head upstairs and jump into the shower while Bridget gets ready in the guest room. As I'm putting on a coat of lip-gloss, she strolls in and I can't help but laugh.

We both have thrown on jean shorts, Chucks and tanks. This is why she's my best friend. We are so in tune with each other that we are actually wearing the same outfit. With the same color hair, we look like twins.

An hour later, and with our bellies full of sweet delicacies, we step into the warm summer air, and walk straight into a large, *familiar* group. My stomach churns at the sight of Matt. Everything inside me rebels at the idea of being close to him.

"Let's go," I say under my breath, pulling on Bridget's arm. At that moment, Matt's eyes meet mine. *Please don't speak to me. Please.*

"Lynn."

*Fuck.*

"Leave me alone, Matt," I huff.

"You don't need to be a complete bitch. I said I was sorry."

He doesn't look sorry. He looks more like a condescending bastard. "Sorry? Yes, okay, because that makes it all fine."

He blatantly rolls his eyes. "Oh, for fuck's sake, Lynn. What did you expect?"

"I don't need to hear this right now, Matt. I get it. You're a big shit college guy now. Go. Have a grand time." And with that, I turn and walk away. Bridget follows behind.

"God, that was awful. He's such a douche," she says with labored breath.

"Was he always that horrible?" I ask her.

"He was the coolest douche in Cranbrook." She shrugs. "Everyone thought it was cute."

"Slap me next time I do something that stupid."

"Deal."

"Let's get real dessert now. Macaroons didn't satisfy me. I need to eat my sorrows."

"Ditto."

At that, I smile. "I don't know what I would do without you."

"Die. You would probably die."

"Yep, that's it." I laugh, and thank God for her because she's the only person I have. I really should tell her about my night with Carson, but not yet.

I will.

Soon.

Eventually.

———————

The weekend passes, and before I know it, it's Tuesday—the official first day of my senior year of high school. As the bell rings, I slide across the hallway, dashing as fast as I can. I can't miss attendance. Cranbrook Prep has a strict tardy policy, and three tardies are equal to cutting a class. My last name starts with an A, so I'm pretty much fucked once the second bell rings.

I glance down at the printed slip of paper in my hand with my class schedule: AP World History. Mr. Blake. Hall B. *Shit.* That's clear across the building from where I currently am. I pick up my gait until I'm at a near sprint. I round the corner . . .

And fly face first into a wall, my notebook falling to the floor.

"Watch where you're going," a voice says.

*Well, maybe not a wall.*

*Fuck.*

*Fuck.*

*Fuck.*

This day just keeps getting better and better.

With a huff, I bend over to grab my notebook. My ass is probably hanging out of my short, pleated, black and red plaid skirt. But I can't force myself to care.

I do my best to make sure I'm decent before opening the door. The squeak is deafening against my ears. *I'm so late.* Just as I take a step forward, I hear my name being called.

"Here, here. Sorry I'm so late," I say, rushing in. Laughter erupts at God knows what, but I can't bring myself to care. I'm so disheveled.

"Miss Adams, will you please take your seat." I roll my eyes at the command. *That's what I'm trying to do, idiot.* I glare up at my teacher, sure to make an even better first impression. My gaze meets his—

And my world stops.

My book drops from my hand again and goes crashing to the floor. The sound reverberates through the room, causing me to be met by another round of laughter. As I bend over and fidget to grab my belongings, I peer up and see Carson looking down at me. His movement's halt as all the muscles in his jaw tighten, causing a small, barely noticeable tic beneath the skin. His mouth turns into a grim line. Lifting my chin, our gazes meet again. He appears stunned. His mouth opens, and then shuts as his eyes probe mine. There are so many unspoken questions in the way he looks at me. Sharp and assessing. There's a lethal calmness to them that makes the oxygen in my lungs feel restricted.

*How is this possible?*

*How can fate be so cruel?*

Through heavy lids threatening to expel tears, I watch as he studies me intently. A student's coughing in the distance has him giving his head a little shake. Righting himself. But the rigidness of his body betrays him. He's as unnerved as I am.

"Lateness will not be tolerated," he stammers before abruptly turning on his heel, heading back to his desk. "Take the first seat in the row and open your book to page one."

# CHAPTER FIVE

## Carson

HOLY SHIT.

This is hell.

If I ever wondered what hell would be like, this is it. I mean, where else could I be?

My teeth grit from the effort to remain silent, to not launch into an attack and demand to know why she's here. Why she's sitting right in front of me. Torturing me with her mere presence. *And Lord, is she torturing me.* From where I'm standing in the class, I can see her creamy thighs peeking out from that scrap of material this hellhole calls a skirt. I can only imagine what she's wearing underneath it. A lace fucking thong. One that could be ripped from her body, exposing . . .

*Head in the game, Carson.*

When I woke up alone on the beach, I was pissed she had snuck out on me, but I knew it was for the best. With her going back to school, and me starting my job, there was no future. But God, she was incredible.

Fuck, how did my day go so wrong so quickly?

Everything seemed to be going great. I came in early on Monday, set up my classroom, and walked the grounds. I was excited to be back here again, not as a student but as a teacher. It was perfect.

Until the moment the fucking door opened and she walked in.

What I'd do to turn back the clock to Saturday night and not have touched—

*Fuck that.*

As much as this situation sucks—*and Lord, does it ever*—I will *not* regret one minute from that night. Being with Lynn, even if only for one night, was incredible. Why would I want to forget it?

My eyes catch her again from across the room. She's gorgeous, and the crazy part is, she doesn't even realize it. Not going there, though. Doesn't matter how much I want to lift up that skirt and . . .

Our eyes lock.

God, what I would do to bend her over my desk and lose myself in her for the rest of the period. Hell, the hour; maybe even the day.

*Fuck.*

She's my student.

With a shake of my head, I try to lure myself out of my perverse thoughts. If I'm lucky, my pants won't tent in front of a classroom full of kids. Kids . . .

*Oh shit.*

How old is this girl? If it's not bad enough I've fucked a student, what the hell will I do if she's not legal? *Shit.* I'm going to get fired from a job I only just started. Hell, I might even be arrested. Not that it would be my first time, but still . . . This is not good. From my peripheral vision, I see that some kid in the first seat is frantically waving his hand in the air to ask a question and I can't even calm down enough to call on him. Instead, under my desk I keep balling my fists and then unclenching them.

I need answers.

I glance up at the clock. Only fifteen more minutes until I get some.

# CHAPTER SIX

## Lynn

I SHOULD BE TAKING NOTES. I SHOULD BE PAYING ATTENTION. But all I notice are his muscles flexing as he writes on the smart board and I can't help remembering how his arms felt when they were bracketed around me. All I can hear when he speaks is the sound of his moans in my ear as he tasted my skin, and all the sinfully delicious words he spoke when he took me on top of the blanket. My face flushes at the memory. I can't think of him like this. *No.* I left for a reason and this cements my reason. It's time I stop daydreaming about him, no matter how hard the memory is to relinquish.

"Miss Michaels?"

His voice breaks through the memory. I glance back up and see he's staring at a girl sitting a few rows away from me. His gaze is paralyzing, his pupils flat and dull. Not at all like the Carson I knew from the beach. I wonder what he's thinking. I wonder what makes him so angry. *Is it me?*

"Yes," she mumbles, flustered from her own daydream she

must have been in. I would feel the same way if he had called on me, but as he refuses to even look in my direction, it doesn't seem as though I'll have to worry about that.

"I asked you a question," he states in an icy-cool tone.

"You did?" she mumbles. *Poor girl.*

"Yes, Miss Michaels. And from the look on your face I can safely assume that you, in fact, were not paying attention."

"I'm sorry, Mr. Blake."

Hearing his last name sounds bitter in my ears. But that's who this man is, and as much as I remember *Carson*, this man is not him. Even thinking his first name now feels like a dirty secret waiting to be expelled.

An audible sigh escapes his lips before he looks down at the seating chart on his desk. "Miss Clarke, can you help Miss Michaels?"

Madison perks up and moves her body in a seductive manner. From the pucker of her lips, I can see she's set her sights on him. An encompassing sickness coils its way into the pit of my stomach. It invades my bloodstream and takes over like venom. I clench my mouth tight, gritting my teeth against the invasion of emotions wreaking havoc in my body. The sound of my foot tapping on the floor makes me realize how badly I'm fidgeting from the anger and jealousy. I shouldn't feel this way. I shouldn't care. But why won't he look at me? I keep staring at him, willing him to look back and praying he won't. Trying to force my conflicting thoughts from emerging, I look down to my desk hoping he never calls on me and this class ends soon.

"The answer is expansion," she says smugly.

"Okay, class. I want you to read to chapter five in your textbooks and be prepared to discuss it tomorrow."

A collective groan emanates through the classroom, and

someone behind me mumbles under his breath, "God, it's the first day of class. Isn't there a no homework rule?"

"Chapter five," he repeats sternly. "Miss Adams, a minute please."

I sit perfectly still in my chair, the ticking of the clock etching away at my nerves. As the last student leaves, I feel my hands shaking, so I slide them under my thighs to hide them as he makes his approach. He stands next to my desk and then, after a beat, pulls a nearby chair around to sit facing me.

"I don't understand how you're here." His eyebrows lower, and a fine line forms between them. He reaches up and tugs at his hair, pulling it at the root. "Are you even eighteen?" His eyes close, then reopen with a flash. "Please God, tell me you're at least legal?"

I boldly meet his eyes, trying desperately to hide the inner turmoil I'm experiencing. "I'm legal."

With a deep breath, his tense shoulders relax. "Thank fuck for that," he mumbles, and I purse my lips, trying my best to not let on that the extraordinary memory is now becoming tarnished.

"So, how are you here? This is an AP class, which is typically filled with juniors. I don't often hear of seniors choosing to take this class as an elective." His body is straight again. The mask of Mr. Blake has returned as quickly as it left.

"One, I needed an elective and my choices for this time slot was this or art. I have no artistic talent at all, and I actually really like history. Two, my mom held me back." I leave it at that. I don't owe him more of an explanation. Maybe in the Hamptons, underneath the canopy of stars as he peppered my skin with kisses, I would have confessed all my sins. But now? I most certainly will not.

"What are we going to do about this?" he muses, and then proceeds to answer his own question. "You will change classes."

As much as my heart wants to stop, and I can feel the familiar sting of tears wanting to expel, I hold back my emotions, straighten my back and meet his eyes. "No, I'm not switching. It never happened," I assert. At my words his face is expressionless but then something flashes beneath the surface of his hardened face. I can't place the emotion.

"Yes. Perfect. We can never talk about what happened. We need to forget it all." He nods to me, and for some reason I'm infuriated that he agreed so easily. First, he acts like I wasn't here, and now the dismissal. Rage, anger, and pain fill me.

"Exactly. This," I motion between us, "will never happen again. I'm sorry it ever did." I jump up and head for the door, my head held high.

*Self-preservation.*

I walk out without a backward glance.

---

I spent the next class period in the bathroom, dry heaving the bile that collected in my stomach after my confrontation with Carson. Correction—*Mr. Blake*. After my third period class, I head over to the lunchroom. As I sit at the table, Bridget plops down and inclines her head to the side and looks at me.

"What up, biatch?"

"Nothing," I mumble back.

She furrows her brow at my one-word answer, then narrows her eyes at me. "Where's your lunch, Lynn? Are you feeling okay? You look a little pale."

"I'm just not hungry." A part of me wants to tell her, but

embarrassment and rejection lock my jaw and make my head pound. I press my fingertips against my temples and start to massage.

"You need to eat something."

I reach across the table and grab an apple off her plate. I take a small nibble, but the taste alone turns my stomach. "See, I ate."

"Great, you licked an apple."

"Bridget, I'm not in the mood. Lay off, okay?" I drop the fruit back on her tray and then hide my hands under the table. They're trembling from the confusion coursing through my veins. *Of course* this is my life. *Of course* this would happen. I never thought I would see him again. And now he's my teacher.

"What crawled up your ass?"

"Nothing, okay?" Blood pounds beneath my temple, and I wonder how I'll make it through the rest of the week, let alone the rest of the semester, when Bridget's voice cuts into my thoughts.

"Sure, whatever." Her lips are thin with what I can only imagine is irritation, but she quickly rights herself with a shrug of her shoulder and then a condescending smile. "So, how's your first day of school so far?"

I can't help the groan that escapes my mouth, eliciting an eyebrow raise from Bridget.

"That great, eh?"

"I have no words to describe my day. Next subject, please." I give a dismissive wave of my hand, hoping that ends the conversation before it starts. It seems to work as Bridget is now staring in the opposite direction. Her mouth drops open.

"Oh, my God. Who is *that*?"

I follow her gaze and my heart races as I locate the object of her dismay. *Mr. Blake.* Obviously it's him. Of all the people to walk into the room and capture my friend's attention, it has to be the one I never told her about. Shit. I need to pull my gaze away but my head won't turn. I can't stand how beautiful he is. It makes everything inside me hurt. She reaches across the table and squeezes my arm until I wince.

"Do you know who he is?" she asks again.

"Mr. Blake." I try to keep my voice flat, but unfortunately my eyes roll of their own accord.

"Um, not a fan?" I pull my arm away from her and slide both hands under the table.

"No." My right hand clenches.

"Lynn, he's fucking gorgeous. How can you not want to worship at his feet?"

*If only she knew I've worshiped more than his feet.*

"He's a dick, Bridge. I was late and he was a complete douche about it."

Her eyebrow lifts. "That's a lot of animosity for a simple tardy."

"He made me stay after, too."

Her mouth forms a perfect circle and her eyes bore into me. She gawks at me like I'm crazy, and I probably am. She reaches across the table and gives me a little squeeze. "I'm sorry that your day is sucking, babe, but I have some good news." Her eyes light up. "Coop's parents are in Europe this week. Big party at his place this Friday. You want to go?"

"No. Not really. Do I have to?" I grumble. I hate Coop. He is a total idiot. The idea of going sounds awful.

"Yes. Oh, come on. Don't be like that. Let's just go have fun." She won't ever drop this. Once Bridget sets her mind to something, she'll keep harping until I give in. With a deep sigh, I do.

"Fine."

"Woohoo!" She bops up and down in her chair. "Okay, we should go get a blowout and have our makeup done before. You in?"

"Yeah, sure."

———— ◡ ————

"Miss Adams! Wait up."

I've managed to avoid Mr. Blake for the rest of the day, but as I make my way out the front door of the school, I hear my name being called from behind me and I know it's him. I'm not sure I can bear speaking to him again, but I discern something in his voice that makes my movements cease. I turn and stare him down. His face, although beautiful, seems worn and tired as if he is hauling the worries of the world on his shoulders. If this were a different time, a different place, my only desire would be to rid him of his pain.

He peers around us and then motions me to keep walking. We're about a block away from the school when his movements cease. I follow suit. With another look around to make sure no one is around, he looks down at his feet, his top teeth biting into his lower lip. "I'm sorry about this morning."

His lack of eye contact pisses me off. "Whatever." If he can't find the decency to look at me when he apologizes, I don't need to find it in me to give a shit.

"Lynn—"

"Oh, I thought I was Miss Adams now?"

He stands silently for a moment, distributing his weight from the ball of one foot to the other as he searches for the words he wants to say.

"You barely acknowledged me in class at all." *Shit.* Did I

really just say that out loud? Yes, I did, and he should know he can't treat me like that.

"Listen, I'm sorry. I was taken aback by your presence. I wasn't prepared to see you, but that doesn't excuse my attitude."

"No, it doesn't."

"You're right. There are no words to tell you how sorry I am for that. How sorry I am for this—*all of this*. I'm not even sure what I'm supposed to do. Can we try this again? The right way?"

My heart hammers in my chest. Can I do that? Start fresh? Pretend nothing happened? "Um . . ."

"It doesn't have to be weird."

I pause for a minute and study his gaze, looking for any false pretense in his words. When I find nothing but a genuine smile, I nod. "If you say so."

"Okay, I'll see you in class tomorrow?" he asks, and I lift my shoulder in a half shrug, and then finally bob my head, *yes*. For a moment he stands frozen in place, before pulling his gaze from me. As he retreats into the distance, my thoughts of what the future will bring spiral out of control. I don't know if I can do this but I will at least try.

The thought makes me uneasy, and the need to be comforted weaves its way through my body. Pulling out my phone, I dial my dad's number even though we haven't been speaking as often as usual. He says he's been busy with work, but something isn't right. I can't quite put my finger on what, but it feels strange. *A bit off.* As if I'm grasping at straws wondering what to talk about, and he sounds awkward—uncomfortable and unsure what to say. Yet at the same time, it feels as if he has a lot to say but just doesn't have it in him. I blame this on my mom. When they got divorced, a fire went out in my father. He's never been the same since. One day he was loving and caring, and then the next he was different. The worst part is that the older I get, the worse it gets. The most noticeable change came when I turned eighteen, almost as if he stopped trying. It makes no sense. But still, I think it's her fault somehow, she killed something inside him. I hate her for it.

The phone goes straight to voicemail.

"Hi. Um . . . Hi, Dad. It's me . . . Um, Lynn." I pause. God, I sound stupid. "I haven't spoken to you in a few weeks, so I . . . I just wanted to see if you wanted to grab dinner. It's been awhile." And now I'm rambling. "Well, I guess I'll try back later. Or you can call me," I add hopefully. I should know better, but I still hope. "Love you, Dad."

I expect to find the brownstone that I live in with my mother quiet, but when I step inside the front foyer I hear a ruckus in the living room. The sound of a drawer opening then slamming shut makes me grimace. Peeking in, my mom's tall, willowy frame comes into focus just as she's about to sit down. Her chocolate locks are perfectly blown out in soft, flowing waves, and she's wearing what I refer to as her Fifth Avenue uniform: tweed Chanel coat with designer jeans. That way she appears sophisticated and young all at the same time. A perfectly Botoxed face helps with the latter.

"Umm. Hi, Mom," I stammer in bewilderment, still not understanding why she's here. "Aren't you supposed to be away?" Her head pops up, and if she could frown she would. Luckily for her, the muscles on her forehead are frozen solid.

"Lynn." That's all she says before rummaging some more in the desk drawer.

"What are you looking for? Do you need help finding it?"

"Just papers from your father. Nothing of your concern." The annoyance is evident in her voice. I stand for a moment, wondering what else I should say, but she gets up with a stack of papers in her hand. They appear to be legal papers, judging by their size.

"Are you staying for dinner?"

"No, I'm leaving now."

That's no surprise. Why would I think differently? "I guess I'll call Bridget and see what her mom is making . . . *again*," I mutter.

"I don't want you going there. That girl . . . she's beneath us. Don't you have any other friends?"

"What's your problem with her?" She's always had an issue with Bridget. Even the first time she met her, there was something in her eyes. A deep, rotten hatred I couldn't understand. A level of disdain that was unfathomable to me. I'll never forget how Bridget held her hand up in introduction and my mom stepped away. Shunned her. My face had turned hot, and tears welled in my eyes. I had never felt so embarrassed. But Bridget had simply laughed it off, vowing that we'd spend more time at her place. So from there on out, that's what we did.

"I don't like that family," she huffs, her face reddening by the second.

"Why? Because they're happy? You know you can't resent everyone whose family is actually happy."

"Don't believe everything you see. Most of the lies and deceit hide beneath the surface."

And with that she storms out of the room, leaving me utterly confused.

———◇———

The next day comes faster than I'd hoped. I spend the period staring at the clock on the wall. *Almost done.* Almost time to leave this hell.

The Mr. Blake from yesterday after school is gone and replaced once more with the somber Mr. Blake. His face is stone again, and he doesn't smile. He goes about his lesson rarely looking at me, and the few times he does, I swear he hates me. His stare is so intense it makes waves of chills run up my body.

"Okay, guys. As you well know, Cranbrook has a mandatory number of community service hours you must complete every year. The school has provided a list of students to be divided into two groups." Most of the hands in the class lift. "Before you ask, no, you can't pick your group, and yes, you can petition to pick your own community service project, but that option requires weekly check-in papers." A few groans emanate around us. "Remember, colleges love good recommendations."

He pauses and pulls out a paper from his desk. "It won't be hard at all. Only a few hours a week for the next few months, and I will write you the shiniest, most kick-ass recommendation to send off with your college applications."

The whines cease. A "kick-ass" recommendation from a faculty member of Cranbrook is solid gold. As much as money can buy you into this school, withholding recommendations is the teachers' silent protest against the wealth and opulence around them.

"Okay, group one. Katie Anderson, Scott Berry . . ." I tune out as he continues to prattle on. "Gwendolyn Adams."

When I hear my name, the muscles in my back go stiff, and I jet my eyes up to meet his gaze. His eyes dark, he forces a smile. He was hoping I wasn't in this group. There is no question.

"Courtney Michaels." He continues to list the students until he is finally done. "Okay, everyone whose name I called out, please stay after class for a minute so I can tell you the incidentals. Thursday will be our first day. If you have any problems, please speak to me after class."

When the bell finally rings, there are ten of us still in the room.

"Once a week, we will meet to go to The Kids' Club on 75th and Second. We can walk together, or if for some reason you are late leaving the school, you can meet the group there at four o'clock. You are required to spend an hour there, but if you want to stay longer, even better. We will be reading to the kids." A hand from the back of the class must go up, because he points and then lifts his chin to signal whoever is raising their hand to ask their question.

"What will we be reading, Mr. Blake?" I turn my head over my shoulder and see that Scott is asking the question from the back of the room. I look back toward Mr. Blake to see how he'll respond. His eyes drift closed, then open and find mine.

"Greek myths."

I suck in a breath at the memory that invades my brain. His hands . . .

*His tongue.*

It's as if Mr. Blake can hear my thoughts, because his features harden. "The kid-friendly versions."

"Like Percy Jackson?" Someone says from the back of the classroom.

"Exactly like that, but these books were written and published for elementary school kids. When we meet after school on Thursday, I will distribute a copy to each of you before we leave, and I will hand you the name of the child you will be reading to. I'll see you all around three on the front step. If you choose to go straight to the club, I'll bring your book with me. Just let me know before the end of class on Thursday." He turns around and starts shuffling papers on his desk.

I move briskly out of the classroom. It's bad enough I have to see Mr. Blake every day in my first period class, but now I have to see him once a week after school as well. What type of fate is this?

# CHAPTER SEVEN

## Carson

Having Lynn in my class every day is starting to grate on me. I hate being the asshole, but I don't know any other way to handle this situation. It sucks that I'm forced to avoid her, and the truth is every time I see the hurt in her eyes, I want to pull her aside and tell her how truly sorry I am. Sometimes the insane notion to resign actually filters through my brain. That would be the easiest way out of this hell, plus, in truth, it'd be the right thing to do. But in the end it doesn't happen. Instead, I build walls. Walls I have no intention of letting her breach.

*Now to keep them up.*

The first test to my armor is approaching, and that's because today is finally Thursday. Today is the first day of the new volunteer program at The Kids' Club, and may officially be the worst thing that could have happened. Why did I bother to volunteer to head up this program? *You did it for the kids.* Plus, you didn't know Lynn would be in your group. But now that I know, I can't shake the feeling that this will be my demise.

A strangled groan escapes. Yep, I'm fucked. I'm having a hard enough time keeping my thoughts straight in the building; add on more temptation, and I'll be itching to get out the tension.

Coffee.

Coffee will not help, but at least it will keep me distracted.

"Well, hello, Carson," Lauren purrs at me when I enter the teacher's lounge. *Great.* Just what I need. School hasn't even been back a week, and I've already been hit on by nearly all the female staff in the building. Don't these women know? Don't shit where you eat. I'm saying this, and yet all I can think about is what color underwear Lynn wears under that skirt.

*Oh, the fucking irony.*

"Hello, Ms. Stuart."

"Oh no, Carson. Call me Lauren, like I told you yesterday." Her arm touches mine. Her fingers are rubbing too close, and I feel my back straightening. I don't like people invading my space; it puts me on edge. Strangely, I didn't feel that way with Lynn the first night we met. *Maybe it was the booze.* Maybe the beach or the stars calming me, but I can't remember anyone ever making me feel so at ease that easily. I take a step back.

"I'll remember for next time." *Not that there will be a next time.* I'm not the type to initiate small talk. In fact, I'm usually the one to end it. I move to walk out the door.

"Oh, are you leaving?"

"I was going to head back to my class and go over notes—"

"Please stay, I haven't gotten a chance to talk to you, and I would love to get to know you better."

*Shit.* "Rain check? I need to be getting back," I say, and she pouts at my words.

"Fine, but you owe me." There is a glint in her eyes and a

small smirk lines her cheek.

*No hiding what she means.*

With a few minutes to kill before my next class, I find my-self searching out someplace to be alone. Any place that's qui-et enough to think and decompress. *Air.* Could definitely use some air. With quick steps, I head toward the door leading out of the building. When I'm about to turn the corner, the sound of approaching footsteps has me halting my own steps, but as the chattering noise grows closer, I hear a voice that has my muscles tensing. It's Lynn and a few other voices I can't place.

Impatiently, I wait for them to pass. Everything inside me feels so rigid, I might snap in half. Time stands still as I wait for her to come in focus, and once she does, a heaviness grows and spreads through my chest. But I can't pull my gaze away. Instead, I watch as one foot steps in front of the other and it leaves me wondering, *Will she look at me?* An odd sense of dis-appointment weaves its way through me when she purposely looks down to the ground, so as not to catch my eyes. But that movement is her undoing, because just as she attempts to look anywhere but at me is the exact moment she missteps and her body rushes forward, about to hit the linoleum. Time seems to slow as I instinctively reach out to catch her, then pull her to-ward me and hold her in my arms.

Her chest rises and falls with each inhale of air. My own quickens.

"Damn, Mr. Blake. Look at you acting like a superhero," her blonde friend laughs. "Will you catch me if I fall?"

The other girl with them—a short brunette—lets out her own giggle, but my eyes are still locked on Lynn, who's safely enclosed in my arms. Her cheeks pale and then she blushes.

"Are you okay?" I grit out, hating how good she feels, how

natural it is to hold her and hating myself even more for thinking this way.

"Yeah." She pushes off me and stands. "I'm fine." Then without another word, she grabs the blonde by her hand and pulls her down the hall, the brunette following closely behind. What the hell was that, and why did my treacherous body have to respond?

———

Hours later and we're finally heading out for the day. Since I held her in my arms earlier, my brain has been working on sensory overload. Like a beacon, everything inside me hums with Lynn's proximity to me. It's strange. Sure, we got on well enough at the beach—okay, more than well. It was fantastic, but still, this incredible need for her that courses through my body, I don't understand it. In the two days since school started, Lynn Adams has been on my mind constantly. To be completely honest, since she left me on the beach she's all I think about, *and it isn't just the sex.*

I shouldn't get excited to see her in class. I shouldn't get excited at the idea of reading her future papers to discover what's going on beneath the surface, and I definitely shouldn't be interested in what she thinks about me. But I am. And that's the scary part.

This is why I have to avoid her.

This is why I can't speak to her.

It's too difficult to keep Lynn out, and in truth I don't want to.

I want to talk to her.

I want someone who listens. Lynn always listens . . . and she hears more than the words I speak.

Her presence in my life is dangerous and this is why having her in my class, and thus having her in my group, is not a good idea.

This is why I have to keep my resolve and shut her out.

# CHAPTER EIGHT

Lynn

ONCE WE STEP INSIDE THE VAST SPACE OF THE KIDS' Club, we're divided into small groups by the age of the children, and then divided off again. I'm assigned a little boy named Toby.

From across the room, I hear the sound of the door creaking open. The scratching of the metal hinges makes my back straighten as I wait for the children to arrive. It sounds like a stampede of animals as they flood into the room. The stomping of their feet hitting the wood floor has me nervous to meet the child I will be reading to for the semester. As they get closer and sit at tables set up against the window, their footsteps stop but chatter and giggles still fills the space. And then I see him. His arm is resting on the shoulder of a little boy who's so small and frail, it's almost as if Mr. Blake is holding him up. As the students greet the other children, I sit back and watch. Mr. Blake's gaze meets mine, and he nods his head at the boy, indicating to me that this is Toby. This is the little boy I have been assigned.

Toby halts his steps, and all the oxygen leaves my body as Mr. Blake gets down on his knee to face him eye to eye. I don't know what he says, but as I watch these two interact, a quick breath leaves my body. He's so different here. So relaxed. He even looks different. Lighter, playful. The tension I've noticed in his shoulders and the dark circles are now gone.

When Toby is finally brought to my table, my smile turns into a frown. His deep brown irises peek out from a mass of what should be gold curls, but instead they appear black as they are matted with dirt and grime, and he's in desperate need of a haircut. When his gaze meets mine, it's unnerving that the shadows appear to spread across his sunken cheekbones, and my heart lurches in my chest.

"Hi, Toby, I'm Lynn. I'll be reading you a story today. Would you like that?"

His expression is guarded, his small features held tight. "I guess," he mutters, and then turns his head away from me. I pull out the book and start to read, filling in the stories with my own dramatizations and adding funny voices until Toby has no choice but to smile and laugh. The sound of his giggles makes me want to cry. When we reach the end of the chapter, I see Toby fidgeting uncomfortably in his chair, his little body bouncing up and down.

"Is everything okay?" I ask.

"I have to go to the bathroom," he whispers.

"I'll just sit here."

After he leaves, I head over to where Mr. Blake is standing. He looks at me, his expression a mask of stone.

"What you do here is amazing."

A small twitch in his cheek tells me he's surprised by my comment. "Thanks. It's a great organization, and I love volunteering

53

here." His eyes brighten and it causes a smile to form on my own face.

"How long do these kids come here?"

"This location only handles kids until fifth grade."

"What happens after that?"

His eyes grow somber. "There used to be another youth center, but it shut down. They just don't have the funding to hire staff, and no one has the time to volunteer."

"It's so sad. My heart breaks for Toby. I mean, you are doing something fantastic but—"

He places his hand on my shoulder, giving it a little squeeze. "I know. Trust me, Lynn, I understand." My heart flutters at the sound of my name on his tongue. He hasn't called me Lynn since the first day of school, when he slipped. Every surface of my skin feels warm.

"Well, if you ever need help raising funds . . ."

"Thank you, but first they would have to find someone to run it, so until that happens, it's a moot point."

The whole thing is disheartening. "I have to go back to Toby, but thanks for telling me."

"You have about twenty-five more minutes. Stop by the desk before you leave," he says before sauntering back down the room to his desk.

A little while later, I hear a cough from above me and realize the rest of my time has flown by. One of the other kids is standing by the table we are sitting at and appears to be waiting for Toby so they can leave. I look up at the clock and realize I have gone over the hour.

"I'll see you next week?" Toby asks in a small voice, and I know he's really asking if I'll be back.

"Yes, Toby. I'll be reading to you for the rest of the year."

With that, a huge smile lines his face.

"Okay, bye. Thank you, Lynn," he squeaks before leaving.

I stand and stretch my arms over my head. From the corner of my eye I see Mr. Blake staring at me, and I realize we're the only two people left in the room. He waves me over, and with slow steps I make my way to him.

"You did great today. I'm impressed with how you handled the responsibility."

"Thank you."

"Do you want to sit?"

"I-I really should be going."

"That's fine." He nods. "I'll see you tomorrow. Again, thank you."

The walk home is effortless. My feet carry me, with muscle memory as I think about the children's center and *Carson* . . . or, well, Mr. Blake. I don't even know what to call him anymore. Seeing him there, watching him with those children, makes this complicated man even more complex. I need to know him. I want to know him. By the time I arrive home, a huge smile lines my face, and when I open the door, it spreads further. The brownstone is quiet and clean, and I thank every star in the sky that it's empty. My mood from earlier this week is looking up, and I don't want my mom ruining it.

---

I'd like to say Mr. Blake has gotten better in class, but alas, the little interaction we had at The Kids' Club was short lived. It's still the same bullshit at school. He doesn't even acknowledge my presence. It's ridiculous that he doesn't, especially since I've spent every night reading the material. When he asks the next question, I raise my hand in the air frantically like a child who is dying to be picked in gym class. His gaze sweeps across all the students, locking on me briefly . . .

And then passes right over me.

Trying to get noticed by him is useless. It's not that I want him to pay attention to me per se. It's simply that I don't want to feel dismissed, and that's how this is starting to feel.

By the time class ends, I'm so ready to head out of there that I don't even wait for him to finish talking before I pop up from my chair. Luckily, the bell rings at the same time so I can't get yelled at.

Without a backward glance, I leave.

---

*One week later . . .*

Thursday: only one more day until the weekend, *thank God.* I'm so ready for the week to be over. I just need to get through community service today, and then tomorrow will be smooth sailing.

When I open the door and head into the rec room, my gaze locks with his. Is he happy? Angry? There's something different in the way he looks at me here. It's almost as if it pains him to look at me, but not out of anger or malice. I don't get it. In school, he barely sees me. Why is it different here? His eyes find me more often and he doesn't turn away as abruptly. I feel this strange sensation that something is lingering in the air. It's like the facade he shows the world melts away and it's just him and me at the beach again. *Wishful thinking.* I shake it off, pulling my gaze away from his, and find Toby, waving at me from a table at the far side of the room.

"Hey, Toby," I say as I take a seat, and the smile he gives me is infectious.

"You came."

"Of course I came. I told you I would."

His little face scrunches up, and his eyes go glassy. "I just . . ." he starts and then stops.

A part of my heart lurches in my chest. "I promise you, if I say I'll be here, I will." I smile. "So, what story do you want to read next?"

"The flying horse story." He bounces eagerly in his chair. His excitement warms my heart.

"Which one?" I flip the pages, looking for the story he's describing.

"You know . . ." He pulls out the picture book and flips through the pages. "This one." He turns the page to show me and my heart stops. Perseus. I shouldn't look, but I can't help it. My head turns toward Mr. Blake. Everything from that night rushes back to me.

The story.

The stars.

The little kisses he placed on my body, and the way his hands traced the curves of my skin, drawing out a delicious torture. And how finally, underneath the stars, underneath the myths, he made me feel . . . *special.*

My cheeks feel warm as our eyes meet from across the room. His gaze is harsh, but then something flashes against his rigid features. A crack in the armor he wears. I wonder if he knows what I'm thinking about. I wonder if he remembers, too. I wonder if he wishes things were different.

As I reminisce about our tryst, he furrows his brow, his eyes growing darker. Then his gaze snaps away from mine, shutting me out and placing that last stone in the wall separating us. I feel cold and confused. *What did I do? Why does he hate me?*

Turning back to Toby, I issue a huge, albeit fake, smile. I make him think I'm okay. This boy has been dealt a bad enough hand, and no way will I let him down. We read the story together, taking turns on each page. When he gets stuck I help him, and the little smiles and giggles he awards me makes the uncomfortable feeling worth it. After the hour passes and we are done he leaves, but not before throwing his arms around my shoulders and giving me a giant hug.

Moving to stand, I resist the urge to search for Mr. Blake. It's nearly impossible. I exhale a giant sigh and the air around me rushes through my system. I'm so happy that I don't have to do this again for a week. As much as I can make it through the tedious forty-five minutes of his looks in school, this is too much.

Once all the children are gone, the Cranbrook students proceed to gather their stuff together. The sound of papers rustling is followed by a cough.

"Hey, everyone. Can I have your attention, please?"

The room goes quiet.

"I just wanted to say, great job today. For some of these kids, there is no consistency in their life at all. As I am sure you can tell, some of the children are finally starting to come around. They are trusting you will be back." His gaze meets mine, and he gives me a reassuring smile. "Others are a little slower to warm up, but when they do it will be the most rewarding experience of your life. Trust me." With one last smile, he moves back to the table he's sitting at and gathers his own papers. As soon as all the volunteers are gone, I make my way over to him.

He looks up at me, his eyes widening in surprise. "Lynn. I

mean Miss Adams." He assesses me with a small incline of his head. "Is there something I can help you with?"

"Mr. Blake, I just wanted to tell you . . . I really like being here."

"Thanks. It means a lot to me that you feel that way." From the look in his eyes, I know he means what he's saying. A deep sigh reverberates from his lips and fills the space between us, passing through his lips with familiarity that reminds me of our time on the beach. "Do you want to sit down?" His gaze skates over to the chair sitting across from him. Even though we have spoken alone, this moment seems different.

I nod and lower my bag to the floor and take a seat. "You mentioned that you picked this charity. It's really special. Do you mind telling me how you got involved with it?"

"Well, as you know I'm a Cranbrook Prep alumni, so I had to do community service hours, too. Most of the students lied about it, hence the reason we need proof now." A smile tips at his lips, and my own mouth can't help but spread as well.

"Wow, really?"

"You'd be surprised the crazy stories people make up to not have to do community service."

"Crazy, but I guess I know people like that. They'd rather party."

"I don't think it's that black and white. Many of the people here are performing a mandated service. Their heart's not in it. They're just looking for their "sentence" to be up, and then they go back to the way they were. Others have good intentions and then life happens. But at the end of the day, no matter what the story is, these kids deserve better. They deserve to know they can rely on us. That they have us."

Listening to him speak, and the passion in his voice, gives

me a new respect for this man. In awe, I watch him for a beat. This is *Carson*. This is the man from the beach. The one who regaled me with stories and spoke with conviction. This isn't the man at school. A new and unexpected warmth rushes through me. No. This is so much more. This is a new Carson. A Carson I want to know. *I need to know.*

He stands. "I should be heading back to the school. I have papers to grade tonight."

"Do you mind . . . " I swallow and he meets my gaze. There's a spark of some indefinable emotion in the crystal blue of his eyes. He watches me with interest and I feel the need to blink to break up the pull he has over me. "Do you mind if I walk back with you? My place is right down the road," I stammer. Instead of being met with indifference, his lips tip up into a small smile.

Soft.

Kind.

Warm.

"No, of course not," he finally says and I let out the air in my lungs I don't even know I'm holding.

He pauses to let me pass, and then steps ahead to hold the door open for me. He's so unlike all the boys who go to Prep. But that makes sense, as he's not a boy at all.

"Thank you," I say as I move through the entrance of the building and out onto the street. Together we fall into step. Even though there is space separating us, he's shortening his gait to keep us on course, and for some reason it warms me to him.

I like this.

He's a different man.

From the corner of my vision, I notice his hands are securely tucked in the pockets of his pants. Looking further up, his brow is set into a straight line as if he's uncomfortable in the silence that has descended as we wait to across Third Avenue. He impatiently shifts his weight back and forth on the balls of his feet, and I decide to break the tension.

"Is this your first year teaching?"

"Yeah, not exactly what I planned but still a good fall back. How's your senior year going so far? Other than my class." He laughs and the sound makes me smile. The comfort I feel isn't forced. There's an energy coursing between us. It's tangible and runs through every muscle in my body, warming me. I wonder if he feels it too?

"It's good. Although I will tell you I don't at all look forward to fifth period with Mr. Anderson."

"Yeah, he's a tough one. Plus, calculus sucks. If you need help learning how to deal with him, let me know." As we continue to make our way down the sidewalk, a giant pothole is etched away in the pavement. Stepping back, he places his hand on the small of my back to guide me out of harm's way. The contact causes my skin to prick with goose bumps. Turning up to him, I catch his stare. There's something different in the way he looks at me. It's as if a veil is lifted and he actually sees me. They smolder with a fire I haven't seen since that first night. We stay locked in each other for a beat before he pulls his gaze away and I pass.

When we finally reach the corner of Fifth, the location in which our paths deviate, we halt our steps.

"Okay, I'm off that way. I'll see you tomorrow." He hesitates as though he wants to say more, but no words leave his mouth. We are both at a standstill. Neither of us wants to take the first step, yet neither of us is ready to stay. Finally, he makes the decision for us, slowly turning and walking in the opposite direction.

I miss him already.

# CHAPTER NINE

## Lynn

*Five days later . . .*

TUESDAY MORNING FINDS ME IN A BETTER MOOD. FIRST period is no longer a drag. Carson has been calling on me in class, and there is no feeling of awkwardness. Sometimes it's actually pleasant.

Stepping inside, I hurry to the front and grab my seat. Even though we've been getting along, the idea of being late and pissing him off scares the heck out of me.

I pull out my papers and then lift my gaze to the front of the classroom. Carson is staring at me, and a small quirk in his cheek shows me he's trying not to smile. The thought makes my heart hammer in my chest. I feel as if we've hit a turning point and the idea invigorates me. My own lips spread in a smile. The intensity of his gaze sharpens, setting off an inferno inside me as warmth spreads against my cheeks.

When all the students are seated, he proceeds to talk about

the rise of Spain and England during the 1700s, and I'm intrigued. Carson is so intense. Passionate. With my eyes open to the different sides of him, I now see the version of him that's not so closed off. The version he shows his kids at the center.

He drifts down the aisle, handing back the papers we had to complete over the weekend from our reading. The paper turned out to be fairly easy, but from the groans that emanated through the class last Friday, you would have thought it was a twenty-page dissertation rather than a brief explanation of one important similarity between the goals of the Spanish and the English in establishing colonies in the Americas. When he reaches my desk, I lift my hand to seize the sheet and our hands touch. Our fingers meet. The rough pad of his thumb draws a small circle on my palm as he pulls away. Then he moves to the next chair without a backward glance. I look away, stare at the ceiling, and will myself to breathe normally again. But the pounding of my heart shows no sign of slowing as it beats frantically in my chest.

Did that just happen?

Or did I imagine it?

I read the notes he marked on my paper. *Great Job* is all it says. I'm a little upset, but was I really expecting him to write something more to single me out? I guess I was expecting something more since . . . since *what*? Just because he's been different at the center doesn't mean he'll be different at school. I raise my chin to look at him, and, as if he has a beacon, he lifts his gaze at the same time. As if we are tethered together by an invisible thread. His lips tip up and give me a smile that tells me, in fact, I really did do a great job and he recognized it.

My cheeks warm. There's a frenzy of sparks igniting beneath my skin, and I quickly drop my gaze back to my paper.

"This Thursday after school I have scheduled a private viewing for the kids at the planetarium. This is a school-sanctioned trip. It is required to attend as part of your community service project. We will be meeting at four o'clock at The Kids' Club and then heading over to the Hayden Planetarium. Please have a permission slip signed prior to the trip. I'll leave them on my desk." His eyes dart to me, and I know he's wondering if my mom will be around to sign it. *Probably not.* Technically, since I'm eighteen, I could fight it, but forging her signature will be easier.

His eyes are dark, his brow furrowed, and he looks pained, even angry. The same look was present in his stare on the beach when we spoke of our parents. With a shake of the head, he turns back to the lesson.

---

The next day passes, and before I know it, the bell to ninth period is ringing on Thursday afternoon, signaling the end of class, the end of the day. It's time to head over to meet the kids. Warm September air drifts against my face as I walk. It's almost October already, but the heat still lingers from the summer, making the trek quite pleasant.

When I arrive I'm met with a large group of students gathered in front of the center; no kids yet. From the looks on all the girls' faces it seems every one of them is waiting on bated breath to see our teacher. No surprise there. With his brooding good looks, it's obvious why they are drawn to him. The boys seem completely vexed about having to wait, obviously eager for this to be over with. When Mr. Blake finally does arrive, he seems a bit frazzled. The group of kids is with him and he's holding Toby's hand. He greets us, and each child finds their buddy. When they arrive at my side, he smiles down at me and Toby takes my hand. Together we follow him down the street to where a small private van is waiting to take us to the Museum of Natural History.

Once we enter the impressive structure, we head to the planetarium and I wait for everyone to sit before I choose a location for me and Toby . . . one that has an empty chair situated next to it. Carson is still standing and I wonder if he'll sit next to me. He catches me staring. Air lodges in my throat as he scans the room. My heart pounds frantically in my chest. Will he reject me? I know it's not rejection, more like self-preservation, but I can't help feeling this is a battle—and the pivotal moment. This will show me where he falls in the sand. With one last glance, his chest heaves slowly as a deep breath escapes and he saunters over to me, or rather to the chair. He doesn't even bother looking at me as he sits.

The lights dim and the video starts.

With my head tilted up to the sky, I watch the screen illuminate with lights . . . stars. The room is eerily quiet as the presentation begins. The only sound comes from the speakers overhead as the commentator details the constellations forming above us. But even though words echo through the vast space, all I hear is *him*. I can hear him breathing. I can smell his cologne wafting through the air. It's too much. His presence is too much. An all-consuming urge to reach out and touch him weaves its way through me. I lay my arm on the armrest. It feels like lead, heavy yet begging me to cross the invisible divide.

I am hyper aware of each of his movements, willing him to cross over. Willing him to move. Willing him to do anything that signals he wants me. That he feels the same way I feel about him. That this is more than one night of sex. The rustle of his shirt makes me pull in a deep breath. He settles his arm on the armrest.

In. Out.

Breathe.

In. Out.

Breathe.

In.

And then it happens.

And I can't breathe.

I can't move.

His pinky touches mine.

Like a whisper, but there it is. *Touching mine.*

I try to concentrate on the sky, I do. But all I can envision is his touch. My hand trembles as I close the gap between us. A soft feather-like caress against my skin apprises me that now our hands are completely touching. A thrill runs through me, time slows between breaths, between wishes, and then I feel it. The slow trailing of circles on the top of my skin. It sends a wave of chills down my body. Making me desperate to have his hands all over me.

It's sweet agony. Exquisite torture.

In the faint distance, amongst the heavy pants of my breath I hear one word. One singular word . . .

*Cassiopeia*

I look up and turn my head to see him. It is almost impossible to see anything in the darkness of the room, but I swear I can see his eyes. And I'm certain they are trained on me. And I wonder if he is as desperate as I am. Desperate for more. Without words, he answers my question as he takes my hand in his, enclosing me in its warmth. He gives me a squeeze, and I know he is. I know he does.

With that, an audible sigh of contentment escapes and I look back to the ceiling, back to the stars, and know that my wish has come true.

When the presentation is over, I stand with Toby and usher him across the room to leave. From the corner of my vision, I catch Carson staring at me. There is an expression in his eyes that sets me ablaze, and then he makes my heart stop when his lips tip up into a mouth-watering smirk.

Carson Blake is as affected by me as I am of him. This isn't an illusion. I didn't imagine this. We both feel it. We both want this. It should scare me, but it doesn't.

Instead, I can finally breathe.

# CHAPTER TEN

Carson

S*HIT.*
 *Shit.*
 *Shit.*

*What the hell was that?* The lines have been blurring these last few weeks, and I need to rein it in.

But I can't.

*How can I?*

In school it's easier to maintain distance, to separate myself, to regulate my thoughts and keep my walls up. But with the kids . . .

Seeing her with Toby . . . Every goddamn wall I've created is gone. Eradicated. They don't just come down. It's like a god-damn bomb blew them to pieces. I don't even know how to re-build them. My fists clench. *Breathe, goddamn it!*

My muscles twitch as anger courses through me. *Why does she have to be my student?* She gets me. Blood pounds through my veins. I want to hit something. I need to.

*Thump*

My heart thunders like a freight train veering off course, ready to crash and explode. Where are my damn shoes? I rip off my shirt. My pants follow. Throwing on shorts and a white T-shirt, I make my way to the foyer and pull on my sneakers. I'm out the door before I do something stupid.

Like punch a hole through my wall.

It feels as if every muscle in my back is corded as I hit the pavement a few minutes later. I don't even remember the elevator ride. The adrenaline weaving its way through me blinds me to everything but my torment.

*Thud*

My feet hit the cement. I'm so damn confused. *Why does she have to be my student?*

*Thud*

My breathing picks up. *Why can't I stop thinking about her?*

*Thud*

The wind crashes against my face, burning me to the point of pain. *Why does she make me feel so much?*

*Thud*

With each stride I take, my muscles become increasingly fluid. My erratic breathing regulates to the proper beat for my pace.

*Thud*

The world around me fades away.

It's just me and the sounds of the city. No tension. No confusion. My gaze tilts up as I enter the pathway through the park. The stars are suddenly illuminating the night sky. And I see it.

*Cassiopeia.*

As the hum of the city traffic fades into the distance, I'm transported back to that night with her. Her face in the moonlight. The warm, smooth touch of her skin on mine. The comfort I found in her body.

Everything I felt. Why am I trying to fight it? *Why should I?*

And although I know there are a million reasons why I should fight it . . . Right here, right now, not one of them matter.

Because under the bright stars in the sky that remind me of her, I can no longer find it in me to care.

# CHAPTER ELEVEN

## Lynn

FTER OUR INTERACTION AT THE PLANETARIUM, I wonder if things will be strange at school, but he seems back to normal. Not cold, but not overly friendly, either. It leaves me confused, unsure how to proceed or act in front of him. It's as if darkness has descended over me and I'm fighting to see the light that shows me which direction I'm to go in.

"Miss Adams, will you stay after class for a second? I have a question about the assignment that was due today."

"My assignment?"

*That's weird, I hadn't even handed it to him yet.* But maybe that's what he wants to discuss. Or he wants to talk about the planetarium? Not that anything happened other than our hands touching. *Did someone see us?* We should probably be more careful. Or maybe he wants to discuss the beach again? Or maybe—

Oh God, I could drive myself crazy wondering what this

man wants to talk about.

I nod at him and throw open my notebook in an attempt to appear to be working. Maybe it's not such a good idea for us to be speaking after class. I should walk right out of the classroom when the bell rings, avoiding him like the plague. Instead, I find myself waiting with bated breath. Finally, it goes off and I move to stand. Carson is beside my desk. *How did he get there so fast?*

"What are you doing tonight?" he whispers in a small voice as the students filter out into the hall.

What am I doing tonight? *Is he serious?* "Um . . . nothing?" I say awkwardly, knowing full well we should not be having this conversation at school.

A smile starts to form on his lips, but I notice his cheeks suck in. "No homework?" He quirks his brow up.

"Nope."

"What about the work you owe me?"

"Work?" I feign ignorance and a small quirk in his cheek tells me he's enjoying the banter.

"You know, the assignment I wrote on the board, Lynn?" My first name slips off his tongue like a soft caress to my skin. It lingers in the air like a private song for my ears alone.

"You put an assignment on the board?" I raise my hand to my chest in a mock act of shock.

He raises an eyebrow, but it doesn't hide the glimmer in his eyes.

"Oh . . . that assignment." When I bat my eyelashes at him, a chuckle escapes. Like this, he looks so young, like the Carson I considered a peer.

"You didn't think I would notice it wasn't in the bunch?"

"No, I knew you would, I just hoped it would be a little later in the day, after I finished it at lunch and I could pretend that I forgot to put it on your desk."

"Very well. How about we say you have it to me by three?" His silky voice holds a challenge as his blue eyes pierce the distance between us.

"It will be on your desk by three o'clock."

"Great. Now, that we have that out of the way, I want to show you something."

"Um, sure," I say half in anticipation, half in dread as to what he wants to show me. I cross my arms in front of my chest and wait for him to say something.

"It will have to be after school. Tonight." He shoots me a penetrating look. "Meet me."

My mouth drops open, and my eyes blink in bewilderment. *He wants to meet me, but why?* I'm so confused by this turn of events I can't muster a complete sentence. I settle for a mere, "Okay . . ."

"Now go, or you'll be late for your next class."

I turn and leave, more confused than when I started. *First, we touch at the planetarium, and now he wants to meet me?* Tonight can't come soon enough.

———

I'm walking to my locker to grab my coat at the end of the day, when I notice a small envelope tucked inside the slot. Pulling it out, my heart jumps at the idea that this could be from Carson.

*Meet me at 945 East 5th. Tell the doorman your name and take the elevator to the top floor.*

That's it. No more information. The top floor? Was I going to his apartment? The thought thrills me until realization has my happiness crumbling. Even if I wanted more, there was little chance it could ever be. He's my teacher. It doesn't matter that I met him before. It doesn't matter that I'm of age. He would lose his job, if not worse. Fate is cruel.

I run my hands down my face, willing myself to pull it together. The truth is, I'll take whatever I can get. If this is all we can ever be, I'm more than happy to oblige.

I head home and freshen up, trying my best to be prepared for anything. Soon, I find myself entering a high-rise on the corner of 70th and Fifth. This is prime Fifth Avenue property, a beautiful location, and I wonder just how much I don't know about Carson. Carson Blake is a puzzle, and every bit of information I find leads me one step closer to solving him. Once I'm inside the lobby, a young man in a morning coat and tie greets me.

"Hi, I'm Gwendolyn Adams, or maybe he put me under Lynn, I'm here to see . . ." I trail off. *Carson or should I call him Mr. Blake?* My cheeks burn until I'm sure my face must be crimson.

"Mr. Blake wanted me to tell you to head on up. Once you reach the top floor, go down the hall and to the door marked exit. There will be a flight of stairs leading to the roof deck."

"Thank you."

*The roof deck?* Why does he want me on the roof deck?

When I reach the top floor, I swing open the exit door and the air leaves my lungs like a soft, gentle breeze. There, in the middle of the deck, is a giant telescope, and crouched next to it is Carson. The whole scene laid out in front of me causes butterflies to swarm in my belly and takes my breath away at the same time.

His gaze lifts and our eyes meet. Against the shadows of the night, the soft glow of the moon shimmers in his blue eyes. They penetrate me. They are vivid and intense; they make me hope. They make me wish. They remind me of the stars he watches, little flecks of bright light in my life.

As he unfolds his body to stand, his muscles flex beneath his gray thermal. He is an Adonis among men, like all the myths and tales he likes to weave.

"Hey." The one word passes from his lips, sending a ripple of excitement and longing through my body. I step closer to him. The faint scent of his cologne drifts through the air. Masculine and fresh. An undertone of salt is present, and it transports me to another time, another place. It's intoxicating. It makes me feel anything is possible.

"Hi."

Our bodies are almost touching. The urge to reach out and feel the heat from his body is a heady sensation that I must shake away.

"What is this?" I ask.

"This is what I wanted to show you." His steady gaze implores me to trust him. To let him show me this. To experience this with him.

He moves to the side and ushers me forward. His hand slides softly down my spine, and the intimacy is unnerving. He must feel my body quivering at the sensation because he pulls his hand away once I'm standing before the eyepiece. "Show me what?" My chest rises and falls, hyper aware of how close we are. My body hums with currents of electricity as his soft breath fans my cheek. I pull away; he aligns his face with the telescope and starts adjusting it.

"There." Taking a step back, he points into the dark horizon. "Do you see those stars? A bit above the buildings?"

"No," I whisper, afraid if I speak louder he will hear the

tremble in my voice.

"It's hard to see with the naked eye. If you squint it will be easier, but with this," He pats the device. "you'll see everything. That's why I brought you here tonight. There are no clouds, just a bit of light from the moon, and this close to the park there aren't many building lights. Okay, so see . . . Here." He repositions my body. His movements are solid and strong, with just enough force and possession to make my heart drum frantically in my chest.

"Yeah, like that . . . There. That's the constellation Capricornus. It's typically one of the dimmest constellations, but in September it's the brightest." Lightly, he fingers a loose tendril of hair lying on my cheek. It's so soft, I wonder if I'm imagining it, but then the rough pad of his thumb trails against my skin.

"Why are you showing me this?" I whisper, still unsure why I'm here. Of what is going on between us.

"Capricorn is your zodiac sign. I saw it on your file and I didn't want you to miss it. It's really only visible in September."

*He looked at my file and thought to show me this?* The last little resistance between us melts. I pull away from the telescope and look back up to the sky. "They're so far away, it's almost like they aren't really there."

"But they are. That's the crazy part about stars. No matter where we are, they're always there, no matter what."

Looking over at him, I incline my head.

"Which is your favorite?"

Carson turns his head toward the sky and points.

"Polaris. Better known as the North Star." His voice is silky smooth. It makes my heart flutter wildly in my chest.

"How come?"

He lowers his head and glances over to me. His steady gaze

travels over my face until I'm staring into his familiar crystal blue eyes. "Because you can always trust it to guide you home."

His words say so much more than he lets on, and my knees nearly give way beneath me as I wait for him to say something more. But he doesn't say anything. Instead, he cups my jaw in his hand and tilts my face up. With his hands on my skin, a strange feeling weaves its way through me; a feeling of being alive.

*Please kiss me.*

And then he does.

His kiss feels like a confession of his need and desire for me. I surrender to it. To him. His tongue sweeps into my mouth. His movements are slow at first, and then deepen. Each stroke pulls me further into the dream. But then I'm ripped away and the illusion fades.

His eyes are troubled. "I don't know what I'm doing. I don't know how to resist you, how to not succumb to you. How to say no—"

I lift my hand. Stopping him. "Please don't say no to this. Don't regret this. I can't bear to hear it." *Not after that kiss.*

"I don't regret it."

All the oxygen in my lungs expels as my lips tip into the biggest smile. A weight lifts from my shoulders, and as I get back into position in front of the telescope, I don't think anything could make this night more perfect.

It isn't a surprise to me when Carson lays out a blanket on the roof deck and the two of us lie down, hand in hand. We lie perfectly still under a dazzling sky. Under stars so brilliant and captivating they hold us prisoner, unable to speak. They capture every thought and transfix me completely. Soon Carson lifts his hand and points into the heavens.

"There are some fantastic stories that have their own

constellations. I can't wait to show them all to you," Carson says with so much conviction that I know he means it. He'll show me every one.

"Which ones can you see now?" I ask, sitting up and balancing my weight on my elbows behind me.

"Over there. It's hard to see now as it's typically gone by end of September, but if you look really carefully, you can see Sagittarius." I squint my eyes, and even though the stars are very dim, a shape is present amongst the darkness cloaking us from above. "This constellation is protected by Artemis."

"Artemis?"

"She was the goddess of the hunt. That amongst other more interesting things." Turning my head to him, a glint of humor crosses his face as he smirks at me. My eyes widen.

"What else?" I plead eagerly.

"Virginity." He laughs and pulls me close to him, and takes my mouth again with his. "I wonder." *Kiss.* "What she would think of this?" *Kiss.* He doesn't let me answer. Instead, he devours me, kissing me with abandon under a starry night sky.

Hours later the whole night plays over and over again like a record on repeat. A favorite song that you never want to stop.

*All we did was kiss*

But those kisses meant everything. He told me he wanted to take it slow. That he wanted to get to know me before we became intimate again.

The night was perfect.

Each kiss was perfect.

As I lie in bed, I replay every last one until my eyes finally drift closed. And for the first time in a long time I'm excited to see what tomorrow will bring.

# CHAPTER TWELVE

## Carson

LAST NIGHT WAS NOT WHAT I EXPECTED BUT MORE THAN I deserved. I knew what inviting her over would lead to, but never did I imagine the night would go so perfectly. That it would mean so much. That's the thing with Lynn—even a mundane evening is so much *more*. When I speak, she listens, but more than that, she cares. She understands. She gets me. As much as I know we are treading in difficult waters, I can't stop the feelings she evokes within me.

I crave it. *Crave her like she's a drug.* My own personal brand, custom made only for me. And even though it's dangerous in school, I still seek her out. I still need my fix. Like a junkie, I watch and there she is . . . walking down the hall, her hips swaying from side to side. She's coming toward me, but she doesn't see me. As she passes, I grab her arm and tug her into the alcove where I am hiding. *Well, maybe not hiding.*

"Oh, my God," she cries. "What are you doing?"

"This." I place my mouth over hers. My tongue sweeps

between her parted lips. She tastes of something sweet. Maybe strawberries? She puts her arms around my neck and deepens the kiss. Her lush body presses against me, making me want more than I can have in the hallway of the school.

I pull away, regret coursing through my blood. I shouldn't have started this, not when I can't finish it.

"What was that?" she asks, and I know I'm a complete dick. Even I'm getting whiplash from my mood swings.

"I couldn't help it. You make me crazy."

"I do?"

"Yes," I grit as if sandpaper is on my tongue; almost hating her for the way my body craves her. If it were left up to me, I would slam her against the wall, lift her skirt, and have her right here and now. But this location isn't safe. The evidence of our tryst is written all over my face, all over my body. If we were to see anyone, they wouldn't have to think too hard to make assumptions.

"You have to go."

"But—"

"Go."

"I don't understand," she whispers, and I feel like the biggest ass.

"Lynn, I want you. Right here. Right now. So you have to go."

Her eyes widen as she straightens her skirt, flattens her top and runs her fingers through her tousled hair. Without another word, she scurries off and I wait a beat to follow, hoping the raging erection I have isn't obvious. As I step from the alcove and back into the hallway, I spot Lauren looking at me, and her eyes widen a fraction. I give her a nod, not a friendly one, but it doesn't stop her from walking up to me.

"Looks like a student has a crush." She laughs.

*Fuck.*

Lifting my brow, I do my best to appear confused. "What?"

"Miss Adams," she clarifies.

"Oh, really? I hadn't noticed." I purposefully raise my shoulder for emphasis. "I need to be going. Good speaking to you." The muscles in my back feel tense as I walk to my classroom. I could snap like a twig at anything. That was close. *Too close.* I need to run, but I can't right now, so I clench my fists over and over again to the point of pain. When my heartbeat returns to normal, I can't help but laugh.

This is going to be a long fucking day. Hell, the way this shit is going, this is going to be a long fucking year.

# CHAPTER THIRTEEN

Lynn

THURSDAY CAME AND WENT. TOBY WAS EXCITED TO SEE me again, and keeping my hands off Carson was no small feat but somehow we endured.

With a few minutes to spare before class, I decide to step into the back hallway of the school by one of the doors. I lift up my phone and try my dad again. We might not see each other often, but we have always spoken on the phone. For a time, our relationship was very strained. It was the worst when they were going through their divorce. I never knew what I did, but it was as if it pained him to even look at me. He didn't petition the court for custody, or even joint custody. Once it was finally over, he started to come around. We spoke every few weeks, but then last year around my eighteenth birthday he started to regress.

The phone rings. I take in a deep breath and will him to answer.

"Hello." His voice is low. Distant.

"Hi, Dad." There's a pause on the line. I can hear him

breathing but he doesn't say anything. "I called you a few weeks ago." It comes out with a lot more bite then I want, but truth is, he never called me back and I'm upset.

"I'm sorry. Yes, I did get your message." He doesn't say anything else and I want to scream through the phone. I want to demand he be my father. I want to cry that I need him, but instead, I inhale.

"Why haven't you called me, Dad? I feel like . . . I—"

"I've been busy," he says before I finish my previous sentence. Tears well in my eyes. I swipe a drop of moisture that trails down my cheek.

"I just wanted to know if I could see you."

"I'm going out of town this week. Plus, I doubt your mom would allow it."

"What does Mom have to do with anything?" I'm confused. This is how it's been ever since I turned eighteen and I don't get it. Why is he being so cold, and why would Mom care? Sure, she despises him, but she always allowed me to see him.

"With the child support done now that you're eighteen, I'd be surprised if she wants you to have anything to do with me."

"But what does that—"

"Listen, Lynn, there are some things going on with your mom and I. Money issues. She's angry that child support stopped but you're still living with her. I wish I could tell you more, but I can't. Besides, my next appointment is here. I have to go." Before I can even say good-bye, the line goes quiet.

My body shakes with the sobs I want to expel but won't let come. As I turn the corner, I run straight into a hard body.

"Lynn, are you all right?" His voice penetrates me, calming me, soothing me. "Come with me," he whispers into my ear as I take a series of choppy inhales. He pulls me along the hall and

leads me into a vacant classroom. My body shakes uncontrollably and he pulls me into his arms. "Shh. I got you." I let it all out,
each pained sob. Torrents of tears expel and he holds me. His
embrace is tight. He takes the burden off me.

"I got you," he whispers as he peppers soft kisses against
my hair, and I believe him. When the tears finally halt, he pulls
back. The concern in his eyes is evident; a fine line forms between his brows. "What happened?"

I move away from him and pull myself together. As I'm
opening my mouth to tell him about the call, the five-minute
warning bell rings through the air. "Fuck," I murmur instead.

"You don't need to rush if you need more time."

I shake my head, deciding I'd rather go to class then relive
the phone call again. "No. I'll be fine." I turn toward the door
and look back over my shoulder. "Thank you, Carson."

He nods at me and I step back into the hallway, needing to
get away from everything. I hurry down the hall until I make
it to where I know Bridget's next class is, scanning the area in
front of me until I finally see her.

"Bridge," I call out from across the hall. She halts and turns
to me.

"What's up?"

I pick up my pace and reach her with labored breath. "I was
looking for you."

"Oh really? Everything cool?"

"Yeah. I just need a distraction."

She arches an eyebrow at me. "Is everything okay? Did something happen?"

"Yes. No. I just—I just need to do something."

"Are you talking now? Like cut out of school early, or can
you make it until three and we can go somewhere after school?"

"I can make it." It's hard being here today, but if I make a big deal and leave early, she'll want the details about what happened. Honestly, she'll want to know details regardless, but this way maybe I can skirt the issue.

"Meet me outside around three. From there we can head to my place, then over to the weekly party at Coop's place." Since the first week of school, Coop's place has been the Friday night hot spot. Surprisingly enough, I don't dread going so much today.

"Cool. Thanks, Bridge."

"What are besties for?" She winks, giving me a salute before heading off in the other direction, leaving me standing in the hall. The bell is about to ring, so I pick up my pace. I make it a point to walk on the far side of the hall from Carson's class. I need to avoid the temptation of peeking in. After the kiss, some distance today might do me some good.

---

When three o'clock comes, I find Bridget standing on the top step of the stairs waiting for me.

"I'm starved," she exclaims. No hello.

"Good to know." I laugh. "So, I take it you want to grab food?"

"No shit, Sherlock, but where to go?"

"Serendipity?"

"I like the way you think, girl. Cab, walk?"

"Well, how hungry are you? At this time of day, it will actually take longer to cab it." I smirk.

"True."

We walk down the steps and once on the sidewalk we fall

into step with one another. She bitches about Mason, who apparently is now her "new boyfriend," and I stay silent about whatever Carson is. By the time we get there, she's in full-fledged rant mode.

"I think he cheated on me."

The desire to clarify that I didn't even know they were dating forms in my throat, but instead, I bite it back. The more I consider the fact she's dating Mason, I really want to blurt out that it doesn't surprise me, that his asshole best friend is a cheater, too. I try to bite my tongue, I really do. "Birds of a feather," I finally say. *Yeah, I couldn't help myself.*

"Right. You are so right. I should have known when you found Matt with his dick in some other girl, there'd be a good chance Mason would do it to me, too."

"Before you get all nuts, how about you present the evidence." I pull the door open and we walk over to the hostess.

"Two, please."

"Lunch or dessert?" she asks from behind the stand.

I look over to Bridget and she puckers her lips and then says, "Both. My boyfriend is cheating." All I can do is shake my head. Only Bridget would tell the hostess her boyfriend is cheating. *God, I love this girl.*

The hostess' jaw drops. "Oh."

*Awkward much.*

"I'll . . . Follow me."

I pull Bridget along and we follow the hostess to a little wrought iron table. "Here are your menus. A waitress should be with you in a minute."

Once seated, we start looking at our options. When a short brunette comes over, Bridget doesn't even wait for her to speak before chiming right in with our order.

"Okay, frozen hot chocolate, foot long hot dog, chili fries?" She turns to me and all I can do is roll my eyes before I laugh.

"Wow, girl. Binge eating?"

"What part of *I think he cheated* did you not understand?"

"Okay, one, you have been dating for like a minute, so how is it even possible he cheated on you, and two . . . You know what? Why don't you tell me what happened?"

"One, he never answers the phone. Two, when he did finally answer I heard a girl in the background. Three, there was a picture of him on Facebook all chummy with a girl."

"Did you confront him?"

"He's in college. What am I supposed to say? I don't want to be that immature high school girl, you know?"

"Yeah, I get it." And I totally do. Maybe it isn't exactly the same thing, but when I'm alone with Carson, I try my hardest to not act like I'm only eighteen.

She emits a loud groan, almost in defeat. "I guess I'll ask him. I am being pretty crazy."

"You think?" The sarcasm drips from my voice, but for added effect I purse my lips and raise my eyebrows.

A boisterous laugh escapes her. "Okay, fine, a lot crazy, but in my defense it's that time of the month."

"TMI much?"

"Oh, shut it, you love me." She blows me a kiss and I can't help but laugh. This is exactly what I needed today after my phone call with my dad. "So, enough about me, what's going on with you? Why are you pissy today? Bad day at school?"

"Not really." How do I tell her I'm upset about my dad, confused about my relationship with my teacher, and just a hot mess in general? There's so much hanging over me, I barely feel I can breathe. "No, things are fine. I'm just annoyed in general over school." Her eyes narrow.

"There's something else . . ."

"I called my dad," I finally admit in a whisper.

Her face instantly grows more somber and she reaches her hands to grasp mine. "Still no headway on that? He still acting weird?"

"No. And yes. But what can I do?" I shrug, hoping the conversation is dropped.

"And there's nothing else?"

"Nope."

*God, it feels so wrong to lie to her.* Like I'm a fraud. If she only knew how on point she is. There is something else going on, but with him being my teacher, I don't know how to broach the topic. A sick feeling weaves its way through my blood. God, how I wish Carson was just another guy in our school and I could tell her everything.

"Come on. There's something else." I shake my head no. "Lynn, I'm not stupid. Whatever is going on, you can tell me. I won't judge you. You're like a sister to me. Honestly, I like you more than my sister, so you're like a sister I would actually choose. Nothing you say will make me think less about you, okay?"

"Okay."

"When you're ready."

"When I'm ready. Promise."

---

After eating our food, we head over to her apartment building, dropping our bags inside before we head up to the blow bar one block over. Afterward, we return to raid her closet for the "perfect weekend party attire." The idea has me wanting to run out of the apartment and pretend I never agreed to it.

"Oh, you have to try this on." Bridget throws a dress at me. I catch it in my right hand and lift it up to examine.

"No way."

"Why the hell not?"

"Um, have you seen it? This is not a dress, it's lingerie."

"Hardly."

"I cannot wear this in public."

"Are you kidding me right now?"

"I can't."

"Can you at least try it on for me?" I roll my eyes and turn to walk toward the bathroom.

"Where are you going?"

"To change."

"You can do it here, you know. We're both girls," she deadpans.

"Hell, no. You're perfect. No way am I getting naked in front of you." Yep. No way am I letting Miss Perfect see me naked. The only person I want to see me naked is Carson.

I shake my head. Nothing good will come from that line of thought.

I look at myself in the mirror and I gasp. This dress is scandalous; it makes me feel and look sexier than I thought possible, but it's completely inappropriate for a party full of horny teens. This dress is for a date with a man who knows what to do with it, *someone like Carson.* No one can see me like this, not unless they're planning to fuck me in it. That's the only thing this dress is appropriate for, and I certainly have no intention of "getting any" at tonight's party.

"What's taking you so long? Come out."

"No," I say through the door.

"Get your ass out here right now or I'm breaking down the door, biatch."

With unsteady hands, I grab at the knob, but it swings open and Bridget is standing in front of me. My arms cross my waist protectively to cover myself.

"Girl, don't cover up. You look hot. Oh, my God. Your body looks smoking."

"I can't wear this."

"You *have* to wear this. I'm not talking to you if you don't. Like ever again." Normally, I might fight harder about not going, but truth is it could do me some good. I need a breather. A distraction.

I roll my eyes. "Fine."

"Don't look so glum. You really do look hot, Lynn. Listen, I know you are not looking for hookups or a boyfriend after what M—"

If she only knew *who* I want to hook up with. I shake my head and raise my hand. "We are not talking about Matt tonight. Let's get dressed and get this over with." The bitterness in my tone rises like bile into my mouth.

Surprisingly though, as Bridget does my makeup, I find myself relaxing. Smiling, and by the time she applies my eyeliner, I need to keep blotting the tears collecting from my laughter. This is exactly what I need. An hour later, when it's finally time to leave, I'm actually excited to spend time with my best friend at a high school party.

As we step out of the elevator, I'm met with a full-length mirror running down the wall. I square my shoulders. The outfit is fine.

I am fine.

Everything is fine.

This night will be great.

———— ⌒ ————

The party is loud and chaotic, and a mixture of cigarette smoke and marijuana lingers in the air. Bodies are everywhere. Across the room, a group surrounds a glass table, one leaning over it with a rolled up bill in their hand. I haven't even been here five minutes and I already need to leave.

"Bridge!" Mason shouts and leans over, planting a wet kiss on her mouth. He pulls away and then heads over to where the bar is set up to grab her a drink.

"Oh, my God, Lynn, I didn't know he would be here. Maybe I was wrong. Maybe he's not cheating on me, and I was just being crazy as usual."

"See. I'm sure that's it. Just you being nuts again." I wink at her and she giggles.

"I wonder who he came with? Or if he's alone."

Matt. *Shit, is Matt here?* The room starts closing in. The idea of seeing him makes my stomach turn. I don't miss or care about him. If anything I hate him, and after our last run-in in East Hampton, I have no interest in ever speaking to that asshole again.

"Lynn, sweetie, I'm sure he's not here." My face must have given me away.

"Who's not here?" Mason asks as he swings his arm around her. "I missed you, babe."

She lets out a giggle. "Cut it out, Mase. You'll mess up my hair." She peers up at him. "She's nervous Matt's here."

"Nah, at least not yet."

"Not yet?" *Shit.*

"Yeah, he had a break from class, so he decided to drive down and hang for a bit."

"And he's coming to a Cranbrook Prep party?" Bridget scrunches her nose.

"Well, *I'm* here."

"That's true, and I'm so happy you are."

"Exactly how happy are you?" he asks as he nibbles at her neck.

"I'll show you later," she whispers under her breath.

*I need to get out of here.* I look around at the throng of people. She'll never know I left. Just need to give it a few more minutes. I think back to the last party I snuck away from. God, how I wish I was at the beach again. The memories are vivid. How one night could be so awful and then turn perfect is beyond me. I grab the vodka sitting on the counter and take a swig. As the liquid caresses my throat my tension loosens, but even with my more relaxed attitude, I know I have to leave before Matt shows up.

"What up, Lynn?" Lifting my gaze, I see Lindsey from school shouting at me from across the room. I can barely hear her words over the loud beat of the music. The bass echoes and shakes the room. I head over to her, leaving Bridget and Mason still flirting with each other. When I'm close enough, she throws her arms around me and pulls me into a giant bear hug.

"Bitch, I missed you. We have no classes together. It sucks we don't even have lunch period at the same time."

"I know, it blows. But isn't it an unwritten rule we can't talk about school at a party?"

"Hell yeah, it is," Bridget says from behind me, throwing her arm around my shoulders. "Linds, what's the good word?"

"Oh, just catching up with Lynn. I'm not lucky enough to see her during the day."

"Yeah, she sucks. She has an extra history class instead of taking an easy art class with us."

"Oh, shit. You're in Mr. Blake's class?" she asks.

I don't think I can even form the word to say yes, afraid my voice will betray me, so I nod.

"Lucky girl, right? But word around town is he's a dick," Bridget exclaims.

"Yeah, I can totally see it, like a hot, smoldering eyes dick. Not that I have a problem with that. He's hot as fuck."

"He's not a dick," I defend. "He's just . . . I don't know, mis-understood. At The Kids Club, he's different." Bridget raises her eyebrow at me, assessing my change of opinion over the last few weeks.

"Cheers to the hot misunderstood teacher," Bridget says, and the two take a drink. "Dude, where's your drink?" she asks me.

"I'm good."

"Hells to the no. Get this girl a drink. Someone get this girl something!" she hollers. As if the alcohol gods were listening, a fresh glass that I imagine is filled with vodka is placed in my hand.

"Bottoms up," Bridget says, putting her glass up to her mouth, and I take the shot, too. The cold liquid burns on the way down, but it also works to relax me. As soon as I'm done, the glass is snatched from my hand and I'm dragged to the makeshift dance floor in the middle of the room. Moving my body with the beat of the music, the rest of my nerves fade away. It feels good to let loose.

After about an hour of dancing, I move out of the center of the room to get air, and someone grabs my arm. Looking over my shoulder, Bridget is staring at me.

"Listen, I'm going to head out of here," I yell over the music.

"Now? But the party just started."

"I'm not feeling so well."

"It's only . . ." She peeks at her phone. "Dude. It's not even ten. You can't—" Her footing slips, and Mason catches her. "Fine. Go. You're a total buzz kill anyway. Good thing I love you."

"I've been hanging with you for hours," I say, defending myself.

"Still a buzz kill." She lifts up her drink as if that will prove her point. "Just kidding, girl. I love you. Go. Feel better."

"Okay, I'll call you later. Have fun."

Taking a few more steps, my arm is yanked again and my whole body goes straight when I see who's holding me.

*Matt.*

Just looking at him gives me a bad taste in my mouth. His eyes are half shut, and the smell of booze radiates off him in waves. It makes my stomach turn over and I feel bile collecting at the back of my throat. *How did I ever find this guy attractive?*

"Youlookhot," he mumbles without even breaking up the words. My eyes roll of their own accord. He steps closer to me, his hand unwrapping and trailing down the skin of my arm instead. "Missyou so." He hiccups. "Bad. Mistake to dump you."

"But you did, and so potently, too," I lash out.

"Want you back, miss fuc—"

Forcefully I push him off me, halting his words as he stumbles to right himself. "Leave. Me. Alone."

Without another word, I head straight for the door, just needing to get out of there. As I make my way outside of the building, I consider hopping in a cab, but instead, I choose to walk. It's a straight shot down Fifth Avenue and I can use the fresh air.

A few blocks later, I see Cranbrook at the corner. I only have a few more blocks until I'm home. My feet are starting to hurt, but I push through the pain as I pass the school.

"Lynn!" someone calls out amid the sounds of the traffic.

Looking up, I see Carson walking toward me. By the time he reaches me, my heart is racing so fast I fear I might pass out.

His eyes sweep across me, taking in my attire. I watch as they darken and dilate, his lips parting. "Wow," he murmurs under his breath, so low I barely hear him.

Heat flashes across my face, down my exposed arms, and continues all the way to my toes. "Hi," I squeak as I try to cover myself.

"Um, you look . . ." His gaze flashes over to the school behind him and he clamps his mouth shut. "What are you doing walking around at this time of night looking like that?" He looks me up and down. The blue of his eyes are dark, his jaw set harshly.

My stomach drops. First Matt implies I'm only good for fucking, and now this. "Like what? Like a slut? Is that what you mean?" My shoulders slouch forward, and I wrap my arms tightly around my waist.

"Shit." He runs his hands through his hair. "I didn't mean it like that, Lynn. You look . . . Fuck." He looks around again and then pulls my arm. "Come on, I'll walk with you. Which way are you going?"

"Don't you think it's inappropriate to walk with me in the middle of the night, Mr. Blake?" I bite out in an overly sarcastic tone. He laughs, and the sound echoes around us, instantly lightening the mood.

"I'm doing my civic duty as a man. A woman as beautiful as you should never walk alone. So, where are we going?"

I expel a big puff of air. "Three more blocks."

We walk the first half block in silence.

"Where were you?" he finally asks.

"A party."

"Ah, the weekly Friday night party for Cranbrook. I remember those." His lips lift into a smirk that makes me want to melt. *Why does he have to be so damn handsome?*

"Oh, yeah, I always forget you went to Cranbrook."

"One of the reasons I was able to get a job there right out of college." His brow furrows. "They treat their alumni rather well." Small crease lines accent his face. "That, and my father is still a large supporter." There's no hiding the disdain in his voice.

"So, why were you still at school?"

"I was catching up. Didn't want to have to work this weekend." He shakes his head back and forth. "It's never-ending though—damn students." He winks as his lips turn up.

"What made you want to be a teacher?"

"I went through a rough time when I was in school. I was a real fuck up. But there was this one teacher my senior year who took me under his wing and changed my life. He helped me channel my emotions."

"How?"

"Running. Mr. O'Brian taught history, but he also coached track. For some reason he decided to help me. He saw something in me that was worth fixing, I guess. He told me to meet him at the track after school, and the rest is history. When I'm running, I lose track of everything. It's just me and the air hitting my face. All my troubles fade away with each drop of my feet, and I feel a euphoric peace."

"I understand. I'm still looking for something to give me that kind of peace. I guess the closest I get to that feeling is heading out east to our house in the Hamptons and watching the ocean."

Silence descends again as we walk the block leading up to my brownstone. Turning to the side, I gesture to the building.

"This is my stop. Thanks for keeping me company." I halt my movements and turn to face him. For some reason I'm nervous. It's like we're a couple kids after a first date, wondering if he'll kiss me while he works up the courage to make the first move. His lips tip up as if he's thinking the same thing and I bounce from foot to foot.

"My mom isn't home. Would you like . . . Do you want to come . . ." I pause and bite my lip.

"I don't think that's such a good idea right now." He doesn't break my gaze, and the words feel like daggers against my heart.

"You don't have to worry, she's out of town."

"I really shouldn't."

Disappointment floods me. I mentally chastise myself for being an idiot. It's one thing for him to kiss me, another for me to think this was more. I turn to head up the stairs, but I can't help myself. I need to see his face one more time, so with a glance over my shoulder, I say, "Good night, Carson." I take another step up without another word, but then I hear him cough and I peer back at him over my shoulder.

"You know what? Actually, yeah . . ."

My mouth drops open.

He smirks at me and takes a step up as my hand shakes to pull the keys out of my bag. We ascend the last steps to the door and then step inside.

The tension is palpable.

When we make it to the living room, I motion for him to sit. Positioning myself on the chair across from him, the room is completely void of sound. Neither of us speaks. In the distance,

I hear the steady beat of a clock.

*God, this is awkward.*

My heart pounds recklessly in my chest.

*Please say something, Carson, or this will be unbearable.*

"Lynn, where's your mom? At the beach you mentioned she's never around, and well, obviously she's not here now."

That was not what I was hoping to discuss. *At all.* "Away." I shrug.

"Yes, I can see that." He smirks and the muscles in my face loosen. "But where?"

"Honestly, I have no clue."

"How is that even possible?" His eyebrow rises, and I can tell he's actually interested to hear this, so I lean back and get comfy in the chair. *This might take awhile.*

"She's dating this new guy, trying to make him husband number four. He's got a boatload of money—obviously, or she wouldn't be with him. She goes everywhere he asks, and I'm not welcome because he doesn't like me." I lower my gaze to my knees and bite my lip. As much as this is my life, and I should be used to it by now, it still hurts.

"I understand."

My head pops up at his admission. There is so much sincerity in his voice. "Are your parents divorced too?" I want to know everything about his man.

"No, my parents are a whole different type." He bites his lower lip.

I can tell he's trying to hold back whatever is bothering him, but I want nothing more than to tear down his walls. "I know it's hard to speak about this stuff, but, um . . ." I meet his eyes. "You can talk to me if you like."

"Like you, my parents weren't around. They worked all the

time. Traveled a lot, and my age was a problem for them. I wasn't old enough to accompany them to wine and dine clients, so they left me behind. They are assholes, to be honest. My dad isn't a good person."

I nod in understanding. Although different situations, we are almost kindred spirits in our upbringing. I let out a deep breath and allow his presence to comfort me. My mom might not be here, but right now Carson is and I'll enjoy it for as long as possible. Still gazing into his eyes, I smile brightly.

"I like having you here. It feels good to be with someone who understands."

He nods his head in agreement. "I like being here, too, and yeah, it does feel good." His lips turn up and a dimple forms. As the comfortable silence stretches between us, I revel in it. Being quiet with someone is nice.

"I'm going to grab a water. Do you want anything?"

"Sure, I'd love one."

He follows me into the kitchen. He stands close, so close that I feel my heart flutter waiting for him to touch me. The mere inches separating us are too much to bear.

"So, what do you want to do?"

He smirks. "Whatever you want."

"We can watch a movie, I guess." I bite my lip, not wanting to watch a movie at all.

"Fuck taking it slow," he groans, pulling me out of my sordid thoughts. He pulls me toward him. Our bodies crash together. His mouth descends, covering mine as his tongue seeks entry and he licks at the seam of my lips. He pulls back and nips on my lower lip, prompting waves of pleasure and heat to spread across my body.

I part my lips on a gasp and he takes full advantage of this moment, thrusting his tongue into my mouth. My tongue sweeps against his and he groans. He pulls back, sucking my lower lip into his mouth. Each breath against his lips comes out in ragged bursts.

"You look incredible. I've been thinking of nothing more than being buried deep inside you since the moment I saw you." His words heat my body, making everything insides me tingle with anticipation.

My arms enclose his neck as he pulls his arms around my body and lifts me into the air. As he carries me, his hand trails circles against me.

*Drifting lower and lower.*

The feeling is intoxicating. It's as if we are under a heady trance. In this moment nothing else matters but the feeling of our bodies pressed together. I wrap my legs around his waist to get closer, burying my head in the crook of his neck and trailing my tongue to the hollow indent in his skin. I'm reckless with need, my teeth scraping against his flesh. Just as I think I can take no more, he sets me on the counter. The chill of the marble does nothing to cool the heat inside me.

He breaks the kiss and looks down at me with a heated stare. My dress is pushed high up my legs and his fingers dig at the fleshy skin of my thighs. Leaning forward, he plunders me again and a primal moan escapes his mouth as he devours me.

He pulls us even closer, and with one final sweep of his tongue, he pushes our faces apart.

"I need to taste you again. It's been too long."

His fingers trail up until he finds my panties, and then swiftly pulls them down. An audible gasp escapes me.

This is passion. Intense and utterly tantalizing.

His gaze breaks with mine and travels down my body,

landing where I need him most. With strong hands, he lifts my legs over his shoulder. He leans forward, his mouth connects to my core, and I quiver with the contact.

He starts slowly, a gentle sweeping of his tongue, and then his movements become more frenzied.

Licking.

Sucking.

Nipping.

He licks me with abandon, like a man starved and desperate for me, and the pressure of his ministrations is almost too much to bear. My body shivers and quakes. My climax is fast approaching.

"Inside me. I want you inside me."

He pulls away and rummages in his pocket.

"You don't need to use a condom." The sound of him tearing the wrapper echoes throughout the kitchen.

"I should. I've never gone bareback."

"I'm on the pill, and neither have I, but with you I want this." I see the hesitation in his eyes. I also see the desire. Each second I wait feels like an eternity until he aligns himself against my core, *bare*. Nothing separating us. With one thrust of his hips, he's fully seated. I feel so full, so completely full and sated. Having him inside me is like coming home. I welcome it. I crave it.

He pulls out, and then enters me again. "I." *Thrust!* "Need." *Thrust!* "You." *Thrust!* "Fucking perfect." He pushes in deeper, his rhythm torturing. He's not making love to me today. Not like at the beach. Tonight he's fucking me at a brutal speed.

"God, so good," he groans, and I fall into my own abyss. Nothing has ever felt more perfect in the world.

When I finally calm from my high, I look into his eyes. They are darker than usual, and lines crease the sides of them.

"Shit," he pants, pulling my bare arm toward him. Angry welts have started to form from where he held me. The skin already turning pink with Carson's fingerprints. "God, I'm sorry. Did I hurt you? I shouldn't have—*Fuck!*"

He pulls out, leaving me empty and desperate. I don't understand what just happened. One minute we were perfect and then . . .

"I'm okay." I whisper out, but Carson just shakes his head back and forth, still muttering to himself. *"I shouldn't have done that."* It's almost like he's in a trance.

Sadness floods my veins. I hate this feeling. I stand fast, missing the comfort of his body already, but I need to distance myself from this rejection. I can't handle the words coming from his mouth.

"I-I think you need to leave," I grit out and he doesn't object. No more words leave my mouth as he leaves.

# CHAPTER FOURTEEN

## Carson

**W**HAT THE FUCK IS WRONG WITH ME?
I was rough. Too rough with her. *There were bruises on her arms.* I should have been gentler. Kept myself in check. But instead I lost myself completely. Got caught up in the moment.

Is she hurt?

*Shit.*

She could be.

I thought I had a better handle on everything, but apparently not. I completely lost control.

It sucks because everything was going well. We were talking, *really* talking. It felt so good to have someone to vent to, and then I messed it up by letting my dick do the thinking.

God! And the way she threw me out . . .

I'm a fucking idiot. Who tells a girl they shouldn't have done that, when he's basically still inside her? *A prick, that's who.* What the hell is it about this girl that makes me act like a complete asshole and a pussy-whipped schoolboy at the same time?

Normally, I'm not like this. I'm not that jerk. Not that I've been acting like anything but that, though. I mean, even knowing she's my student, I still couldn't help touching her.

*That outfit . . .*

*Those legs . . .*

I was done the moment she walked past me.

Shit! Just thinking about her and I'm hard again. She makes me insane with need. I swear, I'll never get enough. If she hadn't kicked me out, I'd be begging for round two at this very moment. *God, I'm a dick.* She's probably upset at home, and me? What am I thinking about? I'm dreaming of round two. I need a run. That's the only thing that will calm my brain.

What is it about Lynn that has me so unhinged? Because that's what I am these days, *completely unhinged.*

It makes no sense. My life isn't that fucked up. But it isn't roses and sunshine either. Maybe that's what it is about her. She understands me. We've lived the same story in parallel. Children of selfish overachievers, learning to never need anyone. Adapting to fend for ourselves. Skilled at living a life of solitude.

But when I'm with her, I don't feel so alone.

Before I can stop myself, I'm turning back. I need to see her. *Can't leave it like this.* Once her brownstone door is in front of me, my knuckles are pounding on the door. It swings open and I'm caught like a deer in headlights. Lynn is standing in front of me, wearing only a small T-shirt but that isn't what makes me stop. What makes me stop is the look in her eyes. The pain I caused her. It's screaming at me through red-rimmed eyes and damp lashes. *Fuck.*

I push past the door, grab her in my arms and press my lips forcefully to her. Losing any semblance of control and lift her up against the wall. My lips press against hers hungrily, covering hers, devouring her.

"I'm sorry," I mumble through sweeps of my mouth against hers. "I don't regret it. I don't regret you. I wasn't thinking."

She answers by meeting and matching my movements, her mouth allowing my tongue entry. I want to take her here. Show her how I feel. That I do want her. But as much as I want that, it's not what she needs right now, so I push away. She twists in my arms, her body begging me not to move. As I lower her back to the floor, I pull my arms away and instead grasp her jaw.

"No, not here."

"Take me to bed." Her voice is husky with need and makes me smirk.

"As you wish." I bend at the waist and throw her over my shoulder. She giggles and squirms at my caveman attack.

*So much for not manhandling her.*

# CHAPTER FIFTEEN

## Lynn

MY EYES FLUTTER OPEN TO THE FEELING OF KISSES being peppered against my skin.

"Mmm," I moan as I wrap my arms around Carson's neck, turning my head so our lips touch. He kisses me with abandon, desperate with a passion that wakes every nerve in my body. Then he pulls away and I want to beg him to come back.

"As much as I would love to spend my day naked in bed with you, I actually have stuff to do today."

A tortured groan escapes my mouth and he laughs, placing a kiss on my lips before rising from the bed.

"Give me a second and I'll show you out."

"Nah, stay in bed, beautiful. I kept you up late last night." He smirks and it makes me melt.

"It's okay, I want to."

Standing up, Carson slowly surveys me. The left side of his lips tug upward, creating a sinful smirk. But it's his eyes that make my heart flutter. He casts a spell over me with the look he sends my way.

I'm so lost in him, that when his hand reaches forward, I'm taken aback when he places a robe in my arms.

"Thanks," I whisper, pushing down the urge to wrap myself around him and beg him not to leave. Instead, I don the robe and together we walk to the front door. We are less than an arm's length apart; the rough pads of his finger stroke my jaw and then lifts to push back a tendril of hair that has fallen forward. His hand trails up and lingers a moment against the soft skin of my lips before he pulls back and replaces his hand with his mouth. Parting my lips, I move against him.

Lingering, savoring the moment.

When we finally separate, he looks me over one last time before giving me a devastating smile, and then opening the door and leaving. As soon as it closes, my eyes flutter closed and my lips spread into a huge grin.

An hour later, my feet drag against the wood floor as I make my way to the kitchen. I swear, small hints of his cologne still linger in the air. I can't help but grin as I think of what we did in this kitchen. *I wish he were here.* My smile fades as I remember the fight, though. I wish I hadn't acted so rashly and thrown him out, but then he came back. *He came back.*

Why does this all have to be so complicated? Why can't he be just another guy? Why does he have to be someone who's forbidden to me? Is that why I'm so fascinated by him? Is it because the idea of a relationship is illicit? I shake my head at the notion. Even before I knew he was my teacher, something pulled me toward him. Something in his eyes tethered me to him. Something about him made me feel understood; was a comfort.

The front door opens, and all the muscles in my back tighten.

"Mom?" I call out and head toward the entrance. She barely registers I'm standing in front of her as she fidgets with her phone. "I didn't expect you back so soon. I thought you were still in Europe." *Thank God, Carson isn't still here.*

"I won't be here long. On my way out east to Richard's house."

"It's Saturday." She raises an eyebrow. "I just figured . . ."

"Lynn, if you're planning to lecture me about staying with you, please don't. You're eighteen years old. You can take care of yourself. When I was your age, I didn't have the luxuries you have. You should count yourself lucky. I have made a lot of sacrifices to provide—"

"Don't you mean you've married a lot of—"

"Stop right there. I will not have you disrespect me in my house. Richard's in the car and I just came to grab a few things."

"Fine. I'll just go to Bridget's for dinner. Surprise, surprise," I huff out.

My mother stops mid-step and turns to me, her eyes narrowing. They are full of anger and rage. "Why do you insist on spending time with that girl?"

"She is my best friend," I deadpan.

"You're better than those people."

"How would you know? You aren't here to be my family, so why do you care if they are?" The scowl on her face makes my blood run cold.

"I'm late, and I don't want to talk about them," she snaps back. Defensively, I step forward and cross my arms over my chest.

"What's your problem? You always say these ridiculous backhanded comments about Bridget, but you've only met her like once. You're never here, and when you are, she avoids this house like the plague because you were such a bitch to her."

"Watch your mouth."

"Why? Why should I? You don't act like my mother. Why should I respect you?" I fire back. The anger inside me is palpable. "Tell me the reason you hate Bridget."

"She comes from them." She stomps away without another word.

*She comes from them?* What the hell does that mean? They have been nothing but nice to me—amazing, in fact.

I'm planted in place, still trying to understand when my mom walks past me, heading toward the foyer to leave. She has her coat and purse, and her keys are dangling from her manicured fingers.

"Mom," I call out so we can finish this discussion before she goes, but she lifts a hand in the air.

"No. I'm not doing this again. You already made me late." She huffs past and soon the door slams shut, leaving me standing alone. A sickening feeling swirls through my empty stomach. Usually I do my best to ignore her hateful comments, but with my father's newfound indifference I'm having a hard time detaching myself from her hate. My head swims with her words, with her dismissal.

*No.*

I won't let her get to me. I don't need to stand here alone and pity myself. I'm wanted somewhere and that's exactly where I'll go. *To Bridget's.*

Later that evening, I find myself chopping cucumbers at Bridget's house.

"Mom, where's the dressing?" Bridget asks from behind the fridge door.

"Open your eyes and look. You're as bad as your father." She laughs.

"Seriously, Mom, there is *no* dressing."

Margo lets out an audible sigh before heading to the fridge and playfully pushing her daughter out of the way. A huge smile spreads across my cheeks. This is what I wish I had.

"Move over," she teases before going to work looking for it. "Really? Do I need to take you to the eye doctor? It's right here."

"What's right where?" Sam, Bridget's dad asks, as he and her sister Olivia saunter into the room. He steps up behind Margo, placing a kiss on her check.

"The dressing. She has your eyesight." Margo rolls her eyes and I can't help but laugh.

Sam turns to me and tips his chin in my direction. "She thinks I can't see, Lynn." He pulls away from his wife and inclines his chin as if he's going to whisper to me. "Little does she know, I play dumb so I don't have to help around the house." He winks.

"Nice, Sam, really nice. And what's your daughter's excuse? Better yet, what's *both* your daughters' excuses? Neither of them can see or help around the house."

"Um, hello, Mom. I *was* just helping," Bridget huffs out playfully, and my cheeks burn from grinning so hard at their banter.

"Don't bring me into this. I just got home. I haven't even been here to be 'blind,'" Olivia air quotes.

"Yeah, why are you home, anyway?" Bridget says, turning her attention to her sister.

"Because damn, is the food bad at school. And Mom's cooking . . . totally worth the drive. Plus, I missed you guys." I can't help but smile at the idea that Olivia drove almost three hours to come home for Mom's dinner. Just to be with her family.

"Well, if you're going to drive all the way here, make yourself useful," Margo teases.

This is why I come here. Because for the little time I have with the Millers, I can pretend I'm part of a *family*.

"At least I have Lynn." Margo puts her arm around me and squeezes.

I can pretend I'm part of their family.

———

Before class, I make my way to the bathroom and freshen up my face, applying a light lip-gloss that Bridget says makes my mouth look fuckable. *Perfect.* It's exactly the look I'm going for.

When I get to class, I take a seat in the front row, giving him the perfect vantage for what I have in mind. His eyes dilate every time he takes me in, and the feeling is all encompassing. No man has ever looked at me like this. It fuels everything inside me. It's powerful to feel wanted.

I uncross my legs and part my thighs as he discusses last night's reading. I'm close enough to hear him stifle a groan. I know I'm not fighting fair, but I don't care.

When the bell rings I stand, walk halfway to the door and stop, turning back to face him.

"What are you still doing here?" He tries to look stern, but the way he bites his cheek gives him away. That and the pulse in his throat leads me to believe he's anything but mad.

"I wanted to speak to you. I needed to see you."

"Don't you have class?" He raises his eyebrow, and I purse my lips seductively.

"Free period."

He runs a hand through his hair and then meets my gaze. His stare penetrates me and makes my whole body shiver. "Close the door. And Lynn . . . lock it." A shiver runs down my spine.

I continue to look at him from under hooded lids. With slow steps, I make my way to the door and close it. The adrenaline coursing through my veins is intoxicating. I'm drunk with it.

"Stop fucking me with your eyes," he growls.

I'm not sure who this man is right now, but I would be remiss to say I wasn't turned on by his authoritative tone.

"Come here," he orders.

Maybe I'm cliché, but there is something hot about a teacher *like him* bossing me around. I saunter over, making sure to swing my hips seductively. From his heated stare, I know it's working.

"Why are you torturing me? Do you think I don't want you? Do you know how hard it is to see you in class? To remember what you taste like? To remember how it felt to push inside you, to have your body wrapped around mine?"

Standing up straighter, he peers into my eyes. "Hands on the desk," he orders, and I turn, placing my hands on the desk. "Is this what you want, Miss Adams?" His hands touch my hip and he pushes me forward, my compliant body bending at the waist. "Do you want to torture me? Is that why you're here?" His fingers lift up the hem of my pleated skirt. "To torture me?"

"No," I breathe.

"Then why are you here?"

"I'm here for you to fuck me."

"*Fuck*," he hisses. His fingers skim up my thighs and land on the elastic of my thong. "You want me to fuck you?" His voice is husky, filled with lust and desire.

"Yes."

He yanks me closer to him, and the hard ridge of his erection presses against me. "Right here?" His fingers tease at the material. They dip inside the lace and like a whisper he lightly cups my core.

"God . . . Oh, God, yes." I push my hips back, forcing his finger inside me.

"I can't think straight around you." He pushes up with his finger, finding the sweet spot inside me. "I can't think of anything but having you. You've fucking bewitched me." He groans as his movements pick up pace, sending me toward my climax.

I pulse around his digits, climbing the edge at a rapid speed. My breathing becomes exhilarated and my vision becomes spotty. I'm going to come, in my classroom, on his hand, and there's nothing I can do to prolong or stop it.

I can feel it.

I can taste it.

It's all consuming.

*On and on . . .*

Until I fall.

As my breathing regulates and I return to myself, he pulls his hand away from my body. I miss the feel of his touch immediately. Looking over my shoulder, I catch a glimpse of his face and it sends a chill down my spine. His lips are puckered.

"We can't finish this here." He shakes his head. "What was I thinking? We're at school. We have to be more careful. But when I'm with you, I lose all reason. Fuck." His fist clenches and then unclenches. "We can't. Not here." He pushes his hands through his hair. "Shit. We have to keep our distance at school."

"I know." I look down at my feet. Suddenly, I feel so small. "I'm sorry. I just . . . I've never felt this way before. When I'm with you it's as though nothing else matters, no consequences."

His eyes soften and he reaches out. Then he pulls his hand back and nods. "We have to try though, okay? We have to be careful."

"Okay."

*I know he's right, but it still breaks my heart that this is the way it has to be.*

# CHAPTER SIXTEEN

## Lynn

THE LAST FEW WEEKS WERE TORTURE. COMPLETE AND utter torture.

Despite agreeing to distance ourselves at school, neither of us is playing by the rules. And even though we said we won't do this at school, I can't help but continue to provoke him here. With every day that passes, I try to entice him.

*Teasing the beast.*

I know I shouldn't, but the high I get from sending him over the edge is one I can't seem to find anywhere else.

Carson avoids being alone with me. Well, at least at school. His place is a whole different story. I often find myself at his apartment, where he shows me over and over again just how much he wants me. Here at school is the opposite. As soon as class ends, he walks out with a student, not allowing me a second alone with him. I would be lying if I said a part of me felt cut by this, but when our gazes meet I can see he's still affected by me.

After three weeks, I'm desperate. I know I see him, touch him, every night, but he's so different at school. It's like being in the shivering cold staring at the flame and knowing I can't feel the warmth. I need him. My desire is unquenchable. Today, everything inside me finally snaps. Against my better judgment, I walk back in as the last of the students leave. He doesn't notice me at first, his attention occupied in a book. When I shut the door, his head snaps up and his eyes go wide.

"Hi, Mr. Blake," I purr as I make my way to the front of his desk.

"We can't be alone together." He rises from his chair.

"Not even for a minute?" I bite my lower lip and dip forward, giving him a full view of the black lace bra I'm wearing under my half-opened button-down. *Definitely not Cranbrook approved.* "Tell me why you don't want to?"

He inhales and exhales, his chest rising and falling as he makes his way around the desk. I turn to face him.

"When I see you." He steps toward me and I back up until I hit the desk. "In your uniform, all I want to do is bend you over my desk and sink so deep inside you I don't know where I end and you begin." A moan escapes my mouth at his words.

"You can't look at me like that. Not when you are so close I can practically taste your need on my tongue." He reaches out and touches my jaw. The soft pad of his finger caresses it and trails up to my lower lip.

"What the fuck am I going to do?"

"Fuck me on your desk?" I purr.

"If only it were that simple."

His mouth tightens, and I think he might just kiss me. *God, I hope he does.* Just as he takes a step forward, the door creaks and he steps back quickly, giving us more distance.

Ms. Stuart pops her head in, and her eyes narrow as she takes us in. "Everything okay in here?"

Carson looks at me, and I see something inside him change. His eyes narrow and he rolls his shoulders, straightening his back. "Yes. Miss Adams has been having some issues with tardiness, but it won't happen again, right?"

His words cut through me. I know what he's saying. His message is coming in loud and clear.

*We can't do this here.*

*I have to stop torturing us.*

"Yes, loud and clear. This will never happen again." The words rush out as I turn my back to him.

Ms. Stuart's brow furrows. "Okay, great." She steps in and moves to the side, allowing a path for me to leave the room. As I'm almost out the door, she speaks. "Carson, would you like to go out for happy hour today?"

My heart beats erratically in my chest. It feels as if it weighs a million pounds.

*Thud.*

*Thud.*

*Thud.*

"Um . . . I can't tonight," he mutters.

"How about this weekend?"

"I'm not sure I can this weekend."

"Sunday? Come on, it will be fun. I'm not taking no for an answer. That is, unless you're . . ."

I peer over my shoulder and wait for him to answer.

*Thud.*

*Thud.*

*Thud.*

"Nope, no other plans. I would love to."

*A part of me dies.*

I run to the bathroom as the pain inside me spreads. My muscles constrict, making my chest tighten and bile collect in the back of my throat. Everything inside me tenses, and as I swing the door to the stall open, I almost don't make it before my stomach empties itself in the toilet. Once I'm done I step in front of the mirror and swipe away the tears that have collected on my cheeks. For a few long seconds I'm unable to move, but finally all my tears dry and I am able to leave the bathroom. It's not even a minute later before Bridget is walking down the hallway. Her eyes widen when she sees me.

"Hey, are you . . . okay?" There's a gentle softness in her voice as if she's afraid I'll break. Little does she know, I'm already broken.

"Um, yeah, must be something I ate. Didn't agree with me," I mumble. Her expression stills and grows serious. *She doesn't believe me.*

"Oh. Um, okay." Her brows pull tightly together. "You sure you're okay? You've been acting a little strange recently."

"Yeah, I'm fine. Listen, I've got to run." I can't stand the idea of her looking at me with pity. I walk out the door without waiting for her to reply and walk right out of the building.

My phone vibrates.

**Carson: I had no choice.**

I don't respond.

I throw my phone in my bag.

I can't be here.

I can't be near him.

*I just can't.*

# CHAPTER SEVENTEEN

## Carson

I CAN'T BELIEVE I HAVE TO HAVE DRINKS WITH THIS WOMAN.

I could clearly see how devastated Lynn was when I said yes to the invitation, but what could I do? More unmistakable than the hurt in her eyes was the speculative flash in Lauren Stuart's eyes. She could see something was up, and that was something I just couldn't have.

Standing outside the bar, I wait for Lauren to arrive. She's five minutes late and I'm already pissed that I have to be here. *This is a bad idea.* I should shoot her a text canceling, but I when we decided the location at school, we never exchanged numbers. That was probably her way of making sure I didn't back out. Checking my watch again, I notice she's now eight minutes late. *Great.* This is going to be a long night.

Just as I decide to head inside to grab a drink, I spy her crossing the street and waving. I have to hand it to her, she does look hot and I hate myself for thinking so. She's dressed in a pair of skin-tight jeans and an off-the-shoulder blouse. If this were a few months ago, I would easily be considering a way to skip right over the formalities of taking her out for a drink and thinking of a way to get her home. Instead, I'm contemplating a way to get out of here as fast as possible.

As we stride into Bar 212, I unlatch myself from Lauren's grasp and make my way to the bar. *Quick and easy.* Maybe I should just go with it. As much as I care about Lynn, the truth is, we really can't be together. I need to get over her, and Lauren might be the perfect distraction.

As we wait for our drinks to be served, I turn my attention back to Lauren. "So, how long have you been teaching at Cranbrook?" I ask, crossing my arms in front of me.

"Only a year. You're alumni, right?"

"Yeah."

"You like it so far?" She inclines her head as she speaks as if she's interested in my answer.

"It has its pros and cons."

"Such as?"

"I'm comfortable there. That's a pro, for sure."

"And con?"

"I guess the students. I grew up with kids like them, so I knew what I was getting, but it's harder when you're the teacher. I know what some of these kids are going through." My thoughts drift back to Lynn again. "I understand them, I was one of them, so I guess it can feel hard to discipline kids that remind you of yourself."

"It will get easier," she says, taking a step closer to me. "I'm happy you decided to join me. I wasn't sure if you were dating anyone." She smiles coyly. "So, are you?"

My eyes widen at her bluntness. *Am I dating anyone?* How do I even answer this? "No one in particular." The words feel bitter as they leave my lips.

"Oh, good." She lays her hand on my arm. "I'm so happy you decided to meet up with me. I know how stressful work can be, and having a drink with someone who understands is always nice. It helps to get the frustration out." She's close to me, her arm brushing against mine. My pulse picks up, a wave of conflicting emotions running through me, making my blood jerk heavily in my veins.

"What do you want?" I ask, and she steps in close, rubbing her body up against me. I know instantly what she wants. *Can I do this?*

She gives me a coy smile as she rubs her hand up my back and then down my arm. "I want *you*," she purrs in my ear. It would be so easy. So effortless for me to just not have to think. To not have to worry. *No consequences.* I shake my head at the thoughts running through my brain, but she lifts her hand anyway. "But if we're talking about drinks, I'll have another glass of Cab."

I wave over the bartender and order our drinks. Once our order is filled, I take a long sip of my scotch and then turn to face her. She's a very attractive woman, but where Lynn is soft and delicate, Lauren is well manicured. She fits the part of a Cranbrook girl better than Lynn does.

*Lynn . . .*

Why can't I get this girl off my mind? *Because apparently I'm a pussy, that's why.*

With another long swig from my glass, thoughts of Lynn recede. Lauren is rambling about something, but through the haze of my drink, I barely make out the words. What I can make out is her hand running up my thigh. My dick twitches in my pants. Evidently, it has a mind of its own and he's made his decision.

She leans in, her breath caressing my lips. But as our mouths are about to touch, it's as though a bucket of cold water rushes through my veins. She smells all wrong. She is all wrong.

*This is all wrong.*

And as much as I want to drown myself in booze and pretend it doesn't matter, the truth is that it does. Because she'll never be *her*.

# CHAPTER EIGHTEEN

## Lynn

A LOUD RACKET WAKES ME. SQUINTING, MY GAZE TRAVels to the clock on my bedside table. Two o'clock. Another loud knock emanates through the quiet. Who could possibly be at my door in the middle of the night? I wipe the sleep from my eyes as I pad across the wood floors to the front door of my brownstone.

"Yes?"

"I need to see you."

*Carson.*

I head over to the console table in the hallway and take in my appearance. I look like a train wreck. I run my hands through my hair to tame my now curled locks. Looking back at my reflection, I grimace just as I hear the pounding at the door again.

"Come on, Lynn. Let me in."

With an exasperated huff, I swing the door open. He leans against the doorframe and stumbles toward me. His eyes blaze with an emotion I can't quite place. He steps forward, his arms wrapping around my torso.

"I needed to see you."

"At two in the morning? After what you said to me?"

"I know it's late. But I needed to see you. I had to tell you I felt like I had no choice. I just—"

I pull back and take in his disheveled appearance. He's drunk and I want to be mad at him for taking her out, for pushing me away, for being cruel. But I can't. I know deep down he's trying to do the right thing.

"Shh, come on, I'm tired. Let's lie down."

Taking his hand, I lead him down the hall and into my room. Once in the bed, he wraps me in his arms.

"I needed to see you," he breathes out again. "I was out with her, but she was all wrong." His words sound hazy and slow. "Can't stand the torture of not . . ."

I peek at him and find his eyes closed. I exhale a breath of contentment and shut my eyes as well; welcoming the bliss I find only when Carson is near me. As the seconds pass, my body calms and our breaths come in tandem.

A perfect rhythm as I drift into a peaceful sleep.

# CHAPTER NINETEEN

## Carson

THE EARLY MORNING SUN PEEKS IN THROUGH THE drapes of Lynn's room, waking me from my sleep. With her body tucked to mine, I think this morning couldn't be more perfect. Other than the hangover still present in my body, I wouldn't mind waking up exactly like this for the foreseeable future. A smile spreads across my face. I might have been drunk last night and I might feel like shit this morning, but nothing could possibly be better than waking up next to her.

Glancing at the clock on the nightstand, I see it's six in the morning. I need to leave and prepare for the day. Carefully as not to wake her, I slide out of bed and stand to retrieve my phone sitting on the desk. Papers lie on the wooden surface next to it. I reach out to grab it and accidently knock a sheet onto the floor. Picking it up, I can't help but take a glimpse. It's a college application to UCLA, dated back to the beginning of the school year. *She wants to go to California?*

But that doesn't make sense. Every time we've spoken about

colleges these last few weeks, she always says she wants to go to NYU. Why hasn't she handed this in? *Why hasn't she mentioned it to me?*

*Shit.*

A thought pops into my head.

*It's me.*

She doesn't want to tell me.

Is this her dream? Is California her dream?

Am I holding her back?

The thought takes root in my psyche and spreads like wildfire.

*Shit.*

I am. Running a hand through my hair, I can't stop staring at the paper that might hold her future. *You know what you have to do?* A voice hums in my brain.

*Walk away.*

I have to end it. I have no choice. I need to step away.

*She deserves better.*

She deserves a chance at happiness, to chase her dreams.

*I can't hold her back.*

The desolation at letting her go is all-consuming. From a burning fire to ice, the two emotions wage war inside me. Eventually, as I struggle to gather my composure, the cold wins out as it pulls tightly around my heart. So tightly I've stopped breathing.

*I have to put her first. I need to let her go.*

Walking back to the bed, I nudge her shoulder to gently wake her. "Lynn." Her lids flicker open in bewilderment as she tries to understand what's happening.

"What's wrong? What time is it?" She rubs frantically at her lids to wring the sleep from her eyes. When she's fully awake, she tilts her head and looks at me. "What's wrong?" she asks again, but her body doesn't move an inch when she speaks. It's as if she's rooted to the spot.

Leaning in to her, I gently trail my finger down her features.

Touching. Memorizing the feel of her skin. Her jaw buckles tightly and I pull my hand away.

"We need to talk."

"About what?" Her mouth begins to tremble. I swallow to steady my words, to hide the emotion in my voice.

"I was wrong. I was wrong about everything. We can't do this. I realize that now. You have your life ahead of you."

"You-you're ending this with me?" she stutters, her eyes filling with unshed tears.

"Lynn, it's for the best." The words fall out of my mouth with conviction. There's no room for hesitation. My mind is already made up. "We can't keep this up. No matter how much I want this, it's not right. We need to stay away from each other." She doesn't speak and the silence stretches between us until I hear a soft, strangled sob escape her lips. "I'm sorry," I say, turning my back, needing air.

Needing space.

But most of all, needing to not see her fall apart. Because if I do, I won't be able to go through with this.

Sometimes you have to put others first, even if it hurts them to do so; that's what I just did. And even though I stand by my decision, it feels as if shrapnel is ripping a hole through my heart. A hole I'm pretty sure will never fully mend.

With no hesitation, I walk out of her room without a backward glance. Shutting the door to that part of my life.

# CHAPTER TWENTY

## Lynn

'M SLOW TO GET TO SCHOOL TODAY; MY RED-RIMMED FACE still shows the telltale signs of my early morning. I dread having to see him, but I have no choice. I need to be strong and walk in the door.

The door creaks behind me as I make my way to my seat, and the sound draws Carson's eyes up to mine. The look he gives me is vacant, unlike anything in the past, and it makes my back stiffen. I continue to stare at him and wait for a change, but when he makes no move to smile or acknowledge me, I slink down at my desk.

*So, that's how it's going to be.*

I'm lost in my thoughts during the entire class but he doesn't call me out on it. It's as though I'm completely invisible. After the bell rings to mark the end, I wait. Once every student leaves, I walk up to his desk. He doesn't look up when he speaks.

"What can I do for you, Miss Adams?"

"Oh, now I'm Miss Adams again? You end things with me

and we go back to that?"

"This is how it has to be. I'm sorry."

"But why?"

"It's for the best. Right now you have to finish school and—"

"No. I get that. You dumped me. But why are you treating me like this again? What the hell happened?" My voice echoes through the room.

His eyes dart up. "Please keep it down, okay?" he whispers.

I shake my head. "I just don't get it." His face hardens. It's as if a mask descends upon him. He's no longer my Carson. The way he looks at me is cold. Detached.

"What's there to get? We can't be together and I need to keep my distance. This is for the best." He halts his movements. "I'm going to speak to the principal about switching—"

I need to get away.

I hurry out of the classroom and down the hall.

# CHAPTER TWENTY-ONE

## Carson

I<small>T KILLED ME TO SAY WHAT</small> I <small>DID, BUT</small> I <small>HAD NO CHOICE.</small> I'<small>M</small> done giving her false hope that this can actually work.

*It can't.*

As much as it pains me to hurt Lynn, this is the only course of action I can take.

I had to let her go, but like an open, festering wound, it stings and burns.

Why does doing the right thing feel so wrong?

Pulling me from my thoughts, Lauren sashays into my room, full of confidence and one hundred percent shaking her hips to show off her assets. I want to groan. I can't deal with this now.

"Hey, Carson, I had so much fun last night."

"Yeah, me too," I respond. She smiles brightly, and I have no clue how she's buying the crap I'm selling.

"We should do it again sometime."

"Sure," I mumble, but I don't even look at her. When I do, I need to get out of here.

The week has put me on edge. Every day that passes gets harder and harder. I'm slipping into old tendencies. Getting angrier more and more, unable to calm myself as easily. It doesn't help that Lynn came to talk to me again today. I wanted to hold her. I wanted to take her pain away, but instead I gave her no solace—unsmiling, never deviating from my plan. Doesn't mean I'm not hurting too, but in order for her to have the life she deserves one of us has to be strong. That responsibility falls on me.

"Hey, Carson." I turn to see Lauren walking up behind me, as I'm about to enter my classroom. "A group of us are going out tonight."

I know where she's going with this and going out tonight is the last thing I want to do. "I've had a long day already and it's not nearly over." I knead at my temples for emphasis.

"Does this have anything to do with Miss Adams? I saw her leaving your class before. She looked ready to cry." Her eyes narrow. "Spending too much time with a student can be misread, Carson. I consider us friends and I—"

I lift my hand. "I'm not sure what you are talking about, Lauren, but maybe you're right. Maybe a drink would do me good. Let me know where you guys are going and I'll stop by."

"Oh, good. This will be fun. Maybe we—"

I look at my watch. "Oh, shit. Is that the time? I have to prepare some papers. Can you let me know where to go before the end of the day?"

"Sure."

"Bye, Lauren," I say as I look at the stack of papers sitting across the room on my desk, basically dismissing her.

Not how I want to spend my evening *at all*, but I guess Lauren has left me no choice.

# CHAPTER TWENTY-TWO

Lynn

OURS LATER, I TURN THE CORNER AFTER LEAVING MY sixth period class and see Carson speaking with Ms. Stuart. She throws her head back into a boisterous laugh as she runs her hands down his arm. Walking past them, I hear her giggle.

"I can't wait for tonight."

*What the fuck is tonight?*

As soon as the last bell of the day rings, I hightail it to Carson's classroom. He's walking toward the door to leave as I step inside.

"I know what you said last week, but what the fuck? Only hours after leaving my bed, you're with her? I know you don't want me, but still. I can't stand watching you talk and flirt. It kills me."

Grabbing my arm, he pulls me deeper into the classroom so no one can see or hear us. "She was asking about you, okay? This morning, right after I rejected her invitation to join a group for happy hour, she implied that she saw—"

"I don't care what she thinks she saw. Every time she touches you—"

"You don't care now, but if it gets back to anyone, it can ruin your chances at college, and my career."

"So, that's what it's about? Your career?"

"Yes. I mean no." He runs his hands through his hair and thinks for a minute. "It's part of the reason, yes, but I also don't want to see you get hurt."

"So, you're going out with Ms. Stuart because you don't want to see me get hurt?"

"There's a group of us."

"Same difference."

"This is the best way."

"But it *does* hurt me." My voice is soft, weak.

"I know, and it hurts me, too, but—"

I shake my head at him. "It's fine. I'll see you around."

*It isn't fine.*

I'm not fine, and I'm not sure I'll ever be, but I won't tell him that.

# CHAPTER TWENTY-THREE

## Carson

THIS IS THE LAST PLACE I WANT TO BE RIGHT NOW. THE idea of socializing with anyone, let alone a group of teachers from Cranbrook, sounds agonizing at best. Like waterboarding or some other form of medieval torture. But I'm here because I can't have Lauren second-guessing my relationship with Lynn. I'm not willing to take that chance.

*That doesn't mean I have to like it.*

Unfortunately, getting out of it isn't an option.

I tried. Lord, did I try. It's not that I don't like the staff at Cranbrook; I just really want to be alone. The thought of having a forced conversation in my current mood sounds awful. But avoiding Lauren throughout the day wasn't in the cards. She eventually found me, and once cornered, informed me we were all meeting at McDougal's for happy hour at six o'clock.

Once school finishes for the day, I don't bother to go home. Instead, I opt to work on my lesson plan to delay the inevitable. An hour and a half later when I finally walk into McDougal's,

I'm taken aback. As much as Lauren said people from work would be here, I wasn't expecting this many people. Nearly all the staff is congregating around the far end of the bar, and it looks as if they already started the party by the way they are laughing.

"Carson," Lauren exclaims when she sees me and waves me over. "We're all doing shots. Want one?"

"Sure." *Why the hell not?* The idea of taking the edge off and being carefree like everyone here is a welcome one.

She lifts her arm to the bartender and a middle-aged man inclines his head to her as he walks over.

"Another round?" he asks.

"Yeah, but this time add one more." The bartender nods and pulls out a bottle of Patron. "Don't forget, extra chilled." Lauren laughs as if this is a running joke. She turns her head back to me and smiles. "It's been a hell of a week. Is it just me or are all the kids crazy?"

I think back to the week, and Lauren is definitely right. Although I can't blame Lynn for her icy demeanor toward me, it still leaves a horrible feeling in my chest. One that hopefully a shot will help wipe away.

"You have no idea," I murmur under my breath and Lauren raises an eyebrow in question. I don't clarify, just shrug. Luckily, the bartender returns with our drinks before she can press the issue. We all make a giant show of clinking our shot glasses and saying, "cheers." The tequila burns my throat as it goes down, coating it and hopefully burying all the shit that's running through my brain.

Five shots later and a happy, faint buzz swirls through my body. Not sure if it's the drinks or the company, but suddenly I'm having the time of my life. It feels as if a huge weight is lifted off my body. I like this feeling.

I turn to Lauren. "We should do this again." Her lips part in a wide smile.

Her eyebrows rise. "Just us?" The underlying sensuality in her words is not lost on me.

*Just us.* Should I do it? Should I go out with Lauren?

This could be the exact distraction I need to get over Lynn.

"I'd like that." And as the words leave my lips, I realize I mean it.

# CHAPTER TWENTY-FOUR

Lynn

MY IMAGINATION IS WREAKING HAVOC ON ME.

I know he's out with her. *Again.* I wonder what they're doing tonight. Will he kiss her? Will he fuck her like he fucked me? Do they have a future?

*No, I won't think about that.*

My head feels as if it's splitting open. I rummage through the medicine cabinet in my bedroom with no luck. *Shit.* I step out of my room and make my way to my mom's bedroom. Hopefully, she had the decency to leave the Advil when she packed her stuff. I look in her medicine cabinet and find little orange bottles lined up, but I'm not sure what they are, so I push open more cabinets. Rip open drawers.

One pill for pain.

One pill for anxiety.

One pill because her husband left her.

One pill for the next husband who left her.

Xanax: to be taken for anxiety. If anyone is anxious, it's me.

I grab a pill, then head to my room and hope it makes tonight fade away.

I need to drown out his voice.

I need to drown out her voice.

I need to drown out all the voices.

---

The week flashed by in a haze. I'm happy it's Saturday because I can't get out of bed. It's as if there is a jackhammer in my head. Last night is a blur. Once I took the pill I no longer cared about Carson or Ms. Stuart. *Maybe my mom is on to something.* From across the bed the sound of my phone ringing burns my ears. It's hard work to grab it, but when I do, text after text comes in.

**Bridget: Morning, biatch! I'm running behind. I'll be fifteen minutes late.**

**Bridget: I hope you got my last text. I'll be there in five now.**

**Bridget: Um . . . Yeah, now I'm waiting for your sorry ass.**

**Bridget: Where are you???**

**Bridget: I'm sick of waiting. I'm hitting up shoes. If you get this text, I'm trying on Loubs ;-)**

**Bridget: You're officially rude!**

**Bridget: ARE YOU ALIVE????**

**Bridget: Well, I had a fabulous day of shopping . . . without you!**

**Bridget: We still on for our standing brunch at Moonstruck Diner tomorrow?**

**Bridget: You better be dying . . . or had your phone run over by a Mack truck and haven't had time to go the phone store because you're being held captive by a smoking hot**

**man in a mask.**

**Bridget: Standing outside Moonstruck and it's official . . . YOU SUCK!**

I hide in my bed.

*Bang!*

*Bang!*

*Bang!*

With a big exhale, I head to the door and swing it open. Bridget is standing there with her hand on her hip and a snarl on her face.

"What the hell? You still haven't answered my texts."

"I'm sick." It's not a complete lie.

She narrows her eyes and cocks her head to the side. "You don't look sick. You look like shit, but not sick."

"I just threw up."

She takes a step back. "Uh, gross."

"Yeah, it was nasty."

"TMI much."

"Sorry I didn't text you back."

"Fine, you get a pass this once. But girl, answer your texts. I was really worried. It's not like you to do that. I thought you died."

*Felt like it.* "I know. I'm sorry. I'll text you back next time, promise."

"You have to know I get nervous about you. You're all alone. What if something happened?" Her eyes soften and I know she means it. I worried her, and I feel awful and selfish, but for some reason it's not enough for me to tell her the truth.

I continue to live in my lies.

---

I didn't go to school yesterday.

Or the day before that.

Or the day before that.

Hell, I didn't even go to school today. The alcohol makes my life bearable. The pills take the edge off completely.

But even though I hid at home today, I still head over to The Kids' Club. I dread seeing Carson, but I made a commitment. When I get to the center and step inside, I'm surprised to notice that Carson's not here yet. Maybe my luck is turning around. Seeing him today might have been too much to bear.

From across the room, Toby is waving to me. Mustering my best fake smile, I head over to him. "Hey, Toby."

His lips part slightly and his cheeks become rosy. Despite that I have been coming here for the last few weeks, he's still shy around me. "Hi," he whispers.

"So, what story do you want read today?"

"Hercules." His eyes are wide and his little body bounces up and down in his chair. It warms my heart and makes me happy that I decided to push down my fear of seeing Carson.

I flip open the book. Toby leans into the table as I regale the adventures. Halfway through my tale, I hear the familiar screech of the door, and my chin lifts to watch. My chest rises and falls as it swings wide. Carson strolls in . . .

But he's not alone.

His head is turned over his shoulder as he smiles at someone. Squinting, I try to make out who he's with, but I can't see. The figure is still hidden behind the door. Time stops as I wait. I feel as though all the oxygen has left my body. Then he steps aside, and sadness coils inside me.

He's here with *her*.

He brought *her* here. To this place. *His place.*

My stomach churns uncomfortably, bile collecting in my throat. The muscles around my heart tighten, slowly breaking. He said he's not with her, but how can I believe him? Look at what Matt did. Men can't be trusted. Carson can't be trusted.

I force myself to stand. I need to say something to Toby, but I'm having trouble finding the words. I place my hand over my mouth. "I think I'm going to be sick," I finally mutter. "Have to go. So sorry."

As I push away from the desk, my chair scratches against the wood floor, and draws all eyes to me. Without another thought, I push past everyone, tears filling my eyes. I think I hear Ms. Stuart speak, but I don't care.

I'm already gone.

---

I wake up the next morning with a bit of a headache, but it fades away with a giant swig of vodka. I can barely get out of bed. *What if they're together now? What if they're holding hands in the hallway?*

I didn't answer Bridget's messages last night when she texted after I got home from the center. Today, she kept texting me again. She wouldn't stop. She mentioned she was worried about all the school I've been missing and did she need to call my mom. Once I realized she was serious, I told her I had the stomach flu and that other than throwing up nonstop, I was okay and just needed to sleep. Surprisingly, she believed me and told me she'd let me rest. Little does she know I'm drinking my sorrows away. The pain starts to recede with each touch of the bottle to my lips.

A laugh escapes as I catch a glimpse of an old family picture beside my bed. Hell, not even Mom can be worse than how I feel right now. My laughs grow until I'm in hysterics. My arm feels like lead and rubber and—

In the distance, I hear the soft hum of my phone buzzing.

*Where's my phone?*

I grab it from next to my bed.

**Unknown number: Why weren't you in class today?**

What the hell? Through heavy squinted eyes, I begin to type.

**Me: Carssoon?**

**Unknown Number: Yes.**

Oh, that's right. I erased his number from my phone last night. Saving the contact, I type in his name . . .

**Douche Face: Are you okay, Lynn?**

My belly hurts, I'm laughing so hard.

**Me: Fit asfiddle**

**Douche Face: Why weren't you in school again today? And we need to speak about what happened yesterday.**

**Me: School today? What time isit**

**Douche Face: It's 5. Are you sure you're fine?**

**Me: Why do you care, Douche Face?**

Oh, shit. Did I just type that? *Fuck.* The phone pings again and I throw it away. I don't want to see what it says. It keeps pinging, but I bury my head under the blanket and drift away. The silence and darkness blanket me like a cozy throw until there's a banging coming from my living room. With shaky legs I stumble toward the disturbing sound. *It's coming from my door.* I can barely look through the peephole, but what I see stops my heart. There he is, Mister Douche Face himself.

I swing the door open. "What are you doing here? And how did you get up?"

"Get up where?"

"The stairs."

"Lynn, there are like five stairs."

As I step back inside, I lose my footing and my arms fly forward. I brace myself on the wall. Thankfully, I don't fall head first into the floor.

"Are you drunk?" There is no hiding the annoyance and judgment in his voice.

"Nah."

"What the fuck, Lynn? Are you high?"

"I don't know what I am. Whyyouhere? Don't you have a girlfriendplay with? I'm tired," I slur out as I start to lie down on the floor.

"What are you doing?"

"Tired," I mumble again.

"Lynn . . . Fuck."

My eyelids flutter shut, and in the distance I hear his voice as I crawl into a ball.

But it all fades away as I fall asleep.

# CHAPTER TWENTY-FIVE

## Lynn

EVERYTHING IS DARK.

I can't see anything in front of me. I groan with pain as I stretch my arms overhead. My hands connect with something and the lump I hit moves.

"Fuck. That hurt."

Prying my eyes open, I move toward the voice. "Carson?"

"Who else would it be? Damn, Lynn. You have quite the left hook. That fucking hurt."

"You're here? You came?"

"I'm here." His voice softens, and for a moment I want to melt, but then I remember his rejection and Ms. Stuart.

"What are you doing here? Why are you in my bed? Don't you have somewhere else you need to be?" The light flickers on, and I squint to avoid the invasion of the harsh contrast from the dark I was recently cocooned in.

"Can you turn the light off?" I groan.

"No. We need to talk."

I slowly sit up, watching him as he paces the room.

"Is this why you haven't been in school?"

"Shh, too loud." I place my hands over my head and shut my eyes.

"Lynn, can you open your eyes?"

"No."

"Stop acting like a child," he grits out.

I pop my eyes open. "A child? Oh, is that what I am now? Why are you even here? You don't give a fuck about me."

"Believe it or not, I do care about you."

"Yeah, so much that you went on a date with Ms. Perfect. That you took her to The Kids' Club."

"Lynn, what do you want me to do? She asked me to go. She wanted to see it. Was I really supposed to tell her no? You know how badly we need volunteers."

"You could have."

"Could have what? This is a no-win situation. Don't you see that? We can't do this. We need to steer clear of each other. I care about you, Lynn, more than I should, but we have to keep our distance. We can't be together."

"Just leave. Please," I plead, my voice cracking with desperation.

He's right. I know he's right. That doesn't stop my heart from breaking, though.

# CHAPTER TWENTY-SIX

## Carson

PULLING AT MY ROOTS, A SENSE OF DREAD WASHES OVER me. Am I doing the right thing? It feels wrong, but what I have with Lynn isn't healthy, especially not for her. As much as I know this, it doesn't make me feel any better. The way our last conversion ended lingers like a dark cloud hanging over my every move—the way she begged me to leave; the pain I caused. An urge to reach out and make things right has me grabbing my phone and shooting off a text.

**Me: I'm sorry it has to be like this. It's for the best.**

The phone vibrates back, and I swipe the screen to read it.

**Lynn: Leave me alone. We are over.**

I stop in my tracks only one block from my destination; I rest my head in my hands. I remain rooted to the spot, frigid air beating against my face as I continue to read and then re-read her response. I'm not sure what I was hoping for, but her words cut into me, ripping at the little shreds still holding me together.

It's over.

We're over.

My legs buckle slightly as my hand meets the cool metal of the door. But I've already made my decision. I know what I need to do.

Get over Lynn.

*Distract myself.*

*Move the fuck on.*

The door pushes open easily, and once inside, my gaze scans the small, intimate room. It's dark . . . sexy. The walls are lined with small tables for bottle service. Everything in the place is plush. *Decadent.* Small crystal chandeliers hang from above each table. With a few drinks, this space could easily invoke desire to course through the veins of the patrons.

"Lauren."

I lean in and place a kiss on her cheek. My voice is rough, fighting my conflicting urges to either grab her and beg her body to make me forget, or just walk away. But I've made my decision. I need to get over Lynn. I need something healthy. Something that doesn't tangle me up on the inside. Something safe. I'm too broken. I'm too fucked up. Lauren is a beautiful woman, and I'd be lying if I said I wasn't attracted to her. I need to exorcise the demons lingering inside me for Lynn, and she is the perfect person.

Call me an asshole for using her, but I don't care. *I need this.* I need the distraction.

I smirk, putting up the mask I show everyone. "Seat?"

"Sure."

Placing my hand on the small of her back, I guide her to a table in the back corner. She looks over her shoulder as my hand hits the material covering her skin. She breathes lightly through parted lips. She takes the seat I pull out for her and I sit across from her with my legs wide. I lean back against the chair and watch her. Her legs cross at the knee and her skirt rises, giving me a perfect view of her thigh. A sigh escapes her mouth, her breasts pushing out as she licks her lips. She's the polar opposite of Lynn. *Sensual and sexy.* She's all woman, and although she doesn't make my heart lurch in my chest the way it does with Lynn, the ivory skin of her thighs makes it beat a little faster.

A waitress appears at the side of the table.

I incline my head. "Same as last time?" She nods, and when I order her drink, her lips part in a wide smile.

"You remembered."

"Of course."

Turning to Lauren, I recline back in my seat and lift my gaze to meet her eyes. "This is a cool place," I tilt my head to the side.

Her gaze takes in the décor around us. "It is. I love it here."

"So, you come here often? Is this your "date" spot?" Her eyes widen. "I'm just playing." I wink, and she lets out a nervous chuckle.

"I like it here because they make the greatest martini," she clarifies. I highly doubt that's the reason, but I nod in agreement. "So, we might work together, but I feel I know nothing about you, Carson." She leans in, giving me an ample view of her cleavage.

"What do you want to know?"

"Well at school, you're quiet. You don't really speak to anyone, so what do you do for fun?"

"Honestly. I'm kind of a loner." I pause for a beat as the waitress approaches and hands us our drinks.

Her eyes light up. "Oh, I'm not. I'm very social," she purrs, and there's no mistaking the innuendo in her voice.

Lifting my glass, I pretend to toast. "To being social," I say and take a swig of my vodka on the rocks. "I do run a lot."

"Oh, cool. I spin, it's my favorite. You don't do anything for fun?"

I'm not even sure how I should respond to this. I wasn't kidding when I said I was a loner. Since graduating from college, I basically stopped talking to my friends. I realized at that last party just how much I hated that shit, and there was no point in pretending I didn't.

"Seriously, I work, I run, and I volunteer."

"Well, that and go out with me." She winks.

"Yes. That, too. But other than going out with you tonight, and going for drinks for happy hour last week, I haven't gone out all year."

"Wait, really? So, what do you do after work?"

"I volunteer. I'm there every day." My back stiffens at talking about this with her. It reminds me too much of Lynn. I need to steer this conversation into safer territory. Leaning into Lauren, I place my elbows on my knees and tilt my head. "So, what about you, Lauren? What do you do for fun?"

"I spin. Play tennis. Do yoga, and I love to go out dancing."

"Any hobbies?"

"Can dancing be considered a hobby?" She laughs. "You?"

"Astronomy." Lynn's words echo through my ears. *Why constellations?*

Lauren laughs. "That's boring. Okay, tell me what you really thought about—"

She starts to talk about something funny that happened at school, and I can't help but laugh. She might not be deep. She might not want to know everything about me, but I like it. I can keep my thoughts and demons to myself. I don't need to delve deeper.

*Easy.*

We sit and laugh as she fills every lull with more chatter. I'm not drunk, not by a longshot. Just relaxed without a fucking care in the world.

*And I really like it.*

After about an hour, I grab the bill. Taking her hand, I help her up. "I had a great time, Lauren." And I did.

She lifts to her tiptoes and places her lips a fraction of an inch from mine. "I'm not ready for the night to be over." Her breath tickles my lips. "Walk me home."

It's not a question.

---

The door to her home doesn't even close before she throws her arms around me and her mouth finds mine. The kiss comes out of nowhere. Blinding me to everything but her. But this.

Her body presses against mine, and I fall into the kiss, closing my mind completely to what this means. I let it take over. I let myself become lost in her. Because this is what I need.

Easy.

Being with Lauren is easy. Simple.

No shit. No anger. No fear of being caught, or consequences, or repercussions for my actions. I just need to lose myself in the simplicity of this.

Not having to give a fuck.

Her hands weave their way through my hair then glide down my back.

I can do this.

This will make me get over Lynn.

And I need to get over her.

We can't be together.

I tighten my arms, holding on tight to the escape. This is pain-free. Meaningless fun.

This . . .

*Fuck.*

It doesn't feel right. Her lips aren't right.

I refuse to push her away. I'll make it right. I can lose myself in her.

Closing my eyes tighter, I shut out the world and all the bull-shit and just try to be here, try to be somewhere else and feel. But as tightly closed as I keep my eyes, I'm here. And as much as I try, my brain won't be fooled. This isn't Lynn.

From the corner of my mind, a sound pulls me out of my haze. It's a soft buzz. She pulls away.

"Hold that thought." She fishes her phone out of her bag. "Hello?"

Her eyes go wide, and her faces pales. "Calm down. Just breathe." She holds up her hand and mouths *sorry* to me. "It's okay. Okay. No, I'm coming over. I'll be there in a minute." She hangs up and bites her lip.

"Is everything okay?"

"My sister just found out her husband cheated on her. She's devastated."

"Go, be with your sister. She shouldn't be alone. No one should be alone when they are that upset." I was always alone, and I wouldn't wish that on anyone. But I don't say that. She doesn't know about my family. Only Lynn knows. Because Lynn knows what it's like to be alone, too.

Lynn.

She's embedded so deeply inside me, there's no chance of escape.

"I'll let myself out," I say.

She steps forward, a piece of hair falling in front of her face. From habit, I reach up to push back her hair, but I catch myself, pull my hand away, and lower it to my side. Neither of us speaks as I swing open the door and take a step toward it.

"Another time," she says, and I turn back to her.

"Hope everything is okay with your sister." I step outside, and the door shuts behind me. My breath is heavy, and my fists tighten until they turn white.

*What the fuck have I done?*

---

I didn't see her all weekend and I find myself anxious today, even worse than when she skipped. When she skipped I was concerned, but now that she's back in my class it's almost impossible to keep from doing something stupid . . . Like grabbing her in front of everyone and declaring she's mine. Or letting her know she doesn't need to be so sad, that she *has* me. But I can't. So instead of pacing in the classroom, I find myself pacing in the alcove. It reminds me of Lynn, of the kiss we shared here, and for some fucked up reason, it calms me.

Closing my eyes, I fill my lungs with oxygen and I try desperately to right my breath. As the air leaves my body, a hand lands on my shoulder. As I'm opening them, lips thrust against mine, making me shut them closed again. I get lost in the feeling, but something is wrong. *This doesn't feel right.*

Jolting my eyes open, platinum blond hair and different features come into focus and I realize I was so absorbed in my own illusion that I forgot where I was and whom I was with. This isn't Lynn. It's Lauren. This is wrong. All wrong. And the feel of Lauren's mouth on mine solidifies that Lynn is the only girl for me. I move to push her away but before I can, I hear a sharp inhale of breath echoing loudly like a freight train from behind me. Everything inside me halts, tensing to the point of pain. I don't need to turn around to know who saw us. To know who was standing behind me. It's written all over Lauren's face.

*Fuck.*

I need to go to her. But I can't. I wish I could hold her, but I won't. I need to stay the course. Pretend she's nothing to me. Convince Lauren that Lynn is nothing. Just another student.

This is for the best. I don't want to let her go. How can I? She's a bright, shining star in my otherwise dull existence. When she's around, it's as though anything is possible. There's not a second of the day that my thoughts don't drift to her. But anything I say is only a hollow promise. I refuse to lie to her, and I refuse to lie to myself. We can't be together. *At least not now.* Until the day comes that she's no longer deemed off limits, we have to tread carefully and live separate lives.

So I let her go.

"What was that about?" Lauren takes a step back at the same time as I do.

"I have no idea what you're talking about."

"Don't you?" Her eyebrow rises. She steps closer, and lifts her hand to touch me.

I grab her wrist, halting her progress. "This isn't appropriate. Us, kissing in school, is not appropriate."

"Is this about Miss Adams?"

"Why are we still talking about her? No, this has nothing to do with Miss Adams," I grit out. I'm mad at myself for sounding so brash, but the way she speaks of Lynn has me ready to break. "Listen, Lauren, you're a great girl. I have fun with you.

But right now in my life, this . . ." I motion between our bodies. "This isn't working for me, and it's not fair to lead you on."

She leans back on her heels and narrows her eyes, studying me, really looking at me. "This is because of your student," she says to herself more to me, her head shaking as she mentally puts everything together.

"I thought we just spoke about this? This has nothing to do with my students. I care about you, but not like that." Pulling my hand through my hair, I exhale harshly and wait for her rebuttal, but she bites her lips and nods once.

"I hope that's the truth, Carson." She gestures behind me to where Lynn was standing. "Because *that* would end your career." She puts her hand on mine and squeezes. "I care about you too, Carson. If anything changes, I'm here."

# CHAPTER TWENTY-SEVEN

## Lynn

EVERYTHING HURTS.

My head, my body, hell, even the hairs on my arms hurt.

For the past week of school, I have been in either a perpetual state of drunkenness or hung over; it's a vicious cycle I can't kick because whenever I try, the pain spreads and festers. I haven't done my schoolwork. I haven't paid attention, and this week I bailed on Toby. I shouldn't have, but I just couldn't muster the strength to go. What if *she* was there again? I wouldn't be able to deal.

As I trudge down the hall, I stop short. About ten feet in front of me is exactly the reason I skipped school last week. Carson is propped against the wall, and he's talking to her.

This is too much. I can't stand it. God, I wish I brought one of my mom's Xanax to school with me, but since I didn't, I turn around and head for the side door. Maybe someone outside has one. The students at this school are prescribed all types of shit.

When I step outside, I spot Bryce Matthews, the resident pill popper at Cranbrook. *Bingo.* "So, Bryce, what do you have for me today? Any Xanax?" I ask him.

"Nah, but I got this. Here," he says as he hands me his water bottle filled with clear liquid. I take a huge gulp, and then chase it with another. *That should make me not care.*

After my fourth or fifth shot, I don't care about anything. Everything is just peachy. I check my watch. *Oh, shit!* Late for class. Wonder what Mr. Jerkface Handsome will think. I bust out laughing.

Within a few minutes, I'm stumbling into class, still laughing. "Miss Adams, thank you for gracing us with your presence today."

"Oh, fuck you, Mr. Perfect." The class erupts into a fit of laughter. Did I just say that out loud? *Oh, shit.*

"Miss Adams, hall—now."

Oh, my God. I totally did. I burst into another fit of giggles.

Once in the hall, Carson turns to face me. There is no trace of emotion on his face. His eyes are vacant. *Hollow. His demeanor like ice.* It feels as if my blood drains from my body as my heart hammers erratically.

"What are you doing, Lynn? What is wrong with you?"

"What's wrong with me? What's wrong with you? You promised. You promi . . ." I trail off as the room starts to spin and bile crawls up my throat.

Then everything goes dark.

———◦———

Light filters in. My body is heavy, weighted to the couch. As my eyes open, I think I see Carson. Through the haze I open my mouth, but my words come out jumbled and confused.

"I was so . . . I scared . . . I lost you. I miss you so . . ."

"What is she talking about, Mr. Blake?" a strange voice says.

My eyes jolt open, and I'm in a strange room on an unfamiliar couch and a woman is standing next to Carson.

"Who are you?"

"Lynn, this is the school nurse. When you passed out, I didn't know if you were okay, so I called her," Carson clarifies.

"A nurse? Did I hurt myself?" My hand travels up my body looking for a wound.

"No, but you were slurring your words and then you passed out. We brought you in here until—"

"Where is she?" My mom storms into the office. "I can't believe I had to drive all the way into the city for this. Are you happy with yourself?"

*God forbid I ruin her little trip.*

I can't look at the disgust in her eyes. The hatred I know will be there. I glare back at Carson. I bite back a tear. "You-you called my mom?" I whisper, my voice catching in my throat. *Please don't cry, don't cry in front of her.*

His hands are fisted by his mouth, but it's his eyes that are almost my undoing. They look so sad, so hurt and broken. "Of course."

"How could you do that? Why do you hate me? Why are you against me?"

"I'm not against you. We're all on the same team here, Lynn."

"I could get kicked out of school. I won't be able to go to NYU if I get kicked out. I won't be able to get away from my mom if I get kicked out," I whisper.

"I won't let that happen. We-I just want you to be okay. I just want you to be happy."

"You might want that, but she doesn't." I slump back on the couch. I want to throw something, but I'm too weak. I can barely hold my head up. "How could you rat me out?" My voice is so low I'm not sure he can hear me over my mother's voice that is rising as she argues with someone on the far side of the room. When he runs his hands through his hair, tugging roughly on the roots, it's obvious he has.

"I had to tell. There needed to be a consequence to your actions. What did you expect would happen? You passed out drunk in the middle of the school. I had no choice." He bows his head and covers his face with his palm. "You can't keep acting like this. What about college?"

"I hate you," I spit out, knowing full well I'm acting like a petulant child. But I don't care. "Second, who are you to say what I need?"

Pulling his hand away, his gaze assesses me. The blue of his irises are almost completely gone, only the black of his pupils is left. He leans in close. "I'm the guy who cares about you." My eyes widen, and he pulls back to a normal distance. "Miss Adams, believe what you want, but everyone at Cranbrook Prep cares what happens to you. We all want you to be healthy, and we want you to be happy, and we want you to graduate and make something of your life."

I lean back and close my eyes, but they soon pop back open when I hear my mom's voice grow louder, followed by Principal Gordon's.

"Please, Mrs. Adams, I don't think this is a good place to discuss—" Mr. Gordon says, but my mom cuts him off, her voice shrill and impatient.

"Where, then? Because I'm running late and have places to be. This incident has already taken too much of my time."

"Please come with me."

Everyone leaves but Carson and me. I don't want to look at him, but I press past my fear and lock eyes with him. The sadness is palpable, but it doesn't stop the anger from boiling in my blood.

"Can you leave, too?" I grit out, and he nods.

"I'm here for you. However long it takes, I'm here if you need me." He looks down at me and his eyes soften.

"What makes you think I'll want to talk to you?" Tears blind my eyes and choke my voice.

"Because I have faith that once your anger fades, you'll realize I'm doing this because you mean something to me."

"I'll never forgive you." My throat constricts, filled with too much sorrow and grief to utter another word.

"I'm willing to take that chance if it means you will be happy in the future."

I sink back into the couch and close my eyes, shutting out the world around me—but not before I hear the steady tread of his footsteps hitting the floor in his retreat.

———

My feet dangle off my bed as I stare up at the ceiling. Confusion clouds my brain as I think back on everything that has transpired. An ache inside me comes and goes as if my heart is missing an integral piece of itself. Days pass and the pain ebbs and flows. I try to concentrate on something else, but with little to pass my time while I'm not allowed in school, I find it near impossible.

As usual, my mother whipped out her checkbook in an attempt to make everything disappear. But the school needed to punish me for drinking on school grounds, so they settled on three short days of suspension and mandatory counseling. Immediately after she made her endowment to the new library, she left. This time she said she was so stressed she needed to go to Canyon Ranch, so she'd hopped in her car service that was parked outside the school and went straight to the airport. Who does that? *A selfish woman, that's who.* I expected my mom to rip into me after the incident at school, but it never came. *She doesn't even care enough to lecture me.*

I can't dwell on her behavior, though. You can't change people unless they want to be changed.

———— ✎ ————

A knock reverberates through my home on day three of my suspension. I haven't left these walls since the incident last Friday, and other than a few texts from Bridget, I haven't spoken to anyone. I'm not sure who would be stopping by.

The last few days have been instrumental in putting me back on track. I've used the time to really think about what I want in life, and what I've realized is I want to graduate in the spring and start NYU as soon as possible. Even though I missed a few reading sessions at the center, Carson apparently came through for me, and gave me a glowing recommendation. I need to thank him. Most of all, I need to make it up to Toby.

I've called the admissions department at NYU and put in my early decision application for summer classes instead of starting in the fall. I also put in my request for housing. My mom's not here to bother me, but in order to get a fresh start I need to distance myself—*from everything*. Right now, I need to concentrate on me.

With brisk steps, I head to the foyer. "Yes?" I answer through the door, too lazy to look through the peephole.

"It's me. Carson."

I groan. Even though I know what he did was right, I'm still annoyed he did it. I wish he had spoken to me first and at least tried to get through to me, without getting my mother involved. I open the door and wait for him to step inside.

"What are you doing here?" I ask as I shut the door behind him. He doesn't respond right away, merely stares at me for a beat. His face is hollow, dark circles shadow his eyes, and there's a few days' worth of hair dusting his face. He's still beautiful but he looks broken.

"I wanted to talk." His hoarse whisper breaks the silence and it pains me to hear the tone. It's as if a raw and primitive grief overwhelms him. He lifts a hand and rakes it through his already unruly hair before stepping farther into the room.

"Talk? *Now* you want to talk? After you got me suspended? You know they're making me see a school counselor?"

He nods once. "What did you want me to do, Lynn?" His shoulders slump and his gaze casts downward.

"It was a dick move," I say and he brings his gaze back up, shaking his head. I gesture toward the living room. We fall into step until he's standing in front of me.

"No, Lynn, it was the *only* move. And if you're too—"

"Too what?" I slam my hands down and they ricochet off my legs.

His eyes widen. "Stubborn. If you're too stubborn to see that, then there's really nothing else for us to talk about."

My back muscles tighten at his words. I have an overwhelming desire to yell at him, but instead, I take a deep breath and calm my nerves.

*Screaming will get me nowhere.*

I sit down on the couch and lower my gaze to stare at my fingers tracing nervous circles on my thigh. "Do you even care about me? Did you ever care about me?"

"Of course I did—*do*. But what do you want me to do? I might have acted as though I didn't care, but I had no choice. I was in an unimaginable situation. You have to know that."

I ran my hands through my hair and then sighed. "I do. I do know that, but so was I."

"I know." The expression on his face is sad and unnerving. As if he's been through a war, and in truth with everything that's gone on . . . he has. "Listen, Lynn, I just want to say I'm sorry. I know you think I sold you out, and I did, but I felt I had no other choice. I was afraid of what would happen to you. You can't do this—the drinking. This won't solve anything. You are more than this."

"I know," I say, meeting his eyes. "And you were only trying to help."

Carson exhales as his body visibly relaxes. "I'm happy you're okay."

"Me too."

A small tentative smile forms across his face. "So, you're back to school on Thursday. Are you planning to transfer out of my class?"

"I think it's for the best, don't you?"

I watch his Adam's apple bob. "Yeah, I guess you're right. I'll miss seeing you there."

"Oh, bullshit." I grin. "I was always a pain in your ass."

He laughs, and little lines grow along his mouth. He looks beautiful.

"But you'll still come to the center, right?"

"I don't know if I *should,* but I know I have to. Does that make sense?"

"Yes, one hundred percent. These kids have been through enough already. They need consistency. Toby needs you. I don't know if he's opened up to you yet, but Toby's father died of a drug overdose. His mother is an addict. Everyone in his life has abandoned him." *Even me.*

My chin quivers at the thought. Toby needs me, and I need to make it up to him. "Do you think he'll forgive me?"

"Eventually. Just give him time." I remain silent, only biting my lip to stop myself from crying. "Well, I've got to go." His eyes appraise me and I sense he wants to say more but he doesn't so I bite back my emotions and say my good-bye.

"See you in school, Mr. Blake."

"See you in school, Miss Adams."

# CHAPTER TWENTY-EIGHT

## Lynn

I TAP MY PENCIL LIGHTLY ON MY NOTEBOOK AS I WAIT FOR Dr. Young to show. Meeting with the school counselor is part of the reason I didn't get suspended for longer than three days. As much as I complained at the time, I realize that meeting with him twice a week is much better than the alternative. I have no doubt if I hadn't agreed to this, there was a good chance NYU would have heard all about it on my transcripts, and I could have potentially lost my chance for acceptance.

The door creaks open, and a man steps into the room. He has salt and pepper hair and a light dusting of gray on his face. "Hello, Lynn. I'm Dr. Young, the school counselor. How are you today?" I shrug, but don't speak. He takes a seat across from me and places a notepad on his lap. "Is there anything you want to ask me before we start?"

"No."

"Well, then I'll jump right in. If you ever feel you need a minute or to stop, please let me know. So . . ." He looks down at the journal. "From what Mr. Blake and Principal Gordon have told me, you were inebriated at school?"

"Yeah."

"Is there anything else I should know?"

"I was also on Xanax," I mutter under my breath.

He scribbles something on his notepad, then sets the paper down. "Are you prescribed Xanax?"

I shake my head.

"Can I assume you took the pills from a friend?"

I don't respond.

"Maybe your mother?"

I furrow my brow.

"Okay, so you took the pills from your mother. What was going on that you felt you needed to take anti-anxiety medication?"

Looking down to the floor, different answers filter through my brain. I *can't* answer this. If I do, I will run the risk of getting Carson in trouble.

"You'll have to trust me for this to work."

"Boy problems," I state matter-of-factly, and hope he doesn't press further.

"It usually is." He gives me a lopsided smile. "So, tell me a little about yourself, Lynn. You grew up with your mom?"

"My mom and my dad—until he left. Then there was Elliot, my mom's second husband. He left, too. After him was David. Bet you can guess what happened to him," I deadpan.

"And how does this make you feel?"

My hands grasp at my skirt, and I pull at a loose thread. "I feel as though everyone keeps leaving me. I have no one," I whisper.

"You had your mother."

"I never had my mother. She was the first to leave."

"Your mom was distant?"

I scoff. "That's an understatement."

"How about we talk about your mom for a bit?"

"I don't think there is enough time to talk about her."

"Since you mentioned self-medicating, let's talk about that first. Does your mother also use coping mechanisms such as drinking or prescription drugs?"

"No, and yes. She doesn't really drink, but she is like a human pill container. She has a pill for everything."

"You were taught to handle sadness one way, but I think it would be beneficial to learn a different way to handle situations. Break the pattern. From here on out, for the foreseeable future, we have a standing date every week. Okay?"

"Okay."

For some reason, knowing I can see Dr. Young each week and he'll listen and be there for me instantly makes me feel as if a huge boulder has been lifted off my shoulders.

———

The time has come, and fear and anxiety coil in my belly. How will I say sorry? How will I make Toby understand that I didn't abandon him? What I did was selfish, but I care and I need him to see that.

He won't meet my eyes. He won't allow himself to open up. I understand. I get it. He's so similar to me, and it breaks my heart that I did this. I didn't show up. I was no better to Toby than my mom was to me.

"Toby."

He ignores me, and continues to play with a toy car on the table. The wheels screech as they turn in the silence that surrounds us.

"Toby, please look at me."

Still nothing. I move to kneel beside his chair so our heads are now at the same level. I reach out my hand and he flinches. "I'm not going to hurt you. I promise."

"You already did," he whispers.

A tear slides down my cheek. "I know I did. And I am so sorry. I understand if you don't want me to be here, but I needed to come. I need to tell you how sorry I am. It was never my intention to hurt you. I was hurting and made a mistake. I know you can't trust me right now, but please, please give me another chance. I will work to regain your trust."

He looks up at me but still says nothing.

"I understand," I say as another tear falls. "I'll be waiting right over there. If you're not ready, I understand, but I'll be here again next week and the week after that."

The time passes, and he never comes. I catch him peeking up from the desk a few times, but I know this won't be an easy fix. It's okay, I'll be back. I won't abandon him again.

# CHAPTER TWENTY-NINE

## Carson

MY FEET HIT THE PAVEMENT, EACH STRIDE RELEAS-ing the endorphins I need to get through all this shit with Lynn. Two weeks have passed since that last time we were alone together, but I still see her every fucking day in the hallways. Even though it's no longer in my classroom, it's too much.

Too fucking much.

So I run.

I make it only a few blocks when I almost trip on my own two feet. There she is, standing outside her brownstone and looking like she walked straight out of my wildest fantasy. I'd be lying if I said I didn't take this route in the hopes of "bumping" into her. Usually, I run through the park, but ever since we ceased our private interactions, I've taken up running Fifth Avenue instead.

She's no longer in her uniform. *Thank God.* But this outfit isn't much better. She's got tight ass jeans on, and boots that go all the way up to her thighs.

I shake the dirty thoughts out of my head and mentally tack on two more miles. She turns her head toward me and our eyes meet. I jog in place as she makes her way to me.

"Hi," she mutters under her breath.

"Hey."

"You do run a lot, don't you?"

"I love it. You can say running is the best thing that ever came out of Cranbrook. Well, second best." *Fuck, did I just say that?* I'm supposed to cut that shit out and give us a clean break.

"What's the best?" she asks. Unshed tears shimmer in her eyes, and my heart lurches in my chest. She's about to cry, and it's my fault.

I shouldn't answer. I shouldn't tell her she's the best thing, but her expression could bring me to my knees. "You." I watch as her mouth opens and shuts with my confession. Her lips tip up, and a small crystal drop drips down her nose.

"Please don't cry," I whisper. My finger touches her soft skin. "Please. Here." I point back to the stairs on her brownstone. She turns around, and I place my hand on the small of her back as I usher us toward the steps.

Once she lowers her body down next to mine, her shoulders fall forward. "I miss you." The quiver in her voice doesn't go unnoticed, and it etches away at the strength I'm trying to maintain.

"I miss you too. More than you know," I say with a sigh.

"You know, I see you running past my building at the same time every night."

"You do?" I take a deep breath. "Is that why you're out here tonight?"

She doesn't answer, but by the way she is biting her lip, I know it is.

"I have a confession. I changed my route. I know I'm supposed to stay away, but seeing your place makes me feel closer to you. Like you're not so far away."

"Why are you running so much? Is it because of me?" I nod. "I'm sorry," she whispers.

"It's not your fault."

"Does it help?" My eyebrows rise at her question, begging her to clarify. "Running? Does it help with the pain?"

"Yeah, it does."

"You said you started in high school, but what happened that was so bad to make you start?"

"I told you my parents were never around. They never came to any events for me. No plays, no curriculum nights. Hell, they didn't even make it to my middle school graduation. As far back as I can remember, it was always my nanny in the audience waving to me and clapping with pride. But no matter how proud my nanny was, it didn't matter because it wasn't them. All I wanted was my parents. Well, really, my mom. I hated my dad."

A muscle in my jaw twitches as I remember this part of my life. It hurts to talk about it, but I find comfort in Lynn's eyes. She understands. "This one time it was supposed to be different. They promised they would be there. She promised she would come. I even made reservations that night for us to go to dinner. I mean, what teenager has to make dinner reservations for their own birthday? Well, suffice it to say, they didn't even bother to call to say they wouldn't make it. I learned from our cleaning lady that they were still in London. For some dumb reason, I thought it would matter to *her* at least. I believed for some reason that *she* would come home—be there for me."

I suck in a sharp breath. "Back then I didn't know how to handle my feelings. I was young and angry at the world. I used to get into a ton of fights. I was one fuck up away from being expelled. The day after my birthday, some guy was in my way, and I pushed him. We were one second away from a full out fight when Mr. O'Brian stepped between us."

"What did he do?"

"He told me I needed to channel my rage and aggression. The track season was already in session, but he said he wouldn't report me to the principal if I came and trained with the team. I didn't. I got into more shit, and then he again stepped in to help me. This time, I knew I had no choice. I was pissed at first, but in the end, it was the best thing I ever did. When I'm running, everything slips away. Plus, I learned some valuable life lessons."

"What did you learn?" Her face tips up at me, her eyes filled with interest.

"I learned that sometimes things get painful, but you have to push through and just keep going. Eventually, you'll hit the finish line."

"Wow . . . So, where is he now?"

"He retired the year after I graduated."

"Fate." She smiles.

"Exactly."

We sit in silence for a few minutes. The sounds of the city are filling the void left by our unspoken words. Lynn lifts her wrist and checks her watch. I know our time is limited, and in a few seconds this moment between friends will disappear.

"I have to go study. It's getting late."

"I know." I stand and jog in place to warm up. "I'll see you around?" She nods at my question, and I take a step backward. Her mouth trembles with the distance I put between us. "This sucks, right?"

"Yeah, it does." Lynn agrees.

"You don't have to be a stranger. Just because we can't be together, doesn't mean we can't be civil. Check in once in a while."

"We can text," she suggests, and I nod in agreement. "It was good seeing you, Carson."

"You too, Lynn."

Turning my back, I hit the corner and turn toward Central Park.

Tonight, I'm going to need a longer run.

# CHAPTER THIRTY

## Lynn

THE LAST WEEK HAS BEEN TRYING. KEEPING A SMILE on my face when I want to cry has been a feat in itself. I know why Carson doesn't speak to me at school, but our interactions with one another have halted completely. Now all I get are little smiles in the halls. I had to switch out of his class for my sanity, but it still breaks my heart to see him pass without being able to talk to him. Even after school at the center, we don't speak. I still keep going no matter how hard it is. I think Toby is coming around, and the thought gives me hope for Carson, too. Yesterday, both of them kept glancing over at me, even though neither said anything. It was hard, but I made it through. Today is even harder. I see him as I walk down the corridor. He turns his head and it feels as if I'm being stabbed in the chest. A few seconds later my cell vibrates in my hand.

**Carson: I'm sorry it has to be like this.**
**Me: Me, too.**
**Carson: I missed you today.**

**Me: I miss you every day.**

**Carson: Today was the worst.**

**Me: How come?**

**Carson: I was discussing a constellation, and it made me think of that night on the beach.**

**Me: It was a pretty special night.**

**Carson: Every second I've had with you was special. I wish it didn't have to be this way.**

My heart tightens and a lone tear drips down my face. I just have to make the best of a crappy situation. Grabbing my books, I head to the library with a new resolve. No more dwelling on my relationship with him. It's time to concentrate on me.

After the library, I plop myself across the lunch table from Bridget. I can feel her eyes boring holes in me, but I can't speak yet. My mouth and brain are working at odds to determine how to say this. I need to just blurt it out, but I can't. The longer we sit, the more tension fills the air. It's suffocating.

"I-I . . ." I stutter.

"Lynn, I have told you time and time again, whatever it is, I have your back. I will not judge you."

"I had an affair with Carson," I whisper so no one around can hear.

"Carson?"

"Mr. Blake."

Her mouth drops open and I have to pull my gaze away. I can't look at her now. I feel so naked and exposed. "You. What?"

"I had an affair with—"

"Your teacher?" She cuts me off mid-sentence, her eyes huge.

"In my defense, it started before I knew he was my teacher."
*Oh shit, did I just say that?*

"Hold up. Let me get this straight. We—me and you—are

best friends? Have been for years, right?"

"Right."

"And you have been having an affair with a man, since before school started, and I didn't know about it?"

"It's not exactly like that." *God, this is bad.*

"Why don't you start from the beginning? I'm thinking that might be a good idea." She narrows her eyes and waits.

"Okay." *How do I say this?* "Before school started, remember the Labor Day party?"

"The one where Matt cheated on you?"

"Yes, ass, that one," I say, and she grimaces at the bite in my voice. Matt has been a thorn in my side this year. Remembering I was once dumb enough to date him makes me pissed.

"Sorry."

"Forgiven. Okay, so after I found him, I wanted to leave, but I saw you hitting it off with Mase and I didn't want to ruin your night."

"You totally should have," she deadpans.

"Are you guys done now?"

"Oh, dear God, yes," she exclaims. "I was such an idiot. He totally was cheating on me, but I guess, as they say, hindsight is twenty-twenty. I should have known after how Matt treated you."

"Next time I think your ex will also be a dick, I'll interrupt you, how about that?"

"Sounds great. You do that."

"Can I continue my story now?" I laugh as I shake my head.

"Oops, sorry."

"So, I decided to leave, and I found a trail that led down to the beach. While I was there, this guy happened to be as not into the party as me, and he was escaping also. We hit it off. We laughed. We drank. We swam, and then under a canopy of stars we—"

"You slut." She laughs. I'm happy that she's not angry, and I'm surprisingly happy that she finds humor in the situation.

"Yes, that happened, but then I freaked out and called your drunk ass, and we went back to my mom's. A few days later, he was my history teacher."

"No shit?"

"No shit."

"Why was he even at the party?"

"Apparently one of his friends was there and he stopped by. And apparently, like me, he couldn't handle the stupidity, so he went to the beach to have a drink and, like me, get air. Well, suffice it to say, we got to talking, and yada yada yada."

"Oh, my God, please don't skip over the good stuff." Her eyes are wide, wanting details.

"Nope, no details."

"Fine, you suck. What happened once you got back to school?" She shifts the position of her body, reclining fully into her chair, getting more comfy. "I feel like I need popcorn for this story."

I ball up a napkin and throw it at her head.

"Hey, what'd I do? This shit is about to get juicy, I can tell."

"Obviously he was as shocked to see me as I was with him. We tried to stay away from each other, Bridget, we really did. But there were all these community service activities . . . And then the planetarium."

Her eyes are huge like saucers by this point. "Oh, I remember that. You were all giddy afterward."

"Yeah, it started up around then. We ended up getting together and kissing, and then we—"

"Oh, please don't leave out the details."

"I'm so not telling you that."

"You suck. Okay, can you tell me this? Did you have sex in school?" I look away, breaking eye contact. "You skank, you did. Oh, now you have to tell me! On his desk?" I refuse to look back. "Oh, my. I need a cold shower just thinking about it. I can't even imagine. He's so stern, and his eyes. Those lips . . . Does he look like he's pissed at the world even when he's fuc—"

"Bridge . . ." I turn my head back toward her and I scowl.

"What? Oh, come on. You know I had to ask. The man looks like he needs to get laid. He's always so damn pissy. Don't get me wrong, he's got this boy next door hot-as-fuck look."

"Yes, okay. He didn't screw me in his classroom, but other stuff happened. Happy?"

"Yep, please go on."

"I am not giving you any more details. That's all you get."

A flash of humor crosses her face. "Jerk," she huffs out before she brings her hand to her mouth to stifle back a laugh.

"Ho."

"Nope, that's you." Her giggles finally escape, and I can't help but chuckle back.

"Back to my story, shit happened. There was some drama with another teacher." I reach forward and take a sip of my water. Bridget's mouth is hanging open again.

"Oh, shit. Which teacher? What happened?"

"I don't want to get into crazy details and to be honest I don't know them, but basically she forced his hand to go out with her. I can't bring myself to ask, but after he broke things off with me he went out with her. I'm not sure what happened or how often, but I can tell you I went a bit crazy. I'm not proud of my actions after that. I got insanely jealous. I started to drink. A lot. It was bad." Her face grows pale and I can tell she's working hard to keep her emotions in check.

"Why didn't you tell me? How did I not know?"

"I was embarrassed, I was hurt, and to be honest, I—you were so happy. I told you I was sick. I lied to you. I'm so sorry. I just didn't want to be a burden." She drops her lashes to hide the hurt behind her eyes, but her lips tremble as she speaks and it breaks my heart.

"How could you ever say that? You are more than a friend. You're family. You are the closest person in my life, Lynn. I could never think of you as a burden."

"I know that. I knew it then, too. I was so depressed and so ashamed, I just couldn't. For what it's worth I'm . . ." It feels like gravel is stuck in my mouth as the notion that I should have told her settles on me. If I had, she would have been there. She would have been a shoulder to cry on. Things might not have gotten so bad.

"I'm sorry. Truly."

There is nothing but compassion in her eyes, and I love her for that. "Don't do it again. No matter what, you tell me. Good or bad. I'm always here for you."

"Thanks, babe. I'm sorry I didn't tell you. I should have. I probably wouldn't have spiraled out of control if I did."

"So now what?"

"Now, I just need to get through school." I shrug. "I guess."

"Mr. Blake?"

"Oh, no, that's done. It's over. He's actually the one who got me in trouble."

"Is this why you got suspended? Do you blame him? I mean, Lynn, you did get caught. I don't know the deets, but word around town is you passed out."

"No, I don't blame him, not at all. But distance is what we need. I need to get my shit together. Whatever happened with Ms. Stuart—I didn't ask him what actually went down; I can't bear to hear it. I don't think anything more will happen there. I did see her talking to Mr. Dan. So maybe . . ." I raise my eyebrow.

"The gym teacher? He's not as hot as Carson." Amusement flickers in her eyes.

"Haha, no, but it makes my life less stressful, so I'll take it. I'll buckle down, though. Mom is impossible, as you know, so I really need to keep my grades up so I can get into NYU. It's my only option to move out." She bows her head and then looks back up to me with clarity in her eyes.

"You can always crash with me this summer." Her voice is full of conviction and I know she means it.

"I know, but your parents already do so much for me. I'm sure they'll want a break from the kid's best friend sometime."

"You know they adore you."

"Yes, but sometimes you need time with just your family. I get it. I wouldn't want to impose. I'll just kick some major ass and move into NYU early."

"I'm your family." And in truth, she really is. She's always been so much more than my best friend, and she always will be no matter what happens in the future. No matter what my mother says.

# CHAPTER THIRTY-ONE

## Lynn

DAYS, WEEKS, AND FINALLY THE MONTH PASSES, AND crisp fall days turn into gray winter nights. December looks promising as Carson and I have shifted into a good routine. Although we aren't together, I'm happy with our weird sort of relationship. It's almost as though we're friends.

One good thing that came of everything is that I really buckled down in school. The fear of getting in trouble again scared me straight. I haven't touched alcohol or pills since the "incident." My grades are phenomenal, and I'm really happy about that. Toby also finally came around, and I now find myself at The Kids' Club more often than the once a week I was originally obligated for.

The best part, though, is that my mom hasn't been around much—or at all. Apparently, Richard proposed right when she arrived at Canyon Ranch. I found out via text. I'm not surprised. Most kids would be angry over the relationship I have with her, but I no longer let it bother me. There was a time when it festered in my soul, but not anymore. Dr. Young has helped me. He showed me that there are too many other things to be excited about.

Today is one of those days. I just received an email from NYU that not only stated I got accepted, but also that I can start school early and I got space in the dorm. I'll be moving out and starting my new life in June. I can't wait to tell Carson and Bridget the news. But first I try calling my dad. He went to NYU, growing up he always told me I should go there. It rings four times before going to voicemail. Maybe he just can't answer a call. I shoot him a text.

**Me: Can you talk?**

**Dad: Sorry, I can't.**

His short answer causes my stomach to knot. I will not let his behavior ruin my mood. I've come too far for that.

**Me: Where you at?**

**Bridget: Outside.**

I leave the school building through a side door to look for her, slipping on my jean jacket before I step outside. It's not very cold, but there's definitely a chill in the air.

I don't make it more than a few feet before I'm face to face with the last person I thought I would see in the alleyway alongside Cranbrook: my asshole ex-boyfriend. He's standing with some straggly guy I recognize as a sophomore. Matt's long, muscular body is leaning against the wall, and he's puffing on a joint as his other hand rummages through his pocket and fishes out a dime bag packed with pot. The kid hands him money and then jets off in the other direction. *God fucking damn it.*

"Well, hello, Lynn." His words slide out lazily because he's high. I want nothing to do with this right now.

"Why are you here, Matt? Were you really just selling drugs

to that kid?"

"I missed you," he draws out, not even bothering to deny my accusations.

"I didn't miss you."

"That's not very nice."

I move to the left to go past him, but with each step I take, he counters to block me in. My eyes narrow and I place my hand on my hip.

"Do you mind?"

"But I miss you," he slurs. "You look smokin' today." A finger grazes the skin of my thigh under the hem of my skirt.

I taste bile in my throat. Again I move, and again, he steps to follow me. All the muscles in my neck tighten, and I have an uneasy feeling in my stomach.

"You're here looking so fine, and I'm here, and we're all alone. It can be like old times when I used to fuck you right here, against the concrete wall between classes." He steps in closer this time.

"That will never happen again." I scan the side of the building for someone passing, but the only people I see are looking to screw or get stoned, and they don't even notice I'm here.

"Oh, I think it will."

He leans in and I smell his tequila-laced breath against my face as he's about to kiss me. With small movements, I clench my fist and pull my hand back, prepared to hit him. Just as I launch my arm, he's suddenly jerked back and a fist flies through the air. Matt drops to the ground.

Carson is standing above him. "Are you okay?" he asks, as he looks me over.

"I could have handled him myself," I bite out, confused by what just happened and why Carson punched him.

"He was going to—"

"Going to what?" My voice shakes from the emotion coursing through me.

"I don't know. Fuck. He might have . . ."

My body begins to shake uncontrollably as the endorphins from the incident flood my system. "Why do you care?" Tears well in my eyes. I need to get out of here before I cry.

"God, Lynn, please don't cry right now." He moves his hand up and it connects softly with my jaw. The warm pads of his fingers caressing my skin makes my jaw rattle as I hold back my sobs. "I thought he was about to hurt you. I *know* he was. I couldn't let anything happen to you."

"Why?"

"Because . . ." He looks down at Matt, who is starting to come awake. "I just—"

A groan emanates from the ground, followed by a series of curses. "What the fuck, man? You're fucking dead. I'll have your job for this."

"I don't think so," I say, moving away from Carson and looking over at the lump still on the ground. "You tried to force yourself on me. He was defending me."

"He's a fucking teacher! He can't touch me. Plus, what the fuck? You know you wanted it."

"No, actually, I didn't."

"It's your word against mine. Let's see who the school will believe."

"Actually, it's your word—a former student who always caused trouble—against a respected teacher, who is also an alumnus of this school, and you're obviously high right now," Carson spits out, not even trying to hide the anger in his voice.

"I—" Matt starts and then clamps his mouth shut.

"That's what I thought."

# CHAPTER THIRTY-TWO

## Carson

*SHIT.*

I fucking punched a former student. Even though he's alumni, he was trespassing and he was trying to assault Lynn.

The room is quiet. Other than my footsteps pacing the space, you could hear a freaking pin drop. What's taking so long?

The door pushes open. Principal Gordon walks in with Matt.

"Carson, take a seat." He motions to offer me a seat and then turns to the piece of shit Matt and offers him the other one. After we both sit, he takes a seat behind his desk. He looks from side to side at us, obviously trying to discern what went down.

"Someone better start explaining and now."

"Hepunchedme," Matt slurs out in word long word, and I smile. Because no matter what this fuck up says, he's drunk or high, and he has no credibility.

"Look at him, he's high as a kite. He's lucky all he got was a punch. He was assaulting a student, trespassed on school grounds. We should call the cops."

Matt blanches at my comment.

"Start explaining now," Principal Gordon orders.

"I walked outside to make a phone call, and that's when I found Miss Adams pushed up against the wall against her will." I clench my fists. The need to hurt him over and over again for touching her spreads through every nerve in my body.

"That's not what—" Matt starts to say, but it seems the principal wants nothing to do with his explanation.

"Out of respect for your father, and the fact I don't want any bad publicity for our school, I'm going to let you leave. But if you ever show up on this property again, I will have you arrested, do you hear me?"

"No way. He can't get away—"

"That's enough. I don't want to hear another word from either of you. Both of you leave my office, and Carson, I'm letting you off with a warning this time. Trespassing or not, you don't lay your hands on anyone in my school, you hear me?"

We leave the room, and as we walk out the door, I hiss out under my breath so only Matt can hear, "You bother Lynn Adams again, and I'll make your life a living hell."

"Not before I ruin you," he threatens in return.

"Try your best." My body is still hopped up on adrenaline as I march my way out of the building. Fuck! Where's Lynn I need to find her, make sure she's okay? *Talk to her.* One thing became clear when I caught that douche pawing at her.

*No one touches her but me.*

I need her. I realize that now.

Fuck what happens. Fuck what anyone thinks. Fuck what's ethically correct or what's expected of me.

I'm not letting her go again.

# CHAPTER THIRTY-THREE

## Lynn

AFTER CARSON PUNCHES MATT, I HIGH TAIL IT RIGHT out of the city and straight for East Hampton. I need time to process it all, and to wrap my head around my life. It's almost too much.

The darkness hovering over the beach is so black that I can't see the ocean. Behind me the lights from the house flicker but in front of me it's bleak. I can only feel the water lapping against my feet, smell the salt in the air, and hear the waves crashing in.

If I take a step back and breathe, I can handle it. I'm a survivor. I can endure it all. With a deep inhale, I let it all out: the animosity, the fear, everything from the past few months. I look around me with new eyes. The beach looks as if no time has passed since the last time I was here. But that's not true.

A lifetime has passed.

And so much has changed.

I hear a cough behind me, and look up to see Carson standing there. The moonlight sparkles off his eyes. There's a softness in them. They are mesmerizing.

"Hi." My voice is low and unsure. "Why are you here?"

"I wanted to make sure you were okay." His gaze sweeps over me, assessing my wellbeing.

"You came all the way out to East Hampton?"

"I would follow you anywhere, Lynn," he comments as if the answer is obvious.

I pinch the bridge of my nose. "How did you know I would be here?"

"You once told me, the beach in the Hamptons is where you think best, but I would be lying if I said this was the first beach I tried. It's actually the third. I stopped by a few of the public beaches before it dawned on me that maybe you would come back here."

My stomach warms with a flutter of butterflies. "What happened with Matt after I left? Will he press charges against you?"

"No, we had a little chat with the principal, and I very clearly informed him of what I saw."

"And what is it you saw?" I look back out into the blackness in front of me. Reliving that moment hurts me. Even though I told Carson I could handle it, deep inside I know it could have gone in a completely different direction. Carson prevented that.

"I saw a girl saying no to a boy." He ground the words out through his teeth.

"And what did Matt say to all this?"

"He was still threatening all types of allegations, but I convinced him to shut up."

"How did you do that?"

"I told him I'd make his life a living fucking hell."

I turn toward him and see he's grinning from ear to ear. "I can't believe you punched him," I mumble under my breath.

"Do you blame me? I could tell in your movements, in your body language, that you didn't want him to kiss you." He looked in my eyes. "To be honest, I would have punched him even if you wanted it."

My mouth drops open. I clamp it shut and shake my head at his admission. "No, he deserved it, but I can't believe you put your job on the line for me."

"After all this time, you still don't know, do you?"

"Know what?" The emotion I see in his eyes makes me want to cry.

"I'm crazy about you, Lynn." My heart flutters with an emotion I have held in for so long. *Hope.*

"I think you're just crazy," I say on a laugh, but everything I'm holding inside pours out as a tear lines my cheek. "Why did you leave me?"

"You have to believe me when I say I never meant to. I thought I was doing the right thing. I didn't want to hold you back from your dreams."

His words confuse me. "My dreams?"

"I saw your application to UCLA. I thought I was holding you back." There's a faint tremor in his voice.

"UCLA was never my dream. I only applied because Bridget wanted me to. I wish you had asked me. Spoken to me. Then you wouldn't have . . ." I pause and my lips begin to tremble. "Why did you go out with . . ." I can't say her name. Pain still lingers at the thought of them together. "Why did you break my heart?"

"She meant nothing. She was never you. She could never be you. I was trying so hard to do the right thing that I didn't realize the damage it did to both of us." He pauses. "I wanted you to have a life. I wanted you to be happy."

"Without you, Carson?"

"Yes, if you need to be away from me to find yourself. To find your happiness, I would let you go."

"And now?"

"Now, I'm too selfish." I shake my head and laugh.

"No, You're just crazy."

He steps toward me and lowers himself to the ground next to where I'm sitting. Warm fingers swipe my tears. "No, just crazy for you. I should be stronger and step away until the end of the year, but I can't. I don't want to."

My breath catches in my throat. I have dreamed of him saying these words, but now that he has, I'm shocked. Rendered speechless.

"See that star over there?" He points up to a bright cluster. One shines more than the rest. "That's Vega. It's the brightest star in the constellation Lyra. As the story goes, a goddess fell in love with a mortal. They were forbidden to see each other, and thus, they were placed in the sky with an obstacle separating them, only to be reunited once a year. I don't want to be like them. I don't want to only see you in passing. I want you, all of you, every day."

He grabs my hand in his. "I'm sure I fucked up all chances with you, but I can't let another minute go by without telling you how I feel. I'm a guy who's falling in love. A guy who doesn't give a shit about the consequences. Because the idea of going the rest of the year without you feels like a fate worse than death."

I gaze at him through tear-stained eyes, and hang on every word. I throw myself into his embrace. "What now?" I whisper. "How do we do this?"

He pulls back so my eyes meet his as he speaks. "We try."

"But what if someone—" One finger lifts to my lips, stopping my words.

"Lynn, stop. Yeah, shit might happen, but together we can get past it. We'll survive. And this time, if we're together, we can make it to the other side."

"You promise?" I lower my gaze but he doesn't allow it. Instead, he tips my jaw up to meet his steely gaze.

"I do."

My lips part in a smile. Our mouths meet, and his lips taste like the crisp winter air, hints of coffee and cinnamon lingering on his breath. His fingers gently run up my spine as he deepens the kiss, each pass of his hand coaxing shivers to spread across my skin. The kiss obliterates every doubt I've ever had about us.

Because this kiss is a promise of endless possibilities.

# CHAPTER THIRTY-FOUR

Lynn

WHITE NOISE FILTERS AROUND ME. THE PESTER-ing sounds of my classmates' idle chatter become louder and louder as I make my way down the hallway to class. My head swims in the sounds, making it impossible to hear myself think.

I can't concentrate.

Everything grates on my last nerve.

*Flick*

*Flick*

*Flick*

The buzz of the fluorescent lights makes my eyelids twitch.

*Mondays.*

Mondays are always like this. But now that I'm finally "officially" in a relationship with Carson, they have gotten worse. Much, much worse. The last two weeks we have spent every free moment together, and every day we fall more and more into a comfortable routine. The only problem is these moments together eventually come to an end, and then I fall from my high into a state of depression because the dreaded Monday comes.

He doesn't acknowledge me. I don't acknowledge him.

Sighing deeply, I pull myself out of my thoughts. In order for this week to pass, I can't dwell. I find when I do I start to come undone. Dr. Young and I have been working diligently on my tendency to self-destruct, but growing up with a mom who sets this example, it's a hard habit to break. I have to try, though, because this feeling creeping inside my blood isn't healthy.

I draw in a deep breath and exhale. *Only six more months of hiding.* I can do this. I have to do this.

With five minutes until first period starts, I walk into the classroom and plop in the chair. I'm the only student here. Not even the teacher has arrived yet. My phone vibrates in my bag, so I pull it out and swipe the screen. My body warms.

**Carson: I missed you this morning.**

I swear my cheeks flush at the mere thought of waking up to him last weekend. The thought of my eyes fluttering open to the soft touch of his hand, and the way his body melded with mine in sweet perfection. If I could wake up like that every day, I would die a happy person.

**Me: Me, too.**

**Carson: I was wondering what your plans are for Christmas Eve?**

**Me: Nothing planned, but usually I spend my holiday with Bridge. Why?**

**Carson: Well, now you have plans with me.**

**Me: What?**

**Carson: My place. Just you and me.**

**Me: That sounds perfect.**

Like a lovesick child, I can't pull my gaze away from the

phone. The idea of spending the holiday with Carson has a wonderful heat dispersing inside me. Images of cooking and celebrating together play out in my mind. I can't help the flutter that spreads inside my belly. After everything that's occurred over the last few months, spending so much time with him sounds amazing.

I hear a cough from the front of the room and realize the teacher has begun her lesson. From the look of the smart board, I haven't missed much. I'm not sure what she's speaking about, and it's quite obvious to her that I, in fact, am not paying attention. I'm so distracted, it's a surprise she hasn't called me out on it. But she has. *The cough.*

I replace my phone and pull my attention back to the lecture, but instead, thoughts of Carson in his own classroom—my old classroom—play out in my mind. *What's he wearing?* His usual casual yet trendy ensemble? *Is his signature smolder lacing his breathtakingly perfect face?* Are his blue eyes hard, as though he won't take shit from anyone?

Carson always looks pissed when he stands up there, as though he's angry at the world, and I wonder if he still holds himself in such a manner when he teaches, or if the snarl was only for me. A small groan slips out, and I clamp my hand over my mouth to stifle it. *It most definitely was just for me.* Since I won't be in his class ever again, I'll never know, but the idea still has me thinking back to a time in the past, and all the feelings it manifested in me.

"Miss Adams." The words drift into my subconscious. *Shit.* I did it again.

"So sorry."

"Do you even know what I asked?" Her eyebrow lifts up. "Do we need to talk about this after class?" It's obvious what she's really asking. She's asking if I'm falling back into old habits.

"No." I shake my head. "No, I'll pay attention." I hate that my previous wrongs hang over me like a black cloud, but what did I expect? Getting drunk at school is bad enough. Getting drunk at school and passing out put me in a whole new category of fuckup.

As the teacher continues to drone on, thoughts and ideas pound my brain, screaming at me to lose myself in the confines of my mind.

*Recipes. What should we eat?*

*I need to make a checklist. Okay, a mental checklist.*

*1) Google recipes.*

*2) Pick out a sexy outfit.*

*Shit. Lynn. Pay attention to what the teacher is saying.*

*Recipes.*

I can't help it. *Fuck it.* I give up trying.

By the time I head into the lunchroom, I have side dishes and a ham recipe planned.

"Hey, girl," Bridget says as I plop down in the chair across from her. "We really should have gone off campus to eat today, but alas, I have too much damn schoolwork." She pulls out her binder and frantically turns the pages.

"Playing catch up, I see," I chide.

"Lord, yes. Olivia came home from college a few days early and shit, is she needy. All she wants to do is shop." She winks. I can't help but laugh. "Speaking of which, dinner is at seven this Thursday."

"What?"

"Christmas Eve, duh. Obviously, you're coming over since your mom sucks." She scrunches her nose. "No. Really. You are coming over, right?" She narrows her eyes at me. "Wait. Is your mom actually going to be a mom and spend a holiday with you?"

I consider what to say. I have yet to tell her about me and Carson getting back together after the beach. It's still so new, so fresh; I'm not sure I'm ready to tell her—especially since we have to be careful. But if I tell her I'm staying home, she will insist I come to her house again.

"Um . . ." I nibble on my top lip, biting so hard I might draw blood. "I'm meeting her. No biggie. It will suck, but at least I won't intrude on your family time." The lie slips from my mouth and I feel horrible, awful, and deplorable, but what else can I do?

"You are never intruding. You're my best friend. My family loves you as if you are part of the family. You know that, right?"

I nod. "So, what homework do you have? Need help?" I say to change the topic, and her eyes go wide.

"Damn, girl. You have done a complete one eighty since you got in trouble. Before, you were cutting school. Now you're what? A 'tutor'?"

"Shut it, ass."

———— ⌒ ————

Monday passes, then Tuesday. By the time Wednesday arrives, I'm a ball of nervous energy. I head to the grocery store and pick up all the essentials I need. I'm about to season the ham, but it dawns on me I'm not sure how I'll get into his place.

**Me: Houston, we have a problem!**

**Carson: And what, pray tell, is our problem?**

**Me: Ham emergency.**

**Carson: Ham emergency . . . Do I even want to know?**

**Me: We need to marinate this bad boy and I can't get into**

**your house. Should we just do Christmas here?**

**Carson: Is that smart?**

**Me: My mom will never come home. She's off gallivanting around the world.**

I leave it at that. He knows what it implies.

**Carson: Why don't we stay at your place, then?**

**Me: Okay, see you tomorrow @ noon?**

**Carson: Can't wait.**

As soon as I put the phone down, I start to prepare. I want to do as little cooking as I can tomorrow because I want to enjoy my time with Carson. It's seldom we have more than a few minutes together, and I miss him. I marinate the ham and prepare the potatoes. The rest we can do together. Excitement courses through me. Tomorrow can't come soon enough.

---

I've spent the morning running around. I'm showered. I did my hair, fixed my makeup, and put on a simple yet sexy flowered dress. The ham is in the oven. The sweet potatoes, too. Everything is prepped and the table is set. All I have to do is light the candles. *The candles.* This very well might be my first "date" with Carson. *How crazy is that?* We spend most of our time together sneaking around, meeting in obscure places. This might even be our first real dinner together.

Butterflies take flight in my belly. I check the clock again. He should be here in five minutes. *Five minutes.* I'm so excited and nervous, I swear I'm shaking. I wash my hands, check my face, and then I hear the knock on the door.

Willing my breathing to calm, I swing it open.

Wow.

Just wow.

*Lord, this man is handsome.*

He's wearing a navy blue sports coat and slacks with a blue pinstripe button-down, and he's holding a beautiful bouquet of mixed flowers. His hair is still slightly damp. The idea of him just getting out of the shower has my knees going weak. His lips tip up to a sexy smirk as he takes in my appearance, his beautiful blue eyes sweeping over me.

Still holding the flowers in one hand, he uses the other to pull me toward him. His lips find mine. His tongue delves into my mouth in firm and steady movements, taking possession of me, owning me, tantalizing me right then and there on the top step of my mother's brownstone.

There is no sense of secrecy here. No thoughts of impropriety. We are desperate for each other. He wants me, and I want him, and if there wasn't a ham in the oven, I would spend the whole day letting him feast on me instead.

Pulling away, his grin spreads and my lips move up of their own accord as well. "Is it time for dessert yet?" he drawls out and I swat at him lightly.

"We haven't even eaten dinner yet."

He pouts and looks nothing like he does at school. There's no smolder. His eyes are still brilliant and piercing, but they are lighter. Full of a range of emotions that he only shows to me.

"I'm only hungry for one thing . . ."

"Seriously, I spent two days cooking. Get in here and keep your hands to yourself." I laugh, and allow him to pass and enter.

"Fine, fine. You're no fun." As we step into the kitchen, the aromas permeate the air. "Smells amazing."

"Thanks. I hope it tastes as good as it smells."

"I'm sure it will. Do you have a vase?" I point to the cabinet that holds them. Carson fills one in the sink and then places the flowers in the water. He walks out of the room and into the dining room, leaving me alone in the kitchen. A few seconds later, I hear him come back in.

"Wow, you really outdid yourself," he says from behind me a moment later as he wraps his arms around my waist. His lips tickle my neck as he places small kisses down my skin. "What can I help you with?"

"Nothing. Everything is already in the oven." I look at him from over my shoulder and can't help but marvel at how perfect this moment is. Carson and me together in my house, making Christmas Eve dinner. Three months ago, I would never have thought we'd be here doing this. Hell, one month ago this was completely outside the realm of possibility, but now . . . standing here . . . being with Carson . . . being domestic . . .

It feels so good. Like I'm home.

"Would you like a glass of wine?" I ask, pulling away from him. We walk back into the kitchen and I kneel down to check the timer on the oven.

"No, it wouldn't be—" I stop him by lifting my hand.

"It's okay if you do. I won't have any." I smile. There was a time a few weeks ago when I would have welcomed the numb feeling the alcohol would bring. But being here, being with Carson . . .

I want to remember every smile, every breath. I don't want to miss a moment of this perfect day.

"So, tell me about school this week," he says, taking a seat at the island. He leans forward, supporting his weight against the marble. A groan escapes me.

"Do I have to?" I mutter.

"No, you don't have to do anything you don't want. But I

would like to know."

"Fine," I huff, pretending to be mad, but he narrows his eyes at me, giving me his stern look, and I swear I go weak in the knees. "It's hard. I try to keep busy. I try to pay attention, but I miss seeing you."

"I know. Only a few more months," he says reassuringly, and I furrow my brow.

"Um, we have over half a school year left," I say beneath my breath. The tightness of his jaw is not lost on me and I desperately plead with my eyes for us to change the conversation.

"You're right. Let's talk about something else." He lets out a sigh before continuing. "How much longer until the food is ready?"

I chuckle and place a kiss on his cheek. "Any second now. It's just heating up." I pop open the oven one last time. "Actually, I think we can eat."

"Think?" He quirks an eyebrow at me. "Will I die of food poisoning?" he chides and I glower at him.

"Very funny."

"I think I'm pretty clever." I like us like this. The playful banter, cooking dinner together. I can envision a future with him, and that future looks pretty damn perfect.

With a smile on my face, I go to grab the food. Carson gets up as well, and together we lay out everything on the dining room table. As he leans across me to lower a dish, our hands brush one another. He smiles warmly, and I can sense a glimmer of something naughty there as well. My body shivers at the thought. It's unnerving how my body needs his touch.

But now is not the time.

"Let's eat."

The air around us is charged with sexual energy. Dinner is

torture. Every look makes me desperate for him, and as I finally set the last dish in the sink he touches me. I look up at him, our eyes locking and conveying a million things.

Need.

Want.

His lips find mine. They devour. They caress. They make sweet passionate love to me. Tell me about forevers, of futures to come. They speak of every promise. Every hope. Every dream. Our lips tell a tale; trace words onto paper. We pull away breathless, panting.

Needy.

Hungry.

Primal hands pull off my skirt. A desperate touch lifts my blouse until I'm naked before him and he lifts me, placing me on the island and spreading my legs.

His gaze sears me. His eyes make love to me. Electric currents tingle down my spine and I open to him. He settles between my parted thighs and slowly—painfully slow—pushes inside my heat.

Spreading me.

Claiming me.

Owning me.

His movements are unhurried at first. They let me adjust, let me feel complete. But as our bodies come together we become more frenzied, we become a storm, and I welcome the fall into the abyss. I welcome the oblivion. I welcome being his. His body trembles within mine until he joins me.

Our hearts beat in tandem.

We whisper words of passion.

His hands fan over my naked back and I shiver. Tiny feathers whisper against my skin as I come down from my high.

"You're cold." He unbuttons his shirt, the one he hadn't taken off during his hasty and desperate assault. "Here," he says as he drapes it over my shoulders and buttons it. His fingers linger too long on my collarbone as he finishes the last closure. It makes me want more. It makes me want him to ravish me all over again. His lips tilt up.

He knows my thoughts.

Reads my mind.

Pulling me toward him, he sweeps his tongue against the seam of my lips. Still seated on the island, I hear the door and scramble to move away. Carson pulls me into his body as his eyes widen. I hear the rasp of his zipper and the rustle of him quickly straightening his pants.

"What the hell is going on in here?" her shriek reverberates through the room.

My shoulders tense. This isn't good. This isn't good at all. Pulling away from the cocoon of warm arms surrounding me, I look over my shoulder and meet her eyes.

"Mom. What are you doing here?"

"What am *I* doing here? This is my house. What the hell are *you* doing here? Naked. In my kitchen. With . . ." she pauses and takes in Carson's appearance from across the kitchen island. His torso is uncovered and his pants hang low on his hips. "Why do you look familiar?" Her eyes narrow.

And I pray.

Pray that she doesn't remember the time at school. Pray that she doesn't put two and two together. Because I know what that would mean. That would be the end of us, and I can't handle that thought right now. He's all I have. I can't lose him again.

"Have we met before?" she asks, and Carson opens his mouth but I clench my arms around his waist and grip tightly to stop him from talking. He can't say anything or we'll both be screwed.

"No. No, you haven't, Mom."

She continues to stare. Waves of emotion pass over her pristine face, and fear passes through my blood. "This is unacceptable behavior."

"Why are you even home, Mom?" I ask again, and silence descends. The room is thick with tension. Finally, my mom tilts her face and opens her mouth.

"This is my house. Where else should I be?"

"Try St. Bart's with . . . What was his name again? Oh, yes, Richard. Soon to be husband number four, right?"

"Not that it's any of your business, but we broke up. Actually it *is* your business," she snarls at me. Her face becomes dark with hate. "I can't wait until you go to college. You're the reason I'm always alone. Even your dad left me because of you. You ruined my life." She pulls her narrow gaze from mine and pins Carson's with disdain.

"I'm going to my bedroom to freshen up. As for your friend, he better be gone when I return." She walks toward the door and then turns around. "This isn't over, Gwendolyn. I'm back now, and things are going to change."

She walks away, and I let out the breath I wasn't even aware I was holding. I don't know what she means by her threat, but it has my whole body on edge. Every limb in my body shakes as the scene plays out for me again, all the hate in her eyes. Carson lifts my face, so our eyes meet. "Are you okay? She said some hurtful things." His fingers work at my jaw until I unclench it.

"Yeah, I'm okay. Nothing she hasn't said before. But fuck, that was close," I say as I let out an audible sigh.

"Too close," Carson murmurs, and my gaze meets his. He

squints at me through hardened eyes, and dread coils in my belly as I see the familiar look taking refuge inside. I wait for him to pull away. I can see it happening.

"I think—" he starts to say, but I lift my hand.

"Do not say anything. I can't go back to before." He blinks at my words and then nods. With a deep breath, his hands bracket my shoulders.

"I wasn't going to say that. Come here." He pulls me toward him.

His lips find mine and press against them in possession. "I won't let you go again. It's you and me. We just might have to find a better place to meet . . . Try my place," he whispers against my lips. I relax into his embrace. We stay like this for only a second longer before he pulls away.

"I should go."

"Yeah."

"I wouldn't if I didn't have to."

"I know, and you're right. She could come out soon and if you're still here . . . Well, we can't risk that."

"No, I *won't* risk that."

"When will I see you again?"

"I'm not sure. It's best if you give your mom some time to cool down, but I am here for you if you need me. Day or night, you call me."

The authoritative nature of his voice has me bobbing my head in agreement. As much as it pains me to agree that we can't see each other, he's right. My mom is a loose cannon who just got dumped. Flaunting our relationship is bad enough, but due to the illicit nature of it, it would be downright stupid to allow her any more details. Including and not limited to Carson's profession.

I walk him out and peek into my mom's room before heading back to mine. *Out cold.* At least I won't have to see her for the rest of the night. But then a distressing thought hits me. There are still two more weeks until break is over and I'm back in school.

I wonder how bad it will be?

# CHAPTER THIRTY-FIVE

## Lynn

**B**AD.

That's how the rest of the weekend went.

Really bad. We didn't even celebrate Christmas Day or my birthday. My ninetieth birthday came and went without any fanfare other than flowers from an anonymous source—*Carson*—and endless texts from Bridget to come over and celebrate with her. I declined. I didn't want to see anyone. I wanted to wallow in my own self-pity.

Mom was in rare form. Hateful words laced with jealousy poured out of her mouth like poisonous venom.

I hid. I only left my room when I needed to, and I hoped and prayed I wouldn't bump into her. Alas, my prayers were not answered as every turn I took, every place I was in our brownstone, she was there with malice in her eyes.

It was almost worse when she didn't speak. When she was silent I didn't know what she was thinking, and the idea that maybe she found out about Carson was too much to bear. The thought that I couldn't live here anymore replayed over and over again until I finally snapped this afternoon as she glared at me one more time and slammed the door to her room.

As Mom sleeps, I find myself quietly opening the door and sneaking out of the place. It isn't late. The slow glimmer of sun still ducks and dances along the skyline. She must have taken something, but it doesn't matter. I won't be there when she wakes. I refuse to be.

I pull out my phone and dial.

"Hello?" His voice is distant, as if wondering what I would want now. And even though he was cold the last time I texted him, I'm desperate, and I need somewhere to go. I might have Carson, but I can't actually be with him.

"Dad."

"Lynn. Merry Christmas. I meant to call you but . . ." He pauses.

He sounds sad. His voice is hesitant, as though he wants to say more but can't. I'm not sure what that's about but I need to talk to him. I need to see him. I need to try to have a family. To have more than what she gives me. I can't stop the tears in my eyes. I can't silence the sob I have buried in my throat. It comes pouring out in deep breaths and strangled weeping.

"I need to see you, Dad."

"Okay."

"Right now."

"That's fine."

"Really?" I sound pathetic. Desperate. It makes me feel weak, but I am weak right now.

"Of course . . ." He pauses and my chest tightens with fear he'll change his mind. "I'll let the doorman know you're coming."

"Thank you," I say on a sigh, relieved he's letting me come.

Maybe everything will be all right after all.

An hour later and shaking from the cold, I enter his building. I could have taken a cab. I didn't need to brave the bitter winter air, but I walk when I need to think, so I walked the forty blocks to his apartment on the Upper West Side.

By the time I get in the elevator, I'm defrosting, but one glance in the mirrored wall of the car and it's obvious I'm far from thawed. My nose is red, my eyes glassy from the wind. I look weathered and beaten.

I pound on his door. The sound is jarring to my ears as I wait to speak my piece, beg and plead, and see what my fate might be. The door swings open just as my hand meets the surface.

"Lynn," he says, but he makes no effort to comfort me, console me, or even greet me. I don't know why he has so much disdain for me, so much indifference, but this is the better option. *He* is the better option.

"Hey, Dad," I mutter, and I see his back tense at my words. He moves aside and I walk past him into the living room.

"Take a seat. Can I get you something? A drink of water maybe?"

"No, I'm okay."

"Are you sure?"

"No. Yes. I don't know."

He nods as if he understands, and he might. Being with Mom is hard. Dealing with her is harder. If anyone understands, it's him.

"Where's your mom?" he asks.

"In bed." I lift an eyebrow, and he gives a knowing nod. "Her fiancé dumped her. She thought . . ." I trail off, looking at him, hoping he understands.

"She finally found happiness. That it would all work out for her." *He does.*

"Yeah, but well, apparently, that wasn't in the cards. She blames me."

"Why would she blame you?" He leans forward with his elbows on his knees and looks at me.

"I got in some trouble first semester at school. I got suspended and she couldn't travel like she planned. I think she thinks that's why he dumped her. Because of me. She thinks it was too much for him to handle."

"That's the most ridiculous thing I ever heard. Typical. Your mother was always overly dramatic."

"I know, but that's Mom."

"So, what can I do for you, Lynn?" He pulls back from his position and straightens his back.

"I—" I don't know how to say what I want. "I want to live with you," I blurt out, and his mouth drops open. Shock. As if this is something he never in his wildest dreams imagined I would say.

He lifts his hand and rubs at his eyes, then pulls at his hair before he gets himself together. "Well, that can't happen."

"I-I don't understand. I know we haven't been close since, well, since you left."

"I had no choice. There is so much you don't know. Your mom threatened me. She threatened to take you completely out of my life if I didn't abide by her rules. I couldn't risk it."

"This makes no sense. What could she possibly have to hold over you? You're my dad. Don't you have rights?"

"There is something I need to tell you." He pauses, and I notice his grip is getting tighter, his knuckles whitening from the tension. "I had hoped your mother would do it, but seeing as she hasn't, I guess I must." His hands tremble as he speaks. It makes me grow cold.

"What are you trying to say?" I feel my throat closing up on each word. His eyes scare me, his unshed tears glistening.

"I'm not your biological father."

My heart stops beating.

White noise rushes in my ears.

I feel as if I might faint.

Instead, a piece of me crumbles as the world I know collapses into a million pieces and smashes to the ground.

This is too much. My whole life is too much.

Everything is a lie.

Nothing is how it seems.

*Not my father.* Anger coils in my belly. The pungent taste of bile works its way up my throat. How can this be? How could I never know?

"What do you mean, you're not my father?"

"I'm not."

"I don't understand. Who is my father?"

"I don't know."

"I-I don't get it," I stutter. The reality of the situation is finally setting in and my eyes well with tears.

"When you were a few years old, I wanted to try for another child and after years of trying, I went to a doctor. It turns out I'm sterile." He looks away. There is a deep rooted sadness in his eyes. I don't know if it's the fact he was lied to, or that he could never have children, but it's there. And as much as I'm angry I never knew, I'm also now angry for him.

"Apparently, I have been since I was a child and acquired measles. It never dawned on me to check because your mother easily got pregnant with you. Looking back, I should have known. Everything at that time was wrong. The way she acted when she found out, her depression. Years later, when I found out, I confronted her. At least she had the decency to not deny having an affair. She told me at the time when she found out she was pregnant she didn't know who the father was.

"I was crushed. I would have done the right thing by you, but she made me leave and so I left. I owed you more than that, but I didn't know how to deal. In some sick twist of fate, I found out there was no way I was your father, that my only child was not mine. How does one deal with that?

"Your mom is greedy. She hung the truth over my head like a bad secret. She threatened to take you away completely. I'm sorry for the way I treated you, but I couldn't handle it. I still can't. It's not your fault, Lynn, but every time I'm around you, I feel her betrayal. It etches away at my soul."

He covers his face with his hands. "It would be one thing if you were my biological daughter, but I just can't get past it. As much as I want to help you, I-I can't."

There isn't anything to say to that. I bite my lip and stifle back a cry. "I understand." And I do. She ruined his life. Her selfish actions killed a part of him, just as they did me. But now I need to know more. I need to know who my father is, and there's only one person to ask. No matter how painful, I deserve an answer. But before I can talk to her, I need to see Carson. Hopefully he can help me find my strength.

———

I knock on his door once, and it flies open before I can place my hand on the heavy wood again.

"What's going on? Are you okay?"

"Yes. No. I'm not sure."

"Come here," he says, and he pulls me into his body. He holds me, the beat of his heart lulling mine to a steadier cadence. "I got you," he says and it causes a dam to break within me.

I held strong as I left Dad's—I mean, *Ronnie's* apartment. I held strong all the way through the park. I even stayed strong as I spun the idea that I knew nothing of my life. I held strong all the way past Carson's doorman, and up in the elevator. But now, in his arms, I don't have to hold it in anymore.

I can let go.

I can fall.

Because I know he will hold me up, and he does. I feel his hands lifting me. He pulls me into a cradle embrace and then walks me through the foyer, into the living room, and onto the couch. I look up through tear-filled eyes.

"I'm okay." I try to smile but my voice gives me away.

"I know you're not, but you will be. I promise you, Lynn. Whatever happens, I will be there for you. I will hold your hand. I will protect you."

My shoulders sink forward. My eyes close of their own accord. The only sound I hear is breathing.

His breathing.

My breathing.

Finally, as my breath calms to beat in tandem with his, I look up at him again. My chin trembles as I find my words. The words I don't want to speak. If I say them they are true, but I have to, nonetheless. "The last couple of days have been bad." The words come out mumbled against the sound of my soft sobs.

His blue eyes narrow, a small line forming on his brow. "What do you . . . I don't understand?"

"He's not my dad."

"Why didn't you tell me? Jesus, Lynn, you didn't have to stay there. You could have—"

"I could have, what? Come here? Stayed with you?"

"Yes." His words are forceful and I don't doubt he believes it, but I know better.

"You know we couldn't. Not with her there." It's one thing for me to stay here when my mom's away, but with her home, she would ask questions. It wasn't worth the risk. His eyes, normally the blue of the ocean as it meets the sky, are darker than usual. Chilling. Angry. Troubled.

"I hate this for you. I hate this for us. I should be able to be with you. To take care of you."

"I know, and I appreciate it more than you will ever know."

The pads of his fingers draw circles on my back and I relax into him.

"Tell me what happened."

"I went to my . . ." I catch myself from saying dad again. It hurt too much to refer to him as *Dad*. Like the name is a dagger in my heart, stabbing me with all the lies. "I went to Ronnie's house. He told me . . . He told me I wasn't his daughter."

"Lynn."

He doesn't say more, just places a soft, comforting kiss on my forehead as his arm tightens and his fingers trail comforting patterns on the exposed skin of my neck. I let him hold me. I'm not sure how much time passes. I'm not sure of much, but as our breaths become one and the beats of hearts are matched, I find the strength to tell him everything that happened. *Everything*.

I tell him how my father left me. How he didn't fight for custody. I tell him how, over the years, he became more distant. How he's been a void in my life since I turned eighteen. I tell him and I cry. And as I tell him everything, it becomes obvious. It all makes sense. He might have just told me I wasn't his daughter, but a part of me always knew. I always felt as if I didn't belong. That there was something amiss, that I never fit in with him. That he never saw me.

"How did you leave things?" Carson asks.

"He doesn't know who my father was. I'll have to ask my mother."

"Do you need me to go with you?"

I lean in, placing a soft kiss across his lips. "No, this is something I have to do alone."

"Will you be okay?"

I shrug, my lips puckering ever so slightly. "I don't know."

"Stay. Let me take care of you at least for tonight." I should go home. I shouldn't risk my mom finding out about us, but I'm not strong enough to confront her right now, so I pull out my phone and shoot off a text. *Staying at Bridget's.* I know after our last confrontation she won't answer. Putting the phone down, my hand shakes. Carson lifts my palm to his lips and places a soft kiss on my skin. "I've got you."

"And tomorrow?"

"I'll be here if you need me."

I want to lean on him. I want to use his strength as my own. But I won't. I can't have a crutch. I need to stand on my own two feet and be strong and brave. If I don't, I might never conquer the obstacles life has in store for me.

# CHAPTER THIRTY-SIX

## Carson

UNDERSTAND WHY SHE HAS TO DO IT ALONE. I DON'T LIKE IT, but I understand. I wish I could be there. Take her pain. Protect her. I wish I could be everything she needs and shield her from anything unpleasant. But that's not how it is. I can't be that for her, and I certainly can't risk her mother putting two and two together and remembering how she knows me. That would be bad. Life altering bad. Not only would I lose my job, but the damage to Lynn and her reputation could be irreparable.

In the silence of my room, I can hear the soft inhale of her breath. It took a while for Lynn to fall asleep, but eventually she did. I don't envy her the shit she's going through. I understand all too well what it's like to feel like your world is ripped out from under you. To feel unloved, that you were never good enough. My parents were awful, but I at least cut ties with them completely. Which makes me much better off than Lynn. Or does it?

How does she do it? After everything that happened to her,

how is she strong enough to want to conquer this battle alone?

In awe, I stare. It takes a lot of to confront this. To confront her mother. I should know. She's stronger than me, that's for sure. Here she is dealing with her whole world being rocked and somehow she's still able to conjure the strength to confront her mom. And me? I pretend my parents don't exist. It makes sense I don't talk to my dad, but my mom . . .

No. I'm not ready to breach that, and I'm not sure I ever will be. Maybe one day I'll be as strong as her. Maybe one day I'll get the answers I've always looked for. The answer to the *why's* that still linger deep down in the darkest crevices of my mind.

Why did she choose him?

Why did she abandon me?

Why wasn't I enough?

# CHAPTER THIRTY-SEVEN

## Lynn

Lights trickle in, dancing across my lids until I'm forced to open my eyes and the room comes into focus. I'm lying in Carson's bed. I don't remember how I got here last night. I only remember crying in his arms.

"Morning." His voice is raspy, still laced with sleep. "What time is it?"

"Eight. Still early. Go back to bed." He pulls me tighter into his body and places his lips against the top of my head.

"I can't. Once I'm up, I'm up."

As many times as we've been together, this is the first time I've ever woken up in bed with him and had no rush to be anywhere. Usually, he leaves super early, the sex fast and frenzied. Always the fear my mom might catch us. But now, in his bed, we have all the time in the world. I'm in no rush to see my mom or tackle that hurdle quite yet.

"Well, if you're up . . ." I drawl out.

His arms bracket me, pulling my body under his. His weight

is welcome. I love the comfort I feel beneath him. His lips fan my jaw and then trail up until he places a kiss on my lips.

"Don't kiss me. I haven't brushed my teeth yet."

"I'll do what I want." He plunders my lips once again.

---

I don't go straight to my mom's and confront her. I don't ask her right away. I basically hide in Carson's apartment for the rest of the holiday break. I know I have to talk to her, but I'm scared. I'm scared of what I'll find out. Who is my father? Does she even know? I'm scared she won't tell me. *Or even worse—that she will.*

What if she tells me and he wants nothing to do with me? What if he has his own family? What if he's dead? *I'm starting to sound insane.*

"What are you thinking over there?" Carson presses a hand on my knee and gives me a little squeeze. I don't look up, though; my vision is trained across the room, my brain still drifting to all my fears and neuroses.

"What do you mean?"

"You have that line." I turn my head toward him and wrinkle my nose.

"What line?"

"The little frown line you get when you're thinking too hard."

My stomach warms at his words. I didn't even know I had a "tell," but he knows. The idea that Carson knows these things—that he pays attention—makes me smile.

"I'm contemplating when I should confront my mom."

His stunning blue eyes cannot hide all the thoughts playing out in his mind that he doesn't want me to see. I see them. I see all the despair he thinks he's hiding, and it's heartbreaking.

"I wish I could be there for you. I wish I could go with you."

"I know."

He gets up and crosses the space that separates us to lift me into his arms. "Do you?"

"Yes, it's in every look you give me, every kiss, every touch of your hand."

"Like this . . ." He plants soft kisses at the hollow of my neck, trailing up my jaw. No words need be spoken. Everything, every action, shows how much I mean to him, how much he loves me, even if he has yet to say the words. *Even if I have yet to say them . . .*

"Yes, like that," I pant.

"What about this?" He places a kiss on my lips, and then consumes my mouth.

"Like that," I mumble and he gives me a hearty laugh. His hands work on my blouse, loosening the buttons one by one until I am bare.

"You are so unbelievably beautiful."

"Thank you," I whisper. My gaze doesn't meet his, and his finger lifts my jaw.

"No matter what happens, from now until forever, I'm here for you."

My eyes fill with tears. Although our time together has been short, I know he means every word he utters. No matter what happens, no matter what we find out, he will be there. We will do this together. We will hold each other up.

He stands with me in his arms and walks us to his room, stretching me out on the bed. I watch him undress, then remove the rest of my clothes. When we are both naked, Carson crawls up my body and places soft kisses until he reaches my mouth. I cradle him between my legs, the evidence of his arousal teasing my seam.

With a breathtaking movement, our eyes meet and he pushes in. Our bodies move together in a perfect symphony. When we're finished, we lay in each other's arms until the beat of our hearts calms.

"Today," I whisper.

"Today?"

"I'll talk to her today."

"Are you sure?"

"No, but I have to. I need to know. And knowing you'll be here afterward is all the strength I need."

He takes my face in his hands, pressing his lips to mine. "I love you."

Those are the only words I'll ever need to hear.

"I love you, too."

The words fill us up, giving us both the strength to let me leave and conquer this hurdle.

———————

The sound of the door opening to the brownstone feels like a painfully brutal song to my ear, but I replay it this morning and push through.

I find my mother in the kitchen. She's disheveled and not like her usual pristine self. "Where have you been?" She glares at me while she props a hand on her right hip and waits impatiently for me to answer.

"I needed some space."

"Space. You needed space? You're nineteen years old. What is so terrible in your life that you need space?"

"I had to think." I close my eyes and reopen them. She has

already dismissed me, and is reaching for a mug in an upper cabinet.

"I saw Dad. Or should I say, *Ronnie*."

I watch as understanding crosses her face and descends down on her, leaving her hand shaking. The mug slips to the floor in a thunderous crash. She looks down to the ground and then shakes her head.

"What are you talking about?"

"You know what I'm talking about. You damn well know." My voice rises higher than I want, but my anger is palpable. My whole life is a lie, and I'm sick and tired of pretending it's not. "He told me everything. How you cheated on him, how you made him raise a daughter he knew wasn't his. He *told* me everything."

"I-I," she stutters, and for the first time she has no snarky comeback. For the first time in nineteen years, I have rendered my mom speechless. "I—"

"Nothing to say? Well, at least you aren't going to deny it."

She turns her back to me.

"So, who is he?" I maneuver my body to block her retreat, caging her in so she has nowhere to go. She looks like a trapped and wounded animal, but I can't find it in me to care. I need answers and I need them now. "No, you don't get to walk away. Not this time. Who is he? Who is my father?"

"I can't," she whispers. Her words are barely audible over the beat of my heart. "I can't." Her head shakes repeatedly and tears well in her eyes.

"Why?"

"He didn't choose me."

"What do you mean?"

"He went back to her. He didn't choose me. They never

choose me. Not even you choose me. You're always with her, with Bridget . . . with them. With *him*."

A gasp escapes my mouth. "Mom. Please. *Please* tell me Sam Miller is not my father." The silence is devastating. She doesn't have to answer. The truth stretches between us, filling in the missing words. "Tell me," I plead. "I need you to say the words."

"I-I can't. He doesn't know."

"So, it's true. You had an affair with Bridget's dad?" She doesn't speak, only nods.

"How could you not tell him?" Her mouth opens and shuts as she tries to figure out what she'll say. Or maybe she's trying to find a way to not answer at all. Finally, on a sigh she answers.

"I didn't know for sure at first. I couldn't risk it. If he wasn't your dad . . . I would have lost everything. By the time I found out, it was too late. And it wouldn't have changed anything for me. He still would have chosen her. Chosen them."

And there it is. Years of deception and lies all based on money and her own wounded ego. I don't even know what to say. There are no words to comprehend what just happened. I was robbed of *my father,* all because she was too selfish to discover the truth, and too hurt once she did to make things right. My father is my best friend's father. Which means Bridget is my half-sister, my younger sister. If I hadn't been held back, we might not be friends, let alone best friends.

My whole body shakes. *Oh, my God,* I have a baby sister, and an older sister, too. Every joke I have ever heard—how much we resemble each other, how much we fit—all comes together in a weird cosmic force—or tragedy when Bridget finds out. Because as much as this has shaken my world, this revelation will change everything for everyone. As I try to make sense of everything, I turn to face my mom but she's gone. She's left me, yet again,

222

filled with millions of unanswered questions. I hear the front door shut, and I know the chance she'll ever tell me narrows.

There is only one person who might have answers, but I'm not sure I have the strength to ask.

---

I find myself walking with no destination in sight, and the cold air bites at my extremities that are exposed to the winter elements. I wasn't prepared for her answer—or lack thereof. The information swirls in my head, pulling at every memory, at everything I know.

If I tell Bridget, her life will forever be changed. Will she hate me? Hate her father? Will it break up his marriage? I'm in a losing situation. As much as I want a dad, as much as I want to get away from my mother, can I really alter her life—her family's life—this much? But don't I deserve a chance at happiness? At having a family?

Each step I take brings me further and further away from where I should be. From lying in Carson's arms for salvation. Each step makes my mind cloudy and allows the bleakness of the situation to hover over me like a dark cloud waiting to spill rain and tears over my body. I want to numb it, bury it deep inside, reach for a state of bliss that will take all my pain away. But I can't. I'm not that person, and never was. I allowed myself to enter that world, weakened by feelings I couldn't understand, but I am and always will be stronger and more than that.

My phone vibrates in my pocket, and I know it's Carson. Hours have passed and I haven't contacted him. This is his third time trying to reach me. The last few times I was unable to form words and sent him to voicemail. I have to answer this time as he's probably going crazy not knowing where I am.

"Hello," I say.

"Oh, thank God. You had me worried."

"I'm sorry."

"Don't be. But when I didn't hear from you, I thought the worst. Did she tell you?"

"Yes." There's a pause but I don't give him a chance to respond. "It's bad. Really bad."

"I'm so sorry. I can't imagine how hard this is for you."

We're both quiet, and all that is heard through the phone is our breathing. Finally, a sigh escapes my mouth.

"It's a horrible situation. But now I have you. It helps." My voice cracks.

"I'm coming to get you."

"No, I'll be okay, I need some time to think."

"Fair enough. I can understand that. I'll be at my place waiting."

"Okay," I whisper before pressing the end button and placing the phone back in my bag. I have a lot to think about. This isn't a case of what to do; more like when. I will go to Sam Miller and deliver the truth my mom withheld from him.

He deserves to know too.

---

I return to my place that night, even though Carson wants me to stay with him. With everything going on, I figure we are better safe than sorry. From across the bedside table, my phone buzzes. Bridget. A strange feeling weaves its way into my blood and collects in my stomach. The cadence of my heartbeat picks up, but then I let out a deep breath. She doesn't know. What am I worried about?

**Bridget: What up? How was your weekend?**

**Me: Interesting to say the least, but too much to type out.**

**Bridget: Problems with Mommy Dearest?**

**Me: Yes.**

**Bridget: Can't wait to hear all the horrid details.**

**Me: Real nice ;-)**

**Bridget: See you tomorrow.**

**Me: Okay.**

Even though I'm not lying or even withholding information, it still leaves a bitter taste in my mouth. But I need to speak to Sam first. *My biological father.* I need to hear what happened from him, how it happened, and how we plan to proceed.

# CHAPTER THIRTY-EIGHT

## Lynn

T'S A NEW YEAR AND A NEW BEGINNING. GOING BACK TO school after the holiday is a bit awkward.

I'm different.

My whole world moved on its axis, and I don't know where I fit now. I'm used to knowing glances from Carson, so I'm prepared for them, but I'm not prepared for seeing Bridget. I've never gone this long without seeing her. Usually I spend my holiday with her when my mom is away, so seeing her and knowing what I do will be difficult.

From across the hall, she waves and skips over to me. The closer she gets, the more my stomach churns. By the time she throws her arms around my neck and gives me a hug, I feel sweat breaking out against my forehead.

"I missed you," she says. Then she pulls back and scans me, her gaze sweeping my body. Her cheeks hollow. "What's going on with you? Everything okay? There's something different."

"Nothing. Well . . . I'm back together with Carson." She

squeals but I grab her arm to silence her. "Shh. Come on, we'll be late. I promise to tell you everything later."

I turn and attempt to pull her, but she doesn't budge. I'm afraid she'll press me and I hope she doesn't, but then she lets out a sigh. It's barely audible but it makes her shoulders lift ever so slightly. She nods and allows me to pull her along. With the change in my schedule, I had no choice but to drop into Bridget's first period elective art class instead of Carson's AP history class. Since it's an elective, no one asked any questions. I mean who really takes an AP class as an elective, anyway? My story was completely plausible to Principal Gordon and anyone else who asked.

We take our seats with a minute to spare. Just as I'm pulling my notebook out of my bag, my phone vibrates.

**Carson: How are you?**

**Me: Ok**

**Carson: If you need me, text. I'll make it happen.**

I know it's not realistic to think we'll have a moment alone together, but I know Carson, and if I really need him, he will move Heaven, Earth, and all the stars in the sky to make it happen.

The class flies by and I welcome the distraction. Hopefully, by the time we go to lunch, I'll stop being so weird in front of Bridget.

Luckily, after the next few periods, it's *almost* as if I don't know I'm talking to my sister. It's *almost* as if there isn't some giant secret hovering between us. *Almost.* But just when I think it's past, I start imagining what my life would have been like if we were raised as sisters. We should have been, and it makes my heart hurt that we weren't. Only by fate and chance did we become best friends. If my mom had her way, we wouldn't be. The thought infuriates me.

All these years that she disapproved of our friendship never made sense, but now that I know, it's so much worse. It's worse than a lie or an omission of the truth, knowing how she tried to separate us. Knowing I have an entire family I didn't know about is the worst betrayal of everything in my life. I was robbed, and a part of me wants to drown the pain of it, but I won't.

Pacing nervously around the living room, I pull my phone out. Today at school with Bridget was hard, and the urge to drown out the noise is almost too much to bear.

**Me: I need you. Please come here. My mom's in the Hamptons again.**

**Carson: Coming**

Within minutes, he's knocking at my door. When I see him, he's sweaty and in running gear. Even disheveled like this, I want him to hold me in his arms and never let go.

"Are you okay?" he asks as he pulls me toward him. I meld my body to him. Sweaty or not, there is no place I'd rather be.

"Today was hard. God, was it hard. I feel like a liar, an imposter. Like I don't know where I belong."

"You belong here. With me. In my arms."

"This is the only place I feel safe these days. The only place I feel like myself."

"So, stay." He laughs.

"If only it was that easy."

"It is. Here, maybe this will help." He reaches for his back pocket and pulls out a small box. "I've been meaning to give this to you for weeks, but with everything that's been happening . . ."

"Oh, I understand, but you didn't have to get me anything."

"It was Christmas and your birthday."

"We've been busy."

"That's an understatement. Here, open it." I take the box from his hand; it's not wrapped so I quickly pull it open.

Inside the box is a tiny gold ring with three small diamonds in the shape of an open triangle. It looks small enough for a child. Carson leans forward and takes the ring.

"Here, let me." He slips it onto my middle finger between the tip of my finger and the knuckle. "It's supposed to represent Vega." An overwhelming onslaught of emotion pours through me. It stretches throughout my whole body warming me, calming me . . . making me feel complete.

"When we aren't together, just look down and know, no matter the distance, I am always with you."

# CHAPTER THIRTY-NINE

## Carson

WITH A LOUD THUD, THE DOOR SHUTS BEHIND me. With Lynn calm inside, I step out of her house to go about my day. There is a lot to prepare for tomorrow's lesson plan. I look left and right out into the street, but a thick fog clings to the brick and mortar surface of the surrounding buildings. It makes it hard to see, but still, I need to look. No one can spot me leaving. It's bad enough that her mom saw me here last week. We can't risk any more questions.

God, it wasn't a good idea to come, but when Lynn needs me I can't think straight. Earlier today when she texted and said her mom went to the Hamptons and she needed me, I went to her. No questions asked. Now I realize how dumb we were.

With hurried steps, I move toward the corner of the street to head back to my place. It's bitter cold, the feel of winter breathing on my skin. I'm only a few steps up the block when I spy that prick ex-boyfriend of hers. He's coming toward me with his lips turned up in an arrogant grin.

*What the hell is he doing here?*

"Fancy seeing you in this part of the city," he chides, ripping me from my thoughts and making my back straighten. "Hmm. I wonder what you're doing a block away from Lynn's." My fists clench, my nails biting into the skin of my palms.

"Why are you here?" I respond through gritted teeth.

"Word around town is she's having mommy issues. I was thinking I'd like to be the shoulder she cries on . . ." As the words tumble out of his mouth, I feel myself getting angrier.

"You're delusional."

"Am I? It wasn't too long ago I was wiping her little tears, not too long ago she was riding my—" I step toward him, blocking his path on the sidewalk.

"Say another word and it will be your last."

"Anger issues?"

"Fuck off."

"Is that appropriate language for a teacher? Hmm. Come to think of it, do you do *anything* appropriate?" He lifts his brow and I take a deep breath to calm myself.

"Is there something I can help you with?" I mutter. Each word tastes like bitter herbs on my tongue.

"As a matter of fact, there is." He lets out a breath and then smiles. "See, I'm having an issue with the camera on my phone. The pictures." His lips tip up further. He's up to something. What, I'm not quite sure, but the idea of him having something on me—on us—has acid churning in my stomach. "Mind taking a look at this?" I shake my head and go to sidestep him as he thrusts his phone in my face.

"Look at this one," he says. "Here is one of a student and her teacher out to dinner. Hmm," he dramatically sighs. "I need help understanding this picture. Is it . . . Maybe I'm wrong, but isn't it frowned upon for a student and their teacher to have dinner?"

*Fuck.*

How was I so stupid to think I could take Lynn out and not get caught?

"Oh, this one is my favorite. . . Lynn and you going to your apartment."

"Did you follow us?"

"Follow you? Why would I follow you? Funny thing about the city . . . It's a small place. Imagine my surprise when I was about to eat at my favorite sushi restaurant and I see Lynn with the teacher who assaulted me. At the time, I wasn't sure about you guys. Maybe you were going over an extra credit assignment." He pauses and I want to wipe his face clean of the smug look. "After seeing this, well, it all made sense."

"What's your fucking point?" That makes him smile.

"You're fucking a student, that's my fucking point. And not just any student. *Your* student." Inhale. *She's not my student anymore, dick.* Don't answer. Exhale. "She really is after some extra credit isn't she?" He winks and I clench my fists tighter.

*Don't do it. You're better than this. Walk away.* But I can't. I need to know what his end game is. What his goal is.

"What do you want?"

"To ruin your life."

"Good luck with that." I turn to walk away.

"I wonder what the school board will think about you having an affair with a student? Do you think they'll press charges? Hmm. Maybe when she's forced to pick up and go to a crappy school after this shit comes out, heck, maybe I'll take her for another spin."

Without thinking, I strike out, squaring him right in the jaw.

His body flops to the ground. The anger coursing through me is intense. It's like a raging inferno with no way to snuff it.

"She really is some lay," he goads. As he spits blood on the ground, I go to kick him, my foot poised to attack, but I stop myself. Instead, I clench and release my hands, over and over again as I try to right my breathing. Finally, he stands and I stalk toward him. He stumbles back until he hits the brick wall of the building.

"You don't look at her. You don't talk about her. You don't threaten her. You hear me? So help me, God, you even think about her and I will fucking end you."

"You're done, Blake." He spits again and then, like the weasel he is, he scurries away.

"Good fucking riddance," I say through a clenched jaw. I'm still not right. I feel like a live wire. I might be in jeans and a coat, but I find my legs have other plans for me on this brisk winter day. Before I know it, I'm taking off down the block, letting my lungs fill with air. Calming each part of me that's lit on fire.

Inhale. My lungs burn. Exhale. It's like glass and fire entering my body. By the time my emotions have calmed, I look up and I'm twenty blocks away from Lynn's. I stop at the corner, my body heaving. *Fuck.*

I almost kicked him. It's bad enough I decked him, but that was a whole other level of anger.

Fuck.

Fuck.

Fuck.

I'm not sure what to do, but Lynn can't be affected. I can't lose control of this situation. I only have one choice. I have to tell the principal. I have to own up to my mistakes. Only then

233

can I spin my actions in a more favorable light. Not that any of this is favorable. But Matthew certainly won't make this easy on me if I let him get the first word out of this incident.

I set off for my apartment. Pulling out my phone, I check my texts.

**Lynn: Miss you already.**

I shove it back in my pocket. I can't talk to her right now. I'm too angry to form a coherent statement. When I finally get home, I fire up my computer and send Principal Gordon an email.

**Hey Barry,**

**Hope your weekend is going well. I need to speak to you about a pressing matter on Monday. Can we meet in your office before or after school?**

I don't expect a quick response, but within five minutes my phone pings.

**Hey Carson,**

**Sure thing. How about after school? Hope everything is okay.**

**Barry**

*I hope it will be.* I start to type that, but then stop to consider a better response. Ultimately it comes down to nothing to say, so I simply agree on the time.

**Afternoon works. Thanks.**

Matthew's a loose cannon; I'm not sure what his end game is. Does he want Lynn back? *Over my dead body.* Does he want to hurt me? *Bring it.* I don't give a shit, but if he thinks I'll just walk away, he has another thing coming.

I grab a tumbler and pour a glass of scotch, debating whether to worry Lynn now or fix shit and then bring her into the loop.

*No, I'll fix this.*

She's got too much going on without having to deal with my shit *and* Matt.

*Matt.*

He's a problem. I need to bring him to heel. I wonder what his father would say about this? That's what I'll do. One, I have to talk to the principal. Two, I have to talk to Matt's dad. That should rein him in.

*One can hope.*

———

I keep myself busy the next day. When I'm not teaching, I'm doing stupid busy work, but it seems almost futile since I know this is it for me. Unfortunately, Lynn is nowhere to be seen today. It's probably a good thing. She tends to be a distraction, and with my meeting with the principal pending, having my wits about me is probably smart. It's still hard to not search her out. In the end, I'm forced to send a text asking her to meet me at my place. She has a key from when she was dealing with all the shit with her mom, and the idea that she will be waiting for me after my future is decided makes me relax some.

*Some.* Not one hundred percent.

I pretty much know what I'll have to do. I put down my pen. *Unless* . . . Maybe I can state my case, explain what happened, and maybe, just maybe, he'll have a different solution. Yeah, maybe this could work out.

Four hours later I realize it was stupid to hope. After briefly describing the ordeal between Lynn and myself and the threat from Matthew, I'm not hopeful about my prospects for a better solution. I find myself growing angry at my own stupidity.

"As I see it, you have a choice," Barry says, leaning over his desk. *Do I really have a choice?*

"And what choice is that?" I take a deep breath to calm my nerves. I can't lose my temper. I need to make the best of this fucking crappy situation, even if that means fisting my palms under the table so he can't see how pissed I am.

"You can resign."

"Or." I huff and he in turn releases a long drawn out sigh.

"I can fire you." His brows draw together and I can tell he's not happy with the prospect of that.

"No other options?"

"Listen, Carson. I like you. I have seen how much you have grown. Hell, I've known you since you were a boy and studying here. You've changed a lot, but you still have some deep-seated anger issues. Running—and yes, I know you run—might channel some of the negative energies that you have, but you still have anger issues you haven't addressed. To be frank, hearing about your fight with Matthew makes you a liability to the student and staff."

"I would never hurt—"

"Yes. Carson, I know you think that. Personally, I know it too, but will the parents? All the parents will hear is that you beat up a former student, and worse than that if he goes public. And I'm not sure he won't. You're carrying on an affair with a student. I understand she's nineteen now. Nevertheless, it doesn't matter. Honestly, you are lucky we aren't a public school. Regardless that the evidence in the picture isn't overly damning, the two together don't look good. If we were a public school, I'd be forced to press charges."

"So, that's my only choice? I'm fucked and without a job either way." He grimaces at my choice of words but in the end, reluctantly nods. I knew the chances were slim to none. "Well,

I guess there's nothing more I can say. Thank you for giving me this opportunity to work for you. Thank you for taking a chance on me. I'll never forget all you've done. Unfortunately, I don't think Cranbrook is a good fit for me anymore. I will be tendering my resignation by the end of the day tomorrow."

"I wish you all the best in the world, Carson, and if you need anything . . . A letter of reference—"

"I won't." He nods and I feel bad for being so candid. But why pretend anything other than the truth. I'll never teach again.

"What will you do?"

"I'm not sure." And I'm not. What I do know, though, is I have time to think. What do I really want to do with my life? I have to figure out this shit. Running is just a Band-Aid.

First thing I need to do is tell Lynn I'll no longer be teaching; second thing is fix my shit. It's not fair to her that I'm a ticking time bomb. I saw the look in her eyes when I fought with Matt the first time.

It doesn't take long to arrive at my apartment. When I open the door and step inside, I find Lynn curled on the couch. She smiles up at me and I hate that in the next few minutes she won't be. My gaze travels up her body until our eyes meet.

Those eyes. God, what those eyes do to me. I can't stop myself, and my hand has a mind of its own. Without freewill I walk over to Lynn and pull her into my embrace. My hand desperately grabs her neck, bringing my lips to hers.

She giggles against my mouth, but I don't stop the thrusts of my tongue. She pulls away and I want to scream *no*, but instead, I attach my mouth to her neck and start sucking.

"Carson." *Lick.* "Carson." *Lick.* "*Carson!*" Her voice is more forceful, and this time her small hands rest on my chest and push me away.

Reluctantly, at least on my part, we separate. I don't apologize. Instead we gaze at each other, getting our breaths back.

Neither of us speaks.

She lets out a deep breath. "What's going on?" I shrug. "Come on. I'm not dumb. I can see something happened. The restless energy is pouring out of you. Just tell me."

"I resigned."

"What!"

"Matt was planning to tell Principal Gordon about us and . . ." I trail off, realizing she might get mad about what I'm about to say. "And I punched him."

"So what? I thought he knew you were defending me." I look away. My eyes skate the distance of the room, looking at the future. Looking everywhere but at her.

"What aren't you telling me?"

"He wasn't talking about that time."

"Wh-Wh-" She pauses to collect her thoughts, deciphering what I just said. "There was another time?"

"Yes."

"I don't understand."

I jump to my feet to pass her, moving away from her completely. Each step made me want to go for a run. I need to tell her, but how will she react? Shit. I don't know what to do. So I pace.

Back and forth.

"You're scaring me," she whispers and my heart tugs in my chest.

"Matt came to me."

"And—"

"He had a picture of us." Her mouth drops open, her blue eyes so wide all I can see is the black of her dilated pupils.

"Before I go on, I need you to know, it wasn't graphic. Hell, it wasn't even that damning."

"So, what's the problem?"

"The problem is how I reacted. I decked him when he told me to end things or he'd show it to the school. The picture alone wouldn't be enough. But the picture combined with my violent track record would. The board *would* have fired me."

"Now what?"

"This way I don't run the risk of this damaging either of us. If the picture leaks, we can spin it that we didn't get together until after I left. That I left to pursue a relationship with you. Yeah, socially we might be ostracized, but they can't press charges."

"But I'm nineteen."

"It doesn't matter, Lynn."

"This is all my fault. You lost your job because of me."

"No." I move toward her and tip her head upward, swiping at the tear sliding down her face. "This isn't your fault. I knew the consequences. I knew the risk. You're worth it. Do you understand me? Even knowing what happened, I would make the same decision again."

"So, will they press charges?"

"No. There is really no evidence, and as it's a private school, they don't follow the same rules as public. With this limited evidence, they run the risk that I could countersue. Instead, Principal Gordon and I came to the decision that the best course of action for all parties is that I resign."

"I'm so sorry."

"Listen. This is a good thing. I became a teacher to help kids, to give them guidance, but maybe I can do that some other way. I'll find something I can do."

"What about the money?"

239

"I own my apartment, and between the trust fund I received when I turned twenty-two and my savings, I'll be okay. This sabbatical will give me time to fix some personal shit, too."

Her brows lowered. "Personal shit?"

"Not you."

"Then what? Carson, I think you need to see someone. One thing I learned from my mandatory appointments with the school therapist is sometimes distraction isn't enough. You spend so much time channeling your feelings through running and through teaching, and you've done a great job, but you still have deep rooted issues. If not therapy or classes, maybe the first step can be a group meeting or something. They have to have *something*, like AA."

"Okay."

"Okay?"

"Yeah. I'll find help."

"Really?"

"Yeah, I promise I will look into talking to someone. But, Lynn, it's been a long day. Can we—"

"Yeah. We can," she said, pulling me to her and burrowing her head in the crook of my neck.

I don't bother to say anything else, instead just bring her mouth to mine while pulling down her pants. I don't even bother with my own clothes.

Just unzip.

Free myself.

We fall to the floor with a soft thud, and then I grab her and position her above my waiting hips, slamming her down. With each move of our bodies, I pick up the pace. Her panting becomes louder and louder, as I pump in and out.

"Carson . . ." she groans.

"Fuck."

I lift my hips again, and then wrap my arms around her, flipping her beneath me so I have control.

I continue to pump in and out at a punishing pace. My hips slam into hers. Her body tightens like a vise at the new angle, her whole body seizing around me, gripping me until that's all it takes to send me over the edge.

"Damn," I mutter out against her neck. She laughs.

This right here makes up for all the earlier bullshit. This right here is perfect.

# CHAPTER FORTY

Lynn

YESTERDAY WAS AWFUL. CARSON LOST HIS JOB. WELL, technically resigned. I wasn't sure if I would see him today, but when I was walking down the hallway, there he was. It took my breath away, but not in a good way. *It gutted me.* He looked so wounded, so hollow. As though the spark in his eyes was gone. As though he had been through a battle and then lost the war. Seeing someone you care about look like that, well, it cuts deep. Especially when you know you're to blame, or at least partially. Even though there is nothing I can do to fix this situation, it still feels horribly wrong for me to walk through the halls as if nothing changed, when in truth everything has.

With everything going on today, Carson is staying late at school so I'm by myself at home. Luckily for me, my mom is not here. I'm not sure where she is, but I'm not questioning it. Just enjoying the peace and tranquility her absence brings. Lying on my bed, I pull out my computer to sort through my PMs on Facebook when I hear a pounding on the door. I check the time on the clock. Nine o'clock. *Who the heck is knocking so late?* Normally, I wouldn't care, but life has been kicking my ass.

Walking out in the hall, I peer into my mom's room. The door is wide open and she's still not there. She's probably out for the night. Maybe she met a new man. We haven't spoken since I found out the truth. Yeah, we bump into each other, but speak . . . not so much. Not that we ever *speak*. More like she tells me where and when to be and how I'm supposed to act. Or she yells what an utter disappointment I am. I hate the idea of living here, but I can't think of any solution. I'll just have to grin and bear it until June. It can't come soon enough. The pounding continues.

I look through the peephole and see Matt standing on the other side. I don't bother to unlock the chain when I open it.

"What do you want?"

"Let me in," he slurs. He's drunk. This is not the Matt I dated. Sure, he was always a selfish prick, but apparently he's now a drunk one.

"You're wasted. I'm not letting you in. Haven't you done enough damage to my life? Can't you leave me alone?"

"You're going to want to hear what I know about him," He braces his hand against the doorframe to balance his weight.

"I highly doubt it."

"I guarantee it."

"Leave me alone. Why are you around all the time? You dumped me, remember? I found you literally fucking someone else and you dumped me."

"I want you back," he says as his hand pulls away from the doorframe and massages the back of his neck.

"Why?" He draws his brows together at my question. He didn't want me once, why in the hell would he want me now?

"I don't know. I just do."

"You only want me 'cause you can't have me. You do believe that, right?" He shrugs, then something flashes in his eyes.

"Where's your boyfriend tonight?" And that's it; he's gone too far.

"You need to leave," I bite out as I cross my arms in front of my chest.

"You know he threatened my life?"

"Yeah, sure." My eyes roll in disbelief.

"He did." My patience is wearing thin, but at the same time I feel the need to stick up for Carson.

"You made him lose his job."

He cocks his head. "Doesn't seem quite enough, does it? The man is fucking crazy. He's a sick and violent pedophile."

"I'm nineteen. I'm legal!" I shout.

"He's still a sick ass fuck."

"What are you talking about?"

"Oh, don't you know?"

"Know what?" He gives me a lopsided smile. One that makes my skin crawl.

"Do you know anything about him from high school? The trouble he got into?" The way his eyes shine tells me he knows something and it's not good.

"He's changed. He reformed. Now he helps people."

"Is getting into fights and taking advantage of little girls helping people?"

"Again, I'm legal and you deserved it. You were the one trying to take advantage of a girl."

"So, he didn't tell you?"

"Tell me what?"

"First off, it wasn't only that one time. He decked me and almost broke my jaw the last time I saw him. Second, well, there's just too much to tell. Maybe you should read this." He throws a printout from an old newspaper at me.

"What the heck is this?" There's no disguising the satisfied look in his eyes. Whatever it is, it's bad.

"Your boy. Yeah, not only is he still violent, but he has a long track record of abusing people." I don't bother listening to any more of what he has to say. Instead, I move to shut the door in his face, but not before he slides the paper all the way in a second before it slams closed. The paper falls to the floor, its threat echoing in the foyer, begging me to read what Matt is gloating about. Begging me to witness the demons Carson is hiding. I lean against the wall, staring at the little sheet of paper I wish I could pretend isn't there.

*I shouldn't.*

I pick it up.

*Don't look.*

I can't help myself.

I open it.

The headline screams at me.

*Violence. Drugs. Rape.*

What the hell is this?

*Students arrested.*

I press my hand against my throat. The page blurs. I continue to read through tears that are falling fast. I swipe them away. The words have no meaning, yet the story screams out at me. The article depicts the story of a young girl at a party, Rohypnol, and an arrest.

None of this makes sense. What the hell does this have to do with the names of the boys arrested?

Mark Bishop.

Carson Blake.

My knees grow weak. They can't hold the weight of my body.

*What is this?*

I don't understand. Could I have been so wrong about Carson? So off-base?

*No.*

This isn't the man I know . . . or is it? I have seen the anger. I have seen the darkness in his eyes. I have felt the palpable energy exuding off him, watched him breathe to calm himself.

I have heard the pounding on the pavement as he exorcised his tremors with each beat of his feet on the path. But the most damning evidence of all—I witnessed the rage in his eyes as his fist connected with Matthew's jaw that day at school. I saw the way he looked. It wasn't him looking back at me. It was a stranger who sounds a lot like the person described in this old news clipping. *Violent. Rage.* It pains me to imagine it, it kills me to admit it, but maybe I am wrong about everything. Maybe I'm clouded by lust and never see just how dark he is. Maybe I never saw the monster living inside him.

*I can't think.*

I need to walk.

Throwing on my coat and shoes, my feet take me right out the door with no destination in mind.

Why didn't he tell me?

*Why would he tell me?*

Would he do that? Would he hurt a girl?

God. My brain. It's like a clamp is grasping every synapse in my head, my mind ceasing to work.

*Think. Think. Think.*

No.

Never.

Not Carson.

But even Carson himself told me he fucked up, that he needed to redeem himself. Change himself? Is this what he was talking about?

My phone rings in my pocket. Speak of the devil. Do I answer? *You need answers.*

"Yes." There is no hiding the bite to my voice.

"Are you okay?"

"I read an article about you," I sneer, unable to control my emotions, my feelings of betrayal.

"What article?"

"Are there that many?" The thought makes me sick. Bile turns in my throat.

"I have no idea what you are talking about." *He doesn't know what I'm talking about?* Who the hell doesn't remember something like that?

"Are you a monster?" I spew out before I can stop myself. A feeling of dread washes over me. *Please say no.* But he doesn't answer and I don't speak. His silence is answer enough for me. I don't know this man at all. "I need to go. I can't do this."

"Lynn . . ." I don't let him finish.

Disconnect. Everything pours out. Every last bit of emotion. Tears drain from my eyes like a torrential rain. Time halts, but my movements do not.

Sometime later, the moisture ceases and my mind clears.

Where am I? Where am I going? With a sudden halting of my steps, I glance from right to left. I'm on his street. Standing in front of his building. My feet brought me here. But why? My mind screams back at me, stop being a petulant child . . . *You need to let him explain.* Shit. What will I say to him?

I nibble on my inner cheek the closer I get to the entrance of his apartment building. When I reach the doorman, I give a nod. Then let myself up.

I know he said I could use my key, let myself in, but I can't. I need to see him before I enter. I need the safety of that. God, I hate myself. I hate these thoughts. Am I really scared of him?

No.

*Yes.*

How can I doubt him?

*Knock.*

*Knock.*

*Knock.*

He opens the door.

His brows are drawn, his eyes hollow. He looks hurt. Wounded. And I feel awful. I don't fear him. I love him.

"Are you coming in?" His words break and there is no doubt this is my doing. What I said is causing him damage and pain.

*What did I do?*

I nod.

He steps away to give me distance. He doesn't touch me. It breaks me apart. Rips and shreds my soul.

When we sit, he buries his face in his hands and the laceration tears further inside of me.

"Will you let me tell you the real story, or have you already damned me?"

I don't answer; I can't because he's right. I have. I have damned him, condemned him without hearing his side, and it's awful. A screech echoes through the space. I jolt at the sound, but it's only Carson pushing his chair back. He stands, not speaking, and I watch as he sulks away. *Where is he going? Am I being dismissed?* A rustling of paper comes from his bedroom and then he reappears, eyes red and glassy. He thrusts a few news clippings in my face. I take them with shaking hands.

There are three.

"This is the original article, the story that was leaked right after the incident. It wasn't the real story. It doesn't tell everything. Read the other two." I look down and then back at him. Lowering the clippings, I emit a deep breath.

"Tell me."

"Why should I?"

"Because even though I didn't hear you at first, you deserve the right to tell your story. And even though I was wrong to attack you, I still deserve to know. I deserve the truth. Your truth. No matter what that means."

He tilts his head back in thought, then looks down without meeting my gaze.

"I told you I got in trouble, but not the extent. It's hard for me to talk about. I thought you understood and respected that. I thought I could withhold that part of myself. But I realize now you're right." His chin tilts up, his eyes penetrating mine. "For this to work you need to know every part of me, trust me and not fear me."

"I don't fear you."

"Yes, you do. And you have every right to. You have seen me lash out."

"That's different. It was deserved."

"Regardless, you have the right to be scared. Without knowing my side of the story, hearing or reading about my past must have terrified you. But I swear on everything, my violence was justified."

"You're not a horrible person."

"I am." He lets out a sigh. "You know I had no guidance in my life. You know my parents weren't around often, that I was raised by nannies. But that's not the whole story. There's more.

So much more. See, my parents *were* around. Not often, but not as little as it became. When I was little they were there. They would take me with them. But then life got stressful and my father started to take his worries out on us. At first it was just yelling, then it escalated . . . a lot."

"Oh, God," I gasp and shake my head, not wanting to believe what I think he's about to tell me.

"When a teacher mentioned a bruise on my arm to my mom, they decided to leave me home. At home, my father was okay. Maybe not okay, but better. But sometimes on the trips . . . Well, they were stressful. Listen, Lynn. I don't want you to fear me. I would never hurt you."

"I know."

"But I also need you to know. They decided to leave me home when they left, and then it became more and more often. It soon became that they were away more than they were not. As I got older I got angrier and angrier. They had abandoned me. Left me to fend for myself.

"I lashed out. I picked on kids in my class. Then I picked fights with them, and as I grew older it escalated, just like my dad, until I found myself fighting more than I wasn't. I was the hothead. The kid with anger issues, abandonment issues. I never let anyone get close. I barely had friends. I was a loner. I was in trouble all the time. But there was no discipline. No one to make me change, and I was too damn foolish to want to change. One night I went to a party and I got into a fight. A bad one. One that should have ruined me. I was arrested, but the papers had it wrong."

"So, you didn't put someone in the hospital." *Please say you didn't*. Please say this was all a big misunderstanding.

"Oh, I did. And I did want to kill him." There was an edge

to his voice. One I had never heard before. It caused a wave of chills to shoot through my extremities.

"I don't . . . I don't understand," I stutter out.

"It was self-defense." His expression grows even more serious.

"But—" I peer up at him, imploring with my determined gaze. I need to know everything.

"Not of me. I walked in on a guy I went to school with trying to rape a girl. His name was Mark Bishop." A chill ran up my spine. *The other name from the article Matt gave me.* "She was drugged, unconscious on the bed. I saw red, and once I started I couldn't stop. Someone called the cops. The story was leaked that there was a fight. That I tried to kill him, and I did, Lynn. You need to understand that I did want him dead, but it wasn't a fight over a girl. I was trying to save her."

My mouth hangs open. I can't speak.

"You have to understand. Growing up . . . " He pauses and takes a deep breath. "God, it wasn't just me he hurt. He hurt her, too."

He doesn't say who he's talking about but I know. I know without a doubt in my bones. He's talking about his mom. About his own twisted youth. About all the anger he holds, and the stress he puts on himself to be better. All of his comments start to make sense. He's not afraid to be arrogant. He's not afraid to be hated. He's afraid he will turn into his abusive father. I think back to the day in the kitchen when he'd left so abruptly. *The bruises . . . He thought he hurt me. He thought he was becoming his father.*

His finger reaches out, gently catching my falling tears, and then his hand trails down until he reaches my jaw. He lifts my chin and our eyes lock. "Look at me. I promise you. I promise I will never hurt you. I will never be him."

"I know."

"Then why are you crying?"

"Because you had to live with that. I-I never imagined it was that bad. I knew you were abandoned like me. But I never knew. I just . . ." I stop as my lids blink out another wave of tears. "I just never . . . I never thought you would hurt me. I-I-I'm not scared of you. I could never be. But why didn't you tell me?"

"I worried you would think I was a monster if I told you—and you did. In the end, you found out and you saw the truth. I was a monster. Maybe I still am. I don't know. I just don't want you to look at me the way you did tonight." I shake my head.

"I don't. I could never."

"But you did. After the fights. After the anger. You did." I move my hand to cover my face, hiding the tears pooling in my eyes. I lower it, still wet, to his hand, and he flinches at the contact.

"No. No, Carson. I was wrong. You are not a monster. That man . . . The man you beat up . . . He was a monster. Your father . . . He was a monster. You. You, Carson, could never be one." He shrugs. He doesn't believe me. Taking his hand, I lift it to my mouth and kiss each knuckle. Each bruised knuckle, one by one.

"You are not a monster, and you never will be."

"How do you know?"

"I won't let you."

"What will you do to stop me?"

"I'll protect you." I say it with conviction. Strong, without a hint of hesitation. "That's what it means to love. Neither of us was shown love by our parents, but I've seen it. I've seen it with

Bridget and her family . . . Well, with my family." My eyes flood again. "I've seen the love they are capable of. Protecting each other, loving each other. You're my family. You're my home. I will protect you with everything I have."

"And I, you." He pulls me to him, crushing his lips to mine. "I don't know." *Kiss.* "What I did to." *Kiss.* "Deserve you." *Kiss.* "But I'm never giving you up."

"Not ever?"

"Not ever."

We continue to kiss, our lips saying every word in our hearts. And when our lips aren't enough, he strips me of my clothes and makes love to me, right there on the couch. Tears stream down my face as he loves me with everything he has. As he shows me everything and tells me everything that no words could ever say.

"Wow," I pant out once I come down from my high. He lets out a chuckle and we simply lay in each other's arms until our breathing regulates.

———

Sometime later, we prepare dinner, set the table and then eat. When we are done, I think about what I said before, about family. About being home.

"Carson," I say from across the room as he washes the dishes. He looks over his shoulder.

"Yeah?"

"I was thinking. I think I'm going to tell him." He puts down the dish and turns around, pulling out a towel to dry the counter. He studies me for a minute. The blue of his eyes widens slightly.

"You're going to tell him?" he finally says.

"Yeah. I'm ready." At my words he gives a nod.

"Do you want me to go with you?"

"Yes, but . . ." I trail off. As much as his presence would calm me, he can't be there.

"I understand. This is something you need to do alone."

"Are you mad?"

"Not at all. I feel the same way about everything with me. So, I understand." My lungs expel the air I didn't even realize I was holding. "I found a group, and they also referred me to a specialist . . . to speak to." He threads a hand through his hair.

"That's good."

"Yeah. I think it is." His head cocks to the side and I smile.

"I'm really proud of you." He smirks. "Is it weird for me to say that?"

"Not at all. I feel the same way about you. You have grown so much this year, Lynn. From the girl I met that day on the beach, to the woman you are now. It's quite remarkable. With everything I am, I know you can handle whatever happens with your father—no matter what. No matter what gets thrown our way, you and I will handle it."

"Now I just have to bite the bullet."

"You will. You just have to decide when."

"I don't know, maybe this week sometime. Maybe next week. Bridget says they are all going out to see a play in a few weeks, but her dad isn't going along. She asked if I wanted to take his ticket. I think I'll visit him then. That way, in case he doesn't take it well . . ."

"He will."

"But in case he doesn't, I don't want Bridge to know quite yet. And depending on how he reacts, if all goes well, he can help with that. We can do it together. And if all goes to shit, you'll help me?"

"Of course. But have faith. It's like the story I told you. You're Artemis. You, like her, are a warrior and her greatest strength was her courage. No matter what happens you will be okay."

# CHAPTER FORTY-ONE

## Lynn

A WEEK PASSES. I STILL HAVEN'T TOLD SAM HE'S MY DAD. I still haven't told Bridget she's my sister, either. Every time I'm ready to tell her, something happens—she has someplace to be or I chicken out. Truth is, it's because I have to tell him first and that's the hard part. Ever since my mom left to go to the Hamptons, I've been hiding at Carson's place. I'm not sure when she's due to return, but until she does I'll continue to live in my pretend bubble where everything is okay. Basically, I'll ignore all the shit I'm supposed to deal with until she's back, and spend all my free time with Carson. Sounds like a good plan to me. Speaking of . . . Where is he? He went to get us a snack twenty minutes ago and hasn't returned.

Pulling on a robe, I head toward the kitchen, but never make it there. Halfway down the hall I spot him sitting at his desk in his office typing furiously on the computer.

"Hey." I step in and he peers up at me and then back down the screen. *Okay.* "What are you doing? Or working on, for that matter."

Without looking up, his voice drifts through the air above the sound of his fingers hitting the keyboard. "I know what I want to do."

"What?" I have no idea what he's talking about.

"I figured it out."

"I don't understand?" He motions me closer. I step behind him and peer at his screen.

"I'm going to do it. I'm going to use some of my trust fund to start a boys' club."

"Where did that come from?" I knew he loved spending time with the kids, but to open a club and manage it?

"It's something I need to do." He hesitates for a minute, and every breath catches in my throat as I wait for him to explain. "Growing up, I needed this, Lynn. I had no one for so long. It wasn't until almost end of high school that I found my outlet. This. Opening this club for boys like me. I need to do it." I watch him warily for a minute to discern if this is the right move for him, but when he peers into my eyes, I see it. This is what he's meant to do.

"Then let's do it." He pulls me onto his lap.

"Thank you for believing in me." It's all he says before he captures my mouth. These words from his lips are everything and more.

---

The next day I receive a text from my mom that she'll be home later that evening. The wedding is back on so she needs to be in the city. Obviously staying at Carson's is out of the question, so I reluctantly head back home. Later that evening as I lay in my bed flipping through the channels, I hear someone knock at the door.

I swing it open without even checking.

*Big mistake.*

Matt. I try to slam it shut, but he thrusts his foot in to block it before I can. The door shoves back open and I stumble back. The smell of booze wafts out at me. He's drunk . . . again. I don't know what his obsession is with me, but this is getting old and a little scary.

"What do you want now? Haven't you caused enough problems?"

"Don't you know?"

"No. No, I don't. Other than you trying to make my life miserable, I'm not sure what you want."

"I want you back."

"Again with this nonsense," I huff out. "Why the hell do you want me back now?"

"I don't want him to have you."

"What the fuck are you going on about? Why can't he 'have me'?" I air quote. "Why do you care? What is your sick obsession with him?"

"No obsession. I just don't like the prick."

"What are you still doing home? Shouldn't you be back at school?"

"I was placed on academic suspension." *Great.* "So now I'm back."

"But that doesn't answer the question. Why are you harassing us? What is your vendetta with Carson? What's your obsession with me?"

He steps into me; my back hits the wall behind me. His breath is in my face, the smell of tequila so strong I swear I can taste it.

"Well, that's easy. He stole what's mine and then he stole my life. Now I want to take one back." His hand snakes out and grasps my wrist. The sharp bite on my skin makes my eyes water.

His other hand runs up the side of my hip and I swear I feel the bile collect in my throat.

"Take your hands off me."

"Now, why would I do that?"

"Because this . . . This isn't you, Matthew. I don't know what's going on with you. But this isn't the guy I dated. The guy I was with didn't drink like this. He didn't hurt and scare girls."

"What would you know about anything?"

"What happened to you? Why are you—"

"Like you don't know. Like you didn't put him up to it." His hand tightens. If he applies any more pressure, I'm sure it will break.

"Put who up to what?"

"Don't play dumb. I know you know. I know you told him to tell my father I was trespassing on school property, that I was touching you."

"I-I don't know what you're talking about."

"Mr. Blake. Your Mr. Blake ran to my father. Told him the school decided not to press charges."

I shake my head in confusion.

"After being expelled from college, that was just the ammunition he needed. He cut me off. Canceled my credit cards. I had to crash at a friend's place. I have nothing. I lost everything because of you." The throbbing in my wrist is screaming at me to pull away.

"I tried to get your boy fired, but lo and behold, my plan didn't work. But maybe this plan will."

"What plan?"

"To hit him where it actually hurts."

"And where's that?"

"With you. I wonder how he'll feel knowing I fucked his girl." His tongue jets out and licks his lips. "Will he even want you afterward? Two birds with one stone, don't you think."

"I'm not going to fuck you. You're delusional and drunk." I try to push him away; my wrist feels like millions of tiny shards of glass as I use my weight to pull back. *If it's not broken it'll be a miracle.* He tightens his hold on my wrist, levering it down to block me in.

His free hand reaches out and grabs hold of my shoulder, and then begins to trail down my torso until it rests on the waistband of my pants.

My eyes lock onto his, but the smoldering stare he gives me has me frozen in front of him, not able to form words from my fear. *I don't know what this Matt is capable of.*

My heart hammers inside my chest as panic starts to grip me. I wonder if he's drunk enough that if I kick him or hit him, I can knock him off.

Just when I'm developing a plan, the door swings open and I let out a deep breath. Surprisingly, it's my mother. I'm not sure what she's doing or what she sees. Her eyes narrow as if she thinks she's walked in on something. I silently plead with her to see me. To see what's behind my eyes.

She looks me up and down, and then her gaze trails to where he's clutching me.

He loosens his grip but maintains his hold. "What is going on here?" With one step she is in front of us, pulling my hand from his. Angry red splotches paint my wrist. "What are you doing touching my daughter?" There is venom in her voice. "I'll say this one time and only one time. No one touches Lynn. I know people. I know a lot of people, and if you ever lay a hand on her again, one phone call and you'll be arrested faster than you ever thought possible." Her teeth are clenched as she grits out the words. Each syllable lashes out like an attack. My mouth hangs open in shock. The air simmers with tension and Matt's eyes are wide in disbelief. He steps back from me.

"Mom, I think it's fine now. Matt was just leaving. Weren't you, Matt?" He swallows and reluctantly bobs his head.

"This isn't over."

"Yes. Yes, it is. You go after Carson again—you say one word to me again. You do anything to us—not only will you lose everything monetarily speaking, but I will also press charges. Do you understand?"

I lift my arm. The color is already changing to a deep crimson.

"I understand," he murmurs.

"Get out, and be lucky I don't have you arrested. Next time, you won't be so lucky."

When he finally leaves, I let out the breath I'm holding.

*Fuck.*

I fall on the floor, tears flowing from my eyes in black rivulets.

Through my sobs I hear the soft patter of footsteps coming closer. "Are you—"

"No. Thank you for sticking up for me, but I can't deal with you right now." I swipe my face. Hold my back up and open the door. She walks out, and without a word I close it.

I need to go to the doctor, or hospital. I need to see if this is broken. I wonder if I should call Carson. Probably, but he's so on edge these days. I'm not sure what to do.

**Me: I need you.**

**Bridget: Are you okay.**

**Me: No. Not really, but I will be.**
**Bridget: Come here.**
**Me: Is your dad there?**
**Bridget: Why do you need my dad?**
**Me: I'm hurt.**
**Bridget: Now you're scaring me.**
**Me: I'll see you soon.**

———○———

Bridget hugs me to her the moment I step through the door. My whole body relaxes into her embrace. *I have to tell her. No. Not like this.* Not when I'm wounded and confused. This isn't the right time. As she hugs me tighter, I wince in pain.

"What happened?" she asks as she pulls away. "Are you okay?" I shrug.

"It's my wrist. I hurt it." I try to downplay the whole situation. But it doesn't work as she frantically takes my arm in hers, and then draws in a long breath.

"It's swollen."

All I can do is nod. Nod and pray she doesn't ask questions.

"Like, *really* swollen."

"Yeah, I know." I jerk my head in the other direction to ward off her inquiry.

"How did this happen?" No such luck.

"I don't want to talk about it." My upper teeth bite into my lower lip. *Please don't push.*

"Bullshit, Lynn. You are going to tell me exactly what happened, and you are going to tell me now. Was it Carson?" She doesn't know much about Carson. She never had him as a teacher, but still. It makes my stomach drop that she would even

262

think it's him.

"No, of course not." I squeeze my eyes shut then reopen them. "How can you think that?"

"Well, what do you want me to think? You've been so weird lately. Distant—"

"So . . ." I look at her intently, then wave my wounded hand at her. "You think I'm a battered girlfriend. Really, Bridge?"

"I'm worried about you. I have no idea what your deal is. Tell me who did this. What happened? If not Carson, then who?"

She's right. I have to tell her. As much as it pains me to admit what happened, it's necessary.

"Matt."

"Matt?" Her eyes are huge. Her mouth hangs open.

"Yes. He's been harassing me."

"I-I don't understand. Why didn't you tell me?"

"I was embarrassed," I whisper out and she pulls me back into her arms.

"You never have to be embarrassed or ashamed with me." I think about coming clean. Of telling her everything. All the secrets I have hidden inside. The relief would be welcome. Maybe I could tell Sam, too.

"What's going on in here?" My back stiffens at the new voice. Speak of the devil . . . It's my father. This is not how I want him to see me, crying in Bridget's arms. I need to be strong to confront him. No, tonight isn't the time or the place. It will have to wait. "Will someone please answer me?"

"Lynn is hurt, Dad. Can you look at her?" I pull away and extend my hand to him.

"Yes, of course," he says as he takes my hand and looks down. He moves my hand, turns my wrist in different directions. "How did this happen?"

"My-my—" I try to say, but a strangled sob comes out instead.

"Her ex-boyfriend," Bridget steps in and informs him.

"You really should file a—"

"No," I blurt out. I can't. I can't run the risk of Matt causing more trouble for Carson and me. "That's not necessary." His eyes narrow. "Please."

"I'm not okay with this. But you're not my daughter, and you're over eighteen, so I can't insist." My stomach clenches. *Not his daughter.* It feels as if my breath is cut off as the sentence plays over and over again in my head. *No. Don't think about it.* With a deep breath, I calm my tattered nerves.

"Thank you."

The tension in the room is palpable as no one speaks. Finally, Sam turns to me. "I still want to document this."

"I—"

"No, Lynn. This, I insist on. Your wrist isn't broken, but the bruising is apparent. If something happens again, we'll have this. Please."

I bite my lip and look away. "Okay."

"Bridget, sweetie. Can you go to the medicine cabinet and grab the prescription Motrin for Lynn?"

"Sure." As Sam wraps my wrist, Bridget steps out of the room.

"Thank you for letting me document this. I'd make Bridget press charges, but since you refuse and I'm not your father, I can't make you. At least we have proof."

*I'm not your father.*

*I'm not your father.*

*I'm not your father.*

The words replay over and over again in my head. They're

my undoing. Something inside me snaps completely at that. Every muscle tenses in my body as he finishes and steps away.

I can't take it. Even though I know he doesn't know, all the lies my mother spewed over the years manifest into a feeling that won't be contained. Misplaced or not, anger coils inside me until it's impossible for the rage not to expel.

"Does she know?" I hiss out.

His whole body stiffens as he turns to me from across the room. "Does who know?" he says awkwardly, clearing his throat.

"Your wife."

Sam flinches at my words. His eyes go round. "I-I don't know what you're talking about?" he stutters, and I know he does and it infuriates me more.

"Don't you?"

He doesn't speak, just rubs at his brow.

"Nothing to say?"

"Listen, I'm not sure what your mother told you, but I can assure you, it's not what you think."

"Not what I think . . . Not what I think," I mumble under my breath, shaking my head. "You disgust me." I don't give him time to defend himself. I'm too angry and too weak to fight anymore. All I can do is find Bridget and cry.

Thirty minutes later, I find myself tucked in Bridget's bed next to her. She insisted. She wouldn't even let me sleep in the guest room. It feels right being here like this, as if we're sisters.

I shouldn't have yelled at Sam. Now that I'm calm I can see that. I was just so angry, I saw red. He needs to know, because it's obvious he doesn't. I need to find the courage to tell him . . . to tell them. With a deep breath, I close my eyes.

I will.

But not today.

———————

The next day, I know I can't put it off any longer. I have to see Carson. He's been texting and calling all day. I can't avoid him, not without hurting him.

I knock on his door with my right hand. Thank God that wasn't the one that was bruised. I was lucky. I was also lucky it wasn't a break. If it was, I don't think I would've been able to convince them not to press charges.

My stomach feels uneasy. I dread facing Carson. I dread what he will say, and truth be told, I'm scared. Not for me, but for him. Heaven knows how he'll control himself knowing Matt touched me. That's something we need to talk about. He would never hurt me, but he still needs to work on his anger issues.

The door swings open and Carson is standing there in his usual casual attire: white T-shirt, ripped jeans, white Converse. A man should never be this sexy. I'm having a hard time speaking as I appraise him.

"What happened to your hand?" he says, pulling me out of my thoughts.

"My hand?" I repeat dumbly, and then snap out of it. I'm not here to have my way with him. I'm here to tell him about Matt.

"Oh, this." I try to make it sound like it's not a big deal. It is, but we are standing in the hallway of his apartment building. This is not the place to have this conversation.

"Yeah . . . this." He glowers at me. It's hard to be evasive when someone knows you so well.

"Can we go inside . . . please?" He must notice my trepidation because his eyes soften.

"Come here first." He gently pulls me into his embrace. It

feels so good. Home. I want to fall into him. I want to cry and let it all go. Every last bit of anger, rage, and sadness for what I went through, for what we went through. But first I need to tell him what happened.

He kisses my hair gently, then moves to tip my chin up and place a soft kiss on my lips. Pulling back he smiles. "Now we can go in."

I follow him into the apartment. Taking a seat on the couch, I look up at him. I know I have to tell him. God, why is this so hard?

He sits adjacent to me and waits. Waits for me to find my strength, my words.

"Matt did this to me." With that, he pushes to stand. His right hand clenches into a fist. I want to go to him. Hold him. Tell him it's okay. But even though I know he won't hurt me, it's better I stay away. All I can do is pray he can control himself, not for me, but for him. "Please listen. Please calm down." His eyes are wild as they take me in. The blue of his irises are completely gone. He looks like a rabid animal.

"Take a deep breath, Carson." I have to fight my visceral reaction to touch him. To make contact with his skin. "Take a deep breath. I'm okay. Do you hear me? I'm okay."

I watch his chest heave. In. Out. In. Out.

"Talk," he says through gritted teeth. He inhales again. "Please. Talk, Lynn." In. Out. In. Out. "I need to know what happened." I swallow with difficulty until I find my voice.

"He showed up at my place. He was drunk. He blamed us for everything. He said you went to his father."

"I did," he admits in a cool tone. As if he's trying to refrain from going over the edge.

"Why didn't you tell me?"

"At the time?" His shoulders lift. "I don't know."

"From now on, you tell me things . . . Okay?" His brows set into a straight line.

"Okay."

"So, he showed up at my place ranting and raving. It was entirely your fault. It was entirely my fault. I tried to walk away and he grabbed my wrist so I'd listen to him. He was so drunk, I'm no—"

"Do not make excuses for him. It's never right to lay a hand on a woman." I want to say on anyone, but this is not the time to bring that up. I'll broach that topic once I get this out.

"He wanted me back, wanted to hurt you through me."

"Did he . . ." I lift my unwounded hand.

"No. He mentioned that, but no, he didn't hurt me like that. He wanted to get back with me to hurt you." Veins have popped up in Carson's neck. Tension is radiating off him. His shoulders lift as he takes a deep breath.

"So, what happened?"

"My mom walked in. Might be the first time I've ever been happy to see her. She threatened him."

"And then what?" He almost sounds like a robot. Stoic.

"I told him I had enough evidence to have him arrested. He backed off after that. I then went to Sam and he treated me. We took pictures, and just in case he didn't heed my warning, I sent Matt a text message with the images. I explained to him he had to stay away or I would go after him. I think he'll leave us alone from now on."

Carson studies me, his gaze hard and penetrating. "When did this happen?"

I wince. "Please don't be mad."

"When?"

"Yesterday." His nostrils flare, and the mask of his rage appears.

"Goddamn, Lynn." I feel sick hearing the tone and anger in his voice. I'm ashamed. I shudder with humiliation. I should have come to him but I was scared. "What were you thinking? Why didn't you call the cops? Why didn't you call me?"

"I was thinking of you. I was saving you."

"He couldn't hurt me." He glares at me.

"I wasn't saving you from him."

"From whom, then?"

"From you. I was saving you from yourself. You have demons. I needed to protect you."

"Lynn, you know I would never hurt you, right? I'm not like Matt. I would never do that. I would rather cut my own heart. I don't want you to fear me."

"I would never fear you." I move to sit on him, placing my lips near his ear. "I love you. I love everything about you. Do you understand?"

"Yes," he says pulling back and crashing his mouth onto mine.

Our mouths collide, teeth gnashing. Frantic. Desperate. I straddle his hips, moving in a circular motion to alleviate the need growing inside me. Frantic hands lift my shirt. Cold air hits my breasts and chills rush over my body. My nipples pebble against his hands. I pull my legs tighter, bracketing myself around him.

I need more.

So much more.

With one hand still wrapped around Carson, I lift my hips, then use my other hand to free him from his pants. I'm struggling because of my wound, so he moves my hand away and I hear the familiar rasp of a zipper. When he's released himself, I feel his fingers pressing against my core. Circling. Teasing.

I want more than his hands. I push down to rub myself against him. He laughs against my mouth and then he repositions me, aligning me with him, pushing me down. Each inch is exquisite.

I pick up my rhythm, pushing up and slamming back down over and over again. It's utter perfection. I feel myself ready to explode, and it's obvious he is about to also. His hands tighten, possessing me and controlling me as he pushes up into me and I ride him. I feel everything; it's so intense, my body stiffens with the need to let go and then it happens. I let go. I lay panting on his chest, my head in the crook of his neck and then he lifts.

One.

Two.

Three more times into me, and he follows me over the edge.

"I love you," he mutters breathily from exertion. I laugh.

We stay panting and breathing heavily for a few minutes before I finally pull my head away to speak.

"I don't think I can get up. I'm jelly."

"Then don't. Let's stay here forever. Let's never leave."

"I would love that, but don't you think that could cause problems?"

"I don't know. I'm sure we could make do for a few weeks . . . at least." He moves his body and I groan. He lets out a chuckle.

"Come on, shower time."

"Shower time, you say?" My body perks up, dirty thoughts of an encore swirling through my mind.

"As much as I would love to have round two, I have a few things to do today. I have a group meeting tomorrow."

"You're still going to that?

"I said I would. And I'll never lie to you."

# CHAPTER FORTY-TWO

## Lynn

I T TAKES ME A FEW WEEKS TO WORK UP THE COURAGE, BUT finally today I decide it's time. With every bit of strength I have, I knock on the door of their brownstone. I know Sam will answer and I'm petrified. What will I say? How will I say it? Fear coils in my stomach. My teeth rattle against each other, making my jaw tremble and shake.

"Lynn." He narrows his eyes. "What are you doing here?" He looks at me with trepidation and I understand why. Last time I was here, I was hurt and I went off on him, screaming and throwing accusations. Why would he feel comfortable around me? I'm like a ticking time bomb. Why he would even want me to be his daughter after that is beyond me, but I can't possibly move forward in my life without trying. "Bridget is not here. She's on her way to the theater."

"I-I know. I actually wanted to talk to you."

"Okay." He pulls the door open wider and steps aside for me to pass. "Do you want to talk in my office or . . ."

"Your office is fine."

I follow him inside and down the hall into the office on the main floor. He motions to a chair, and as he sits I take a seat across from him.

My knee shakes uncontrollably. My hands tremble in my lap.

"What's this about?"

"First, I want to say how sorry I am about . . . Well, how sorry I am about the last time. I shouldn't have attacked you like that."

"You're right. You shouldn't have. And not that it's any of your business, Lynn, but Margo and I were legally separated. I was not cheating on her. The relationship I had with your mother was short and wrong. Very wrong. I knew she was married. I should never have taken part, but I was hurt and lonely. Margo had left me. And not that it's an excuse, but when your mom came around, she was a beautiful woman who accepted me.

"In the end, I went back to Margo. I realized how much I loved her and Olivia and that I needed to change for them. At the time I was a different man, selfish, and my career came first. Your mother was appealing, she didn't ask of my time, nothing more than I could give. But it was shallow and I realized I had a choice. Continue down that path and be with a woman like your mom, or value my wife, my marriage, and be happy. So, I went back to my wife. We halted the divorce proceedings, and I never looked back. And my wife knows. We have no secrets. I'm not sure why I have to justify it to you or why you feel you deserve to know, but that's the story."

"But that's the thing. I *do* have the right to know."

"I don't see how this affects you. This was before you were born."

"Yes, but how many months before I was born?" He stops, his face paling. I might not be able to hear it from his chair, but I can imagine him counting. He's thinking of every moment, putting the pieces of the puzzle together.

"But that . . . Are you saying . . . No, that can't be."

"It's true."

"No. Your mother is . . . How can that be? You're Bridget's age."

"I'm not. I'm actually a year older."

"I . . ." His mouth opens and shuts.

"I was held back. I'm a year older than Bridget. My birthday is in December. I just turned nineteen."

Lines form across his face. My own heart races as I watch him. As he does the math. Counts backward. Figures it all out. I don't think I can breathe. It's all too much. My body is a live wire and I'm about to fall apart.

His jaw begins to tremble, his nose scrunching in a way I have never seen before. It looks as though his eyes are glassy, and then, with no warning or understanding of what's happening, I'm in his arms. I feel my own tears falling, and my heart seizes. He is giving me more love in this embrace than I have ever had from a parent in my life.

"My daughter," he says into my hair, and his own body shakes against mine in silent sobs. It makes my tears fall even heavier.

"I have another daughter?" he mutters out almost in question, trying to understand. He holds me tighter. "You're my daughter," he confirms with conviction.

"You're his *what*?" Our cries stop. We are frozen. Both of us peer with tear soaked eyes to Bridget, who stands in the doorway. Her body is rigid at the sight in front of her. "What the hell is going on?" she asks, and we step away from each other. I wipe the tears off my face.

"What are you doing here?" he asks.

"What am I doing here? That's what you say to me, Dad? I walk in to find you hugging my best friend, calling her your daughter, and you have the nerve to ask what I'm doing here?"

"I can explain," he says again. He reaches for her but she pushes him away.

"Bridge," I say to gain her attention.

"No, you don't say anything. You're my best friend. I have no clue what the fuck is going on around here."

"I know and—"

Sam steps closer to Bridget. "Lynn, let me. Bridget, sweetie, I need to start by explaining that I wasn't always the man you know me to be. There was a time when I wasn't a good husband."

"Oh, my God." She clutches her chest.

"No, sweetie. I never cheated on your mother, but I might as well have. Before you were born, your mother left me. She gave me a choice, and when I chose myself first, she left. At first I was selfish and I was okay with that. Then I grew lonely and depressed. I'm not proud of what happened. I carried on an affair with a married woman."

"You cheated on Mom." She looks crestfallen or like she might throw up. "I can't believe—" He reaches out to her but she swats his hand away. "No. Don't touch me."

"You don't understand." He runs his hand frantically through his hair. "God, this is coming out all wrong."

He stops talking and I think she might do something. Maybe cry? But she looks like a statue, waiting to hear more. She's built a wall around herself so she doesn't suffer from whatever's about to be dumped on her.

"Can you please sit?" he asks nervously. "Please," he implores.

For the first time since this whole thing began, she pulls her eyes away from me. No matter what is going on, I'm her friend.

I nod toward the chair, willing her to understand that she needs to listen. That he's not the villain in this whole mess. That the only villain is my mom.

She sits and he lets out a deep breath. Folding himself into the seat next to her, he takes her hand in his. She looks as if she'll pull away but Bridget is stronger than that. I feel an immense level of pride rush through me as I look at her . . . as I look at my younger sister.

"Okay. I'll listen."

"I wasn't a good husband. I worked non-stop. I was never home, and when I was . . . I wasn't, if you understand. The father you know is not the husband I was in the past. I wouldn't speak to her; I was a void in this house. A ghost. One day she gave me an ultimatum. Shape up or ship out. But I was young. A hotshot orthopedic surgeon. I didn't need anyone telling me what to do. So, when she kicked me out I didn't fight, I just left." Bridget's body grows rigid at his words.

"It was a stupid and selfish thing to do, but I didn't see it at the time. I moved out. And, well, a few weeks later, after no contact, I was served with divorce papers. I was angry. Remember, I thought I was some god. How dare she divorce me? So I did something I'm not proud of—I started an affair with Lynn's mom. I met her at the gym of all places. Cliché, I know, but there she was, miserable and unhappy. And there I was, an asshole who needed my ego stocked. It didn't last long. We snuck around because she was married. But as time went on and I got to know her, I realized I didn't want to be with her. I wanted my family. I wanted love. So, I ended things. I told her never to contact me again, and even if I had to beg and plead, I would get my wife back. And I did."

The room is silent. Only the sound of breathing is in the air.

I don't know what to say, how to broach the next part of this conversation. I implore with my eyes for Sam . . . for my father to do it.

Bridget stands. She starts to pace, trying to work out this story, and then she turns to me. Her eyes are full of so much pain and hurt and sadness. When her gaze meets mine, tears welling, and my own fill as well.

"And you're . . ." She stops as a sob breaks from her throat. My heart thunders in my chest like a freight train. I bob my head yes. "Oh, my God!" Her tears burst out like a levee broke. "You're my . . ." She seems to be hyperventilating. "How long have you kn-known?" she stutters.

"Since around Christmas."

"And you never told me. Why didn't you tell me?"

I step closer to her, but she steps back, holding up a hand, not allowing me to comfort her. "No. You're my best friend. God, you're my sister. You should have told me."

"I know. I just . . . I wasn't sure if you . . ." I turn toward my father. "If he would reject me."

"I was your best friend."

"Was?"

"I-I . . . I need to get out of here. I need to think." And with that she storms out of the room. I fall into the nearest chair.

"It will be okay. She will be okay and understand and love you. She won't reject you. I won't reject you. Give her time. We all need some time."

"Okay," I say, rising to stand.

"Don't leave. I need to talk to Margo, but you're my daughter. And although we've always cared about you, this is your home now. We are your family, and we will get through this together. So, stay. You rest. I have a feeling this will be a long night." He smiles. It's reassuring and it washes over me with love. I believe him. Bridget might be upset and hurt but everything will be okay. I have faith.

He gives me a hug and then leaves the room. I pull out my phone and dial Carson.

"Are you okay?" he asks before I can even say hello.

"Yes. I think I am." I emit the air filling my lungs. Maybe not at this moment, but the weight lifted off my shoulders by telling Bridget, by telling my dad, is immeasurable.

"What happened?"

"I have a family," I say.

"You always had a family." And he was right. Regardless of what happened here tonight, I did have Carson. But now having this family . . . I feel complete. I never knew this part was missing, but I see it now, it floods me and brings on another round of sobs.

"I love you," he says between my cries. "I love you."

"And I you. Where are you?"

"Home. Are you coming here? Can you tell me what happened?"

"I can't come right now. Things are complicated over here at Bridget's. She heard . . . my fa-father," I stutter. "He's going to call Margo to come home."

"How's Bridget taking it?"

"Not well. She's hurt. She doesn't understand why I didn't tell her."

"She will understand. Give her time." His voice is reassuring and I know he's right.

"I will. But depending on how things go, I might not see you until tomorrow."

"Take all the time you need, and know if you need me, I'll

be there."

"I know."

"Keep me posted, okay?"

"I will." I disconnect the call and lie back into the chair and close my eyes. It will be a long night. *I'm Artemis.* I'm strong. I have gone to battle and lived through it. Whatever happens, I will be okay.

———

Some time passes. Minutes, maybe hours. I'm not sure how many, but I haven't moved the entire time. Everything is surreal and I'm not sure how to process it. As if lead has been poured through my entire body, I'm grounded to the couch. My eyelids are heavy.

Lord, did I cry tonight. I'm physically and emotionally exhausted.

There's a soft knock on the door. It opens slightly and I see Bridget pop her face in.

"Can I come in?" Her voice is low, her head down.

"It is your house," I say and she lifts her face to meet my gaze. I'm not sure how this will go, but I want her to know that even though I'm now her sister, I still respect her boundaries.

"It's your house now, too," she says. Those words are my undoing. My shoulders slump forward as I let out a strangled sob and tears pour down my face. She runs over to me, sits next to me on the couch, and pulls me toward her. Sob after sob, the dam bursts and I'm not sure I can stop it.

She begins to cry too, and we cry so hard that eventually we laugh.

"Wow, we're a mess," she says, wiping at her nose. "Need a

tissue?" She reaches for the box behind her.

"Oh, God, yes," I exclaim. She hands me one and we set out to wipe our noses. When I'm done, I ball it up and look up at her. Now that we're not crying or laughing, an awkward silence descends. In all the years I've known her, it's never been weird.

"So." She obviously wants to address the giant elephant in the room. "We're sisters."

"We're sisters," I affirm. "Are you okay with it?"

"Of course I'm okay with it." She nibbles on her lip. "Listen, I'm sorry I handled it the way I did."

"No, I understand. It must have come as quite a shock."

"It did, but still, you didn't deserve that. I spoke to my parents. Actually, I kind of went nuts on Dad. But he explained everything to me. I'm still very hurt, but I do know and understand why my parents never told me about Dad having an affair with your mom. The whole thing is just so complicated right now. But I didn't want you to think I was mad at you for this. I'm sure this has been . . . I know all you've been through, and for me to treat you as anything less than my sister, for you to ever think I wouldn't be happy, that I wouldn't love you and want you in my family . . . I'm sorry. I love you. You have always been a sister to me. Now, it's official."

"Thanks, Bridge. You have no idea how much it means to me. This has been hard . . . Really hard. But I finally feel okay. It has been a giant boulder on my shoulders since I found out. I wasn't sure how to handle it. I was scared. I didn't think I could handle any more rejection. But Carson really helped, and, well, same with Dr. Young."

"Carson knew?" I can't tell if she's hurt or just asking, so I just give a slight tip of my chin to say yes. "I'm happy you have him."

"You are?"

"Now that he's resigned and I'm not scared you'll get kicked out of school, I'm happy. It's not that I wasn't happy for you before. More like I was scared. With everything with your mom, Matt, and then the fear of what could happen at school, I was worried about you. But now that the threat is over, I'm happy. You deserve it."

"You deserve it, too."

"Maybe. I have quite the track record, don't I?"

"Ha!"

"Maybe one day I'll find my Carson. Just not my teacher." She winks.

"I'm sure you will. And knowing you, it will be even more dramatic." She swats at me as the door opens.

Her mom is standing there looking at us giggling on the couch. I can see her eyes are glassy as her lips turn up into a huge grin.

"Hi, Mom," Bridget says.

"I was going to make sure you girls were okay, but I see everything worked out. I knew it would."

"You did?" I whisper.

"Of course, darling. You have always been part of this family. Why would anything change it? Now I get to spoil you even more." Moisture drips down my nose.

"God, I can't keep crying like this." I laugh, and the rest follow suit. I swipe across my cheeks and tilt my head. "Are you sure you guys are okay with this? I don't want you to think I—"

"Stop right there. You are now mine, just as Bridget is mine. Do you understand me? I spoke to your dad." She pauses with a giant grin on her face. Her smile is contagious as she says that word and I grin back. "Sounds good, doesn't it?" She winks. I nod. "Okay, what was I saying? Oh, yes. I spoke to your dad. We both feel strongly that we have been robbed of your youth. Yes, we spend every weekend with you, and most holidays, but still, we want to make some changes starting now. We want you to know that this is your house. We will change the guest room to your room, and if you want—if you want, Lynn—you have a place here."

"What?"

"What I'm trying to say not so eloquently." She wipes her eye. "Is you're our daughter, this is your home, and we would like you to live with us." My chin rattles, my nose twitches, and my eyes well.

"Okay." I'm so emotional I don't think I can say more than that.

"Okay," she says and Bridget joins in our hug.

"Okay."

# CHAPTER FORTY-THREE

## Carson

LYNN IS BUSY WITH HER FAMILY, SO TODAY IS THE PER-
fect day to start working on my own stuff. I made her
a promise and I intend to keep it. Walking into the
brightly lit office is my first step. Once inside, a desk sits in front
of me. A young woman typing at a computer smiles up at me.

"Hi, how can I help you?" she asks.

"I have an appointment with Mitch Johnson."

"Please, take a seat." Once in the chair, I fold my hands in my
lap to keep them from tapping nervously on the wooden armrest of the chair. This is my first appointment for one-on-one
counseling, and a small part of me is excited yet nervous to see
what he has to say.

A few minutes later, an older man, probably in his early six-
ties, walks out. He reminds me a little of my high school track
coach.

"Carson Blake?"

"Yeah," I stand and walk over to him.

"I'm Mitch. Pleasure to meet you." I reach my hand out and give his a shake. "Follow me to my office. Can I get you something? Water? Coffee?"

"No, I'm fine. But thank you."

I follow him down the hallway and into an office in the corner of the suite. He motions for me to take a seat and I do. He takes a seat in a leather wingback across from me.

"So, what brings you here today, Carson?"

"I was at a group meeting for anger management, and one of the members mentioned how much you helped him."

"Very good. I strongly encourage going to group meetings. Can you tell me a little about your triggers and give me some background information?"

I proceed to tell him about my father. How he beat my mother. How when, I got old enough, he hurt me as well and how it continued like that until questions arose. How I was raised by nannies when it became obvious something was going on. I then told him how I started fights in high school, and how I had been lashing out recently. And I told him about Matthew and Lynn.

"Are you afraid you will hurt her?" he asks, and I sit forward in my seat. My hands rest on my thighs.

"No, never." There is no doubt or waver in my voice, and he bobs his head pensively.

"What are you afraid of, then?" *What am I afraid of?* Good question. My teeth gnaw on the inside of my cheek.

"Losing control. I'm not afraid about her, but I hurt her ex and I'm afraid of *that* rage," I finally admit.

"How do you currently channel your emotions?"

"I run." His head gives a little shake and then he smiles.

"Which is harder in the winter."

283

"Yep."

"So you haven't been able to get those emotions out."

"Not really. Normally it's not an issue, but recently . . ." I stop and inhale.

"I understand. Well, the first thing is not really a fix, but maybe you should consider joining a gym." He laughs.

"Good idea." I chuckle back.

"Second thing that will help is talking about it."

"Okay."

"Going to the support groups will help, and coming here. And if you think Lynn is supportive . . ." He lifts an eyebrow and waits for me to respond.

"Yes, one hundred percent."

"Okay, good. Now, the next thing to do is learn techniques that you can use in place of running, since you obviously can't run all the time."

"No, I guess you're right. That would be a smart idea." I sit back in my chair again. I imagine I should get comfortable for this.

"Okay, let's start simple. Relaxation tools. I think this could be very helpful for you. Not only will you be able to take this coping mechanism anywhere, but it's a relatively easy method." I raise my eyebrow at him in question.

"Basically it's as simple as deep breathing and relaxing imagery. It might sound silly, but I promise it can really help calm angry feelings. I will give you a list of books, that teach relaxation techniques, and once you learn the techniques, you can call upon them in any situation. Also, it might be a good idea for your significant other to read the books as well. That way she can help you if need be. It might feel awkward at first, but over time it will become second nature."

"So, what does it consist of? Can you give me an example?"

"It's really as easy as . . . Okay, here. Breathe deeply, from your diaphragm. Breathing from your chest won't relax you. Picture your breath coming up from your gut. Slowly repeat a calm word or phrase such as 'relax,' or 'take it easy.' Repeat it to yourself while breathing deeply. Use imagery. Visualize a relaxing experience from either your memory or your imagination." He waits for me to acknowledge that I understand. After I do, he continues.

"The next part is cognitive restructuring." I lift a brow, because this I don't understand. "Change the way you think. This is harder than breathing." He smiles. "Basically, I want you to work on changing your angry thoughts with rational ones. Remind yourself that getting angry won't fix anything. You will also have to learn better problem solving. I'll give you some reading material for that also. Not every problem has an easy solution, so concentrate more on how to face it rather than solve it.

"It seems you have had stressors recently and have fallen back, but over time you'll have had a good handle on them. I think staying with a course of group meetings as well as open communication with Lynn will be rather helpful. And read the books. I don't feel you will need weekly therapy, but how about a monthly check in?"

"I think that's a great idea." And I do. It sounds perfect. The idea of seeing him once a month feels like a huge burden has been lifted off me.

"I really think the breathing techniques will help. It's basically what you have been doing with running all these years, but more appropriate for work. I also think you need to determine where this all stems from." I know where it stems from. My dad.

My mom. The abuse. But I don't say it out loud. His eyes narrow. "If you know, maybe it's time you confront the issue and try to work through it. You'll never be able to move on without closure, and please, whatever it is that troubles you, keep an open mind. Nothing is ever as it seems."

We continue to talk, and once I have a list of books I set off for the store to pick them up. I feel a sense of relief.

For the first time in a long time, I feel I can handle things. Maybe it's because I finally opened up about my childhood. Even in high school I never talked about it, but being open and meeting once a month to discuss everything might be exactly what I need to move forward with Lynn without the fear of my past rearing its ugly head. I have held so much rage for so long it's time I finally let it all go. Maybe Mitch Johnson is right. Maybe it's time I look at the big picture. Maybe my mom wasn't abandoning me; maybe she was protecting me from him. I might never know her motives, but it's time I forgive her.

I pick up the phone and dial.

"Hello?"

"Mom."

"Carson?" she speaks in a broken whisper.

"Yeah, it's me. Are you alone?"

"Kind of," I hear a muffling sound and a door close. "Your dad's not here. He's in the other room."

"I wanted to talk to you. I've been doing a lot of thinking, and I wanted to talk to you about something."

"I-I," she stutters.

"You don't have to say anything. Just listen to me, please." My voice cracks on the word *please*. Showing me how desperate I am to get this out and start moving forward in my life. "I've been thinking a lot about this, and I want to forgive you. I need to forgive you." Through the phone, she takes in a sharp breath. "I just want to let you know if you need anything, I'm always here for you.

"Thank you. I-I have to g—"

"I know."

"For what it's worth, Carson . . . I'm sorry." The phone clicks and I know she hung up. I'm not sure what will happen next, but I do know I'll be okay.

I dial Lynn's number next. We haven't spoken much this week. She's been dealing with all that surrounds moving into her new home. Luckily for Lynn, since she's now nineteen, there's nothing her mom can do. And seeing as she can still attend Cranbrook, and she now has a live-in study partner in the way of a sister and best friend, she's been very happy.

The phone rings once before I hear her voice.

"Hey you," she says into the phone. "How did everything go?"

"Really good. Any chance we can meet up and I'll tell you everything.

"Yes, of course."

"Okay, great. Tonight. Dinner at my place.

"That would be perfect. See you later."

# CHAPTER FORTY-FOUR

## Lynn

A FEW DAYS LATER I'M STANDING IN THE KITCHEN AT Bridget's when I realize I don't have another set of pajamas. "I need to go home and get some stuff."

"You don't have to go tonight. You can borrow—"

"I just need . . ." I pause, hating the idea of having to go back there.

"Your own things. I get it."

Sam steps forward, his brow furrowed. "Is your mom home?"

"I don't know. Maybe, but who knows with my mom," I mumble under my breath.

"Can you find out?" With a nod, I pull out my phone and send a text.

**Me: Are you home?**
**Mom: Why?**
**Me: Just wanted to know.**
**Mom: Yes.**

I turn to Sam. "Yes."

The thing is, she never asked where I was or if I was coming home. Usually it cut, but as I stand amongst my new family, I realize she has no power over me anymore.

"I'm coming with you," he announces.

"Sam, you don't have to—"

"Yes, I do." He reaches his hand out and takes mine in his. "I'm your dad, Lynn. If it would be okay . . ." He pauses. His Adam's apple bobs in his throat as he tries to find his words. "If it's okay, I want you to call me Dad."

My heart seizes.

"Okay . . . Dad."

When we reach my mom's place, I turn the key and my dad steps forward and pushes the door open. He takes me by the hand, and as we step farther inside he gives me a reassuring squeeze.

"So you're gracing me with your presence tonight," she draws out as I step into the room, but her eyes widen as she sees Sam Miller enter the room.

All the color drains from her face.

"S-Sam," she stutters.

Protectively, he steps in front of me, his hand still holding mine. My mom catches the meaning of this. Revelation dawns on her perfect face, manifesting in a slight twitch in her left eyebrow. Most wouldn't notice, but I have always been so desperate to know her that I'm aware of her facial cues.

She's scared; more like petrified.

None of us speak. Time stretches between us in an awkward silence.

"How could you?" My mom flinches at the tone in my dad's voice. "How could you keep my child from me."

"I-I . . . I didn't know if she was yours."

"You still should have told me. We would have found out and then made a decision how to raise her."

"You wanted your wife. You wanted your family back. You told me never to speak to you again. To leave you alone. You didn't want me." Her jaw trembles, her teeth chattering together. "You didn't love me like I loved you," she cries out. Her body shakes from pent up emotion she must have been harboring for years.

"It wasn't your choice to make." His voice is softer now, broken from the lies, from the loss, from the past being relived.

"I'm sorry. I'm so sorry. I was so jealous, so hurt. I . . ." Deep sobs tear through her as tears stream down her face.

I couldn't speak. I've never seen her like this. So little. So lost. My stomach knots as her body shakes. Time seems to stand still as she lets the pain and emotion flow out and dissolves in heartbreaking despair I've never witnessed before. Finally, her cries lessen and then as if a curtain is dropped, she stands tall and swipes away the dampness that has collected on her cheek.

"Now what?" she asks.

"You have had Lynn for nineteen years. I've come to take her home." His meaning is clear and she doesn't speak. She nods her head once and turns away down the hall and into her room.

"I'm sorry you had to see that," my dad says.

"I'm not." He raises a curious eyebrow, but I don't respond. I just head into my room to gather my belongings.

I'm happy I saw that. Watching my mom break gave me the strangest feeling of hope. Maybe, just maybe, there's a chance for my mom and me after all.

"I feel like I haven't seen you in years," I whisper against his lips a few days later.

"I know exactly what you mean." I feel his tongue sweep against my mouth and I open to him, allowing him passage. It swirls against mine, and then he pulls away with a sigh. "I want to be inside you so bad, but first we have to talk," he groans.

"Fine," I huff and he laughs. "What's so important that we have to stop?" I ask playfully.

"I want to hear everything. I know we spoke, but only about small details. Tell me everything."

"Oh, okay." I roll my eyes in mock annoyance. "It's been wonderful. It's crazy. I never really understood what I was missing. I guess I never thought to dream it could happen. But it has and it's incredible. First, my dad came with me to see mom. We decided it was best not to bombard her. I wasn't sure what to expect, but surprisingly, she seemed somewhat remorseful. Well, for her, at least. She said she was sorry for withholding the information but then she made it about herself, so basically, she said he broke her heart and that's why she wouldn't tell him. She felt bad. I've never seen her like that before. She was sobbing. In the end, though, my dad told her I was coming to live with him and his family now. That she owed him that much. She didn't argue or object." I pause and give a small, sad smile and he nods in understanding.

"You wanted her to fight for you."

"Yeah. I guess. But I still held a glimmer of hope that she would fight for me to stay with her."

"I'm so sorry."

"I know, but it's okay. I promise. My new family—you, my father, my sisters—Ronnie—you all make up for her. I spoke to him, *Ronnie.*" Carson's jaw tightens. I shake my head and give a reassuring smile. "It went well. Really well. I told him every-thing, and then I told him no matter what . . . No matter what blood runs through my veins, he'll always be part of my life. He'll always be my dad. I even joked I should call him pops so not to confuse anyone. He laughed and then he started to cry and I felt so bad for the pain my mom caused him.

After I left I was happy to go back home." I smile at the word. God, it feels good to say that. "When I got back home, I think my dad must have told them about my mom. I had my clothes packed and they were all waiting for me in the living room with hugs. They had a Welcome Home banner set up, they'd deco-rated my room, and they even had a homemade meal prepared. Bridget told them all my favorite foods. She told them I once said when her mom made lasagna it felt like family, and so they prepared it. It was beautiful." Tears fill my eyes at the thought.

"I'm so happy for you. You deserve this and so much more. You deserve everything."

"Not sure what I did to deserve you."

"You deserve much more than me. *I'm* not sure what I did to get lucky enough to have you pick me."

"You think we pick our fate?"

"You know how I actually feel about this, about us. It's pre-destined. Absolute. It's written in the stars."

"Are we written in the stars?"

"In the stars and beyond, to whatever is past infinity." We kiss again and this time I pull back.

"What about you?" I ask him.

"So much has happened, I don't even know what to tell you."

"Start from the beginning."

"I can do that." He drums his fingers on his lap, and then begins. "After we parted, I went to one of my meetings, and it had some great information. One of the members referred me to a counselor."

"Will you start seeing him?"

"I did, actually." The huge smile on his face tells me it went well and I'm so happy and relieved. But I'm a little sad that I missed so much of his life this past week.

"Wow, it has been a busy week."

"Yeah, tell me about it," he lets out.

"So, what did he have to say?"

"I have some books to read. He also encouraged you, my significant other, to read them." Significant other . . . *I like that.*

"When do you see him again?"

"I'll only be seeing him once a month. I'll continue going to the support group, but mainly speaking about my past and learning new coping mechanisms."

"I'm so proud of you," I say, and he smiles.

"Thanks, baby." He pulls me onto his lap.

"Now what?" I whisper into his chest.

"The future is infinite, *our* future is infinite, and I'm excited to see where it leads."

# EPILOGUE

## Lynn

MY EYES SCAN THE VAST DISTANCE IN FRONT OF ME. A sea of faces smile back. There they are. All of them: Ronnie, Margo, Sam, Olivia—my new family—and Carson . . . *my soul.*

My mom hasn't shown up, but I guess I never really expected her. I imagine she and her new husband are off traveling, but I don't care. I have everyone I need right in front of me.

Bridget squeezes my hand.

Strong. Reassuring.

Through the air, names echo around me and then I hear Bridget. She steps forward, a wave of cheers echoing as she moves toward the podium. I watch as she takes her diploma. I can't believe we actually got here. My heart rattles in my chest, waiting for my own name to be read.

Gwendolyn Miller. A few weeks ago, all the paperwork came through. I am now legally and emotionally a Miller. They took me in, loved me, and now I'm officially part of their family. Not that I need a piece of paper, but it's wonderful anyway.

Hearing my name, I stand, tears rolling down my face. It always happens when I hear my name. It also doesn't help that my dad is standing and clapping loudly. It's infectious.

I make my way to the principal, and I hold my diploma up to show Carson, who mouths *I love you.* The love I have for him has only grown. I now know that love is infinite. That there is no limit to how much a person can love, and there is no boundary to one's happiness. It crosses right past the stars to all infinity. That's what Carson taught me, and for the rest of my life, I will be forever grateful.

After all the students have walked the stage, we throw our caps in the air. Then together, Bridget and I find our family, and we each throw arms around each other. From the corner of my eye, I see a familiar face come into focus. Stepping away from the crowd, I walk over to her.

"I'm really proud of you." She swallows hard as if she is biting back tears.

"What are you doing here?"

"I know I haven't been the best mom to you. I blamed you for everything, and for that I'm sorry. It isn't your fault your father left me, just like it isn't Bridget's fault that Sam decided to go back to his family. I realize that now. I've carried a lot of hatred and misplaced emotions inside me all these years, and the only person I have to blame is myself. I know you probably can't forgive me, but I want to do better. Do you think—"

"I really don't know, Mom."

I watch her lower lip tremble as she tries to hold back tears. It must have been hard for her to admit her mistakes. I take a deep breath. She's strong enough to tell me the truth, so I can be brave enough to learn to forgive.

"I guess we can take it day by day."

She wipes an escaped tear as she smiles. "Day by day sounds good."

I hug my arms around myself and nod, not trusting my voice. She gives me a small, tentative smile and then walks away. From behind her retreating body, I see my father approaching.

"Are you okay?" he asks.

"Yeah. I really am." He pulls me into a long embrace.

Once we make it back to *our* home. Margo has a catered lunch prepared and is waiting for us to celebrate—*just for family*. Carson is there. He's become a permanent fixture in this house, and he's as much a part of this family as I am. When he's not here, he's at The Polaris Boys' Club. With the assistance of Sam, who has business knowledge, Carson used his trust fund to start a group to help troubled boys who have aged out of The Kids' Club. Boys like him who need guidance and an outlet for their rage.

"I have a surprise to show you." The rich timber of Carson's voice pulls me out from my thoughts with intrigue.

"A surprise?"

"Actually, two."

"Two?"

"Yes, I think it's the perfect way to celebrate . . ." He trails off and heat spreads across my cheeks.

Together, hand in hand, we walk the three blocks until we reach our destination. A large retail space that I've become very familiar with over the last few weeks. There's a giant red bow in front and he hands me scissors.

"It's ready?"

"It is, and I want you to cut the ribbon."

From the corner of my eye, I notice a crowd has surrounded

us. Toby and his friends are among the familiar faces smiling at me as I cut the ribbon. When I lower the scissors, I notice a small box in Carson hand. "This is a promise. Not only for now, but for the future. A promise to love you forever and to always be there for you. In a few years I'll replace it." He winks as I open the box. A diamond gleams up at me as bright as the sunlight that glitters across the ocean; like the stars against a perfect night sky. He slips the ring onto my left hand and I look down to take in the design.

"The North Star?" He nods and pulls me toward him.

"To new beginnings." He leans in and places a soft kiss on my lips "To daring to dream . . ."

"To finding home," I whisper back.

So much has changed in the course of the last school year and I realize that every moment brought me here. Every hardship prepared me for all the extraordinary things that are now in store for me.

And most of all . . .

I learned that even in the darkest of nights, the stars will always shine.

The End

# ACKNOWLEDGMENTS

I want to thank my entire family. I love you all. Thank you to my husband and my kids for always loving me, I love you so much!

Thank you to all the amazing indie companies that helped mold my words.

Love N. Books

Write Girl Editing Services

Indie After Hours

Champagne Formats

Hang Le

Marla Selkow Esposito

Thank you to Melissa Saneholtz PR for your help with EVERYTHING! I would be lost with out you!

Thank you Give Me Books.

Thanks to Wong Sim and Chad Hurst.

Thank you to my beta team! Melissa, Leigh, Liv, Trish, Mia (for the plotting phone calls) Thank you for your wonderful and extremely helpful feedback.

Thank you to my test readers! Christine, Vanessa, Jacquie, Marie.

I want to thank to ALL my friends for putting up with me. I know it's no easy task!

To all of my author friends, thank you for giving me great advice and being my friend!

Thank you to all the ladies I sprint with! I would never have finished this book without you pushing me.

To the ladies in the Ava Harrison Support Group, I couldn't have done this without your support!

Please consider joining: http://bit.ly/2e67NYi

Thanks to all the bloggers! Thanks for your excitement and love of books!

Last but certainly not least . . .

Thank you to the readers!

Thank you so much for taking this journey with me.

For future release information please sign up here to be alerted: http://bit.ly/2fnQQ1n

# BY AVA HARRISON

*Imperfect Truth*

*Through Her Eyes*

*trans-fer-ence*

# ABOUT THE AUTHOR

Ava Harrison is a New Yorker, born and bred. When she's not journaling her life, you can find her window shopping, cooking dinner for her family, or curled up on her couch reading a book.

Connect with Ava

Newsletter Sign Up: http://bit.ly/2fnQQ1n
Facebook Author Page: http://bit.ly/2eshd1h
Facebook Reader Group: http://bit.ly/2e67NYi
Goodreads Author Page: http://bit.ly/2eNjYwX
Twitter: http://bit.ly/2fnRP1v
Instagram: http://bit.ly/2f5H5RT
Amazon Author Page: http://amzn.to/2fnVJHF

Made in United States
North Haven, CT
18 November 2022

26903681R00183